ECL

Best Wishes

www.leascott.com

Also by the same author

The NED KELLY Game

Australia's most infamous murdering bushranger, Ned Kelly, has been dead for more than 100 years since he was hanged in Old Melbourne Gaol. Now it seems he's back from the dead - and he can't stop killing!

He starts with the four youths who stole his skull from the museum as part of a teenage prank. They're grown men now, and one by one they're picked off and 'hanged by the neck until dead', just as Kelly was. Felicity Simons, the one girl in on the teenage prank, is now a history lecturer at Australia's oldest university. When warning messages from Kelly start to appear she embarks on a quest to grant his dying wish, hoping to put mad Ned's spirit to rest.

But *has* Ned Kelly returned, or is there a real killer out there? As the police begin to hunt the killer, Felicity soon discovers she could be his next victim…

ECLIPSED

Lea Scott

First published in 2010 in the United States of America.

1

ISBN 978 1449 574666

Typeset in Australia
Printed and bound in the United States of America.

Cover design by J Cannell.

To Michael Hutchence (1960-1997) for his gift of songwriting,

a star whose light will never fade.

*'Every single one of us the devil inside'**

* Lyrics from *Devil Inside*, written by Andrew Farriss & Michael Hutchence, recorded by INXS 1987

Acknowledgements

I am greatly indebted to all those who read and praised my first published novel, *The Ned Kelly Game*, and gave me the heart and courage to follow my path of being a writer. I owe a special thank you for encouragement and advice to the members of the writing groups, W.O.W. and W.O.O. who listened with enthusiasm and gave me invaluable feedback for some of the important scenes in this novel. Thanks also to fellow W.O.O member, Jade Cannell for helping with the cover design.

For their technical help over the period of writing this novel, I thank Dr Daryl Dodt for his medical advice and assistance, lawyer Simon Hart for his evaluation of my legal and courtroom scenes, and retired police detective Neal Freier for his procedural review and candid stories on policing in Queensland.

To those that helped edit this and earlier drafts of the story and thereby helped to shape what it has become, I sincerely thank for their time and skills, Ian Jay, Kerry Martin and Joan Lockwood, and last but not least my partner Rob, who added the final touches and whose loving support set me in motion to publish this book.

ECLIPSED

PROLOGUE

Kings Cross, Sydney

She looked like she could be someone's wife, young, attractive and evidently new to the game. She stood apart from the veteran hookers who strutted together on the strip, wailing to passing motorists like packs of banshees. He rounded the block once more then slowly inched the car up beside her.

'Fifty up, before I get in,' she stated in a voice lacking emotion. Icy coldness, combined with business sense. He liked that. Maybe this time he had found her.

For weeks, Angelo had searched for the one who would help him carry off his carefully schemed plan. He had thought about the traits she would need to have. Did she need to be unfeeling, shallow and greedy; someone with whom he could part company once they had finished the job? Or should she have a little more depth of character, someone fearless, with whom he could share the challenge and enjoy the game? She would have to be willing to cut all ties, change her identity and lie low for some time. To succeed, he needed to know he could trust her.

As she brushed the wisps of hair from her face, he could see her impatience growing. He removed his wallet then opened the clip, pausing so she could see the wad of cash within its bulging confines. As she gazed into his eyes, he sensed her aroused interest. His confidence grew. From beneath the larger notes, he slipped a fifty and offered it to her with a throaty laugh. She did not break their gaze, as she swung herself into the late-model green Saab and wrenched the door closed behind her.

PART ONE

PARTIAL ECLIPSE…

For a long time there was only the light…impenetrable white light, shining like a beacon through the surrounding darkness.

A slip in time…

The shadow began its inevitable path across the light. At first it just nudged the edges, causing only the slightest blur against that which had shone pure for so long. The slight change was hardly detectable except by those closest to the light.

ONE

Everything that deceives also enchants.
Plato

Jade Sheffield held her mobile phone in her hand wondering if she should try to call her younger sister back. She had just missed the call but she was on her way out the door for an important function that her law firm was hosting. She was already running late so she decided it could wait until tomorrow. Amy was probably just calling about some trivial boy problem she was going through again. She dropped her phone into her handbag as she raced out the door.

Detective Brent Hunter watched the lights of the Gold Coast glitter strip fade from his rear vision mirror as he drove west toward the foothills of Nerang. He barely acknowledged his partner in the seat beside him as he cursed his rotten luck. How long would this night end up lasting? It was mid-week so he had expected a routine evening. Maybe a few drunk and disorderly pick-ups on the beach then an early end to the night so he could be up with the sun for his morning surf. This callout was outside of the usual run of things.

The harsh lights from the ambulance cut through the darkness alerting him that he had reached his destination. He pulled up behind it then stepped from the car. A tall lithe figure in his dark jacket, his wavy blonde hair glowed alternately red and blue each time the flashing lights illuminated it. His shorter and stockier partner, Martin Andrews, stepped from the other side of the car then without a word, headed directly for the house.

Hunter took a soft pack of Marlboro Lights from his pocket and gave the bottom of the packet two practiced flicks with his thumb. A cigarette popped up and he took it between his fingers. Smoking was the only vice in his otherwise healthy lifestyle. As he lit it and looked toward the house, he braced himself for the scene he was about to witness. His father, a career cop, had been able to detach himself in these situations. He had discouraged the show of emotions in his son under his guise of 'tough love'. If his father were still alive, he would have been disappointed in his son's progress. In the few years since his promotion to detective, it had never become easy for Hunter.

While he waited for the nicotine to settle him, he looked up and down the street. There was movement behind some of the curtains but the neighbourhood remained behind closed doors. It was a typical suburban street where everyone seemed to be content to mind their own business. He watched as Andrews exited the house then sidled up the street and knocked on one of the doors. He took a final drag on the cigarette, crushed it under his foot then headed toward the crime scene.

The first thing he noticed as he entered the house was the distinctive smell of blood. Its metallic scent reached his nostrils, and something else. The faint smell of burnt meat. He had a momentary flashback to backyard family barbeques, when his father frequently spent more time drinking beer and socialising than attending to the steaks. He glanced toward the kitchen and saw a wok on the stovetop with strips of blackened beef in it. A wooden spoon lay abandoned in the middle of the white floor like a blemish on porcelain skin. Someone had turned off the gas and the meat sat unattended, part of a meal that the family would never consume.

He turned his attention to the grisly scene in the living room. There was blood everywhere. Red splatters had ascended the pale walls and sprayed across the white tiled floor. The family were Asian; though he could tell more from the décor of the room and the women's traditional dress, than from any recognition of their disfigured faces. A man sat slumped in a chair in the centre of the living room, his body tethered by loose ropes. He wore dark trousers and a threadbare white business shirt. What was once the back of his head was now a gaping hole of bloodstained black hair and cranial matter. Blood pooled around his chair in stark contrast with the white floor.

Around him, the rest of the family formed an audience-like circle as if witnesses to his demise. An older Asian woman dressed in a red silk kimono slumped forward from the futon sofa, the remains of her grey head lolling between her legs. Beside her, the lifeless arm of a younger woman reached across her shoulder. The woman's head was thrust against the back of the sofa, a red halo soaking the fabric around it. He could tell from the entry wound on her forehead that the gunman had shot her at point blank range. Hunter's eyes moved slowly around the circle, taking in the positions of the victims and trying to make sense of the carnage. He averted his eyes quickly when his glance first fell upon the children but forced himself to look back with a trained eye. The other victims appeared to be in the positions in which they had fallen, but there was something more posed about the positions of the children. The two small boys lay sideways on the floor, their eyes open, staring.

Had they been forced to witness the brutal slaying of their parents? Or had their lives been taken first while their family watched on? He hoped the latter was the case, and was slightly heartened that it was the most likely scenario given the nature of the crime. It appeared to him to be some kind of retribution killing so it was more probable that the man of the household was the last to perish, after the gunman forced him to watch the execution of his entire family.

Hunter took a deep breath and stepped further into the room. A neighbour had phoned in the report of screams, so the crime scene was still fresh. He was relieved in that sense. The smell of decomposing human bodies was not something he thought he would ever become accustomed to no matter how many times he encountered it. He turned to a forensic officer who was inspecting one of the corpses.

'Whatcha make of it Mac?'

'Looks like he was mixed up in some pretty nasty shit. Mafia hit I reckon. Probably the work of those Russian bastards.'

'Hmm. Fits their trademark.'

'Yeah, they're a ruthless bunch. Cross them and they'll take your whole bloody family out, quick as look at ya.' He pointed out an area of bruising on the younger woman's cheek. 'Gun butt I'd say, unless they had another weapon. She must've given them some lip.'

Hunter leant over to inspect the area more closely but shied away as the odour of death became stronger. 'What do we know about the family?'

'Hardworking restaurant owners, according to the neighbours. Never any trouble. Worked long hours. Kept pretty much to themselves.'

'No form?'

'Nothing we've been able to pull up so far.'

Hunter shook his head. 'Which means squat. They come over here in the hundreds under fake names and visas.'

'No, these ones seem legit. The boys found all their papers neatly filed away. They look pretty genuine.'

Hunter shrugged. He had nothing against the Asian immigrants who did things legally and came through the right channels but the others, in Hunter's view, left themselves open to exploitation and aided the corruption and mess that he and his colleagues were left to clean up.

He looked up as Andrews entered the room. His senior partner started speaking before he had even reached Hunter so that he was almost shouting. 'Got a lead on a black sedan. Neighbours that phoned in the screams watched it pull away. Two occupants but they couldn't make them in the dark. I'm taking them to the station to get a statement and try to identify the car.'

'Good work Ands,' he said but his partner was already out the door and was probably taking the damn squad car. Hunter had never found him much of a team player. He had an ardour for advancement that motivated him to take the credit for most of their work. He didn't mind that so much. His motivation was to uphold the law and put away the criminals. But sometimes the guy just got under his skin, and tonight had been one of those nights. Now he would have to find another way to get home on top of everything else he had to deal with.

He turned back to Mac. 'Think I'll take a look around.'

Mac nodded his head and went back to his task of working the body.

Hunter walked down the hall glancing left and right as he went. Nothing seemed out of the ordinary, in contrast to the scene in the living room. The walls were bare except for one silk wall hanging strung lengthways down the wall. Symbols adorned the fabric from a language he was unable to read, although he was familiar with it. Many of the street signs and shop signage across the Gold Coast appeared in both English and Japanese to cater for the high level of Asian tourists that the area attracted.

He nudged open the door to the first bedroom and switched on the light. Bunk beds against the wall. Neat and tidy games and books lined the shelves. It in no way resembled his childhood bedroom of toy guns, dress ups and general bedlam. He moved toward the closet and opened the door. Neatly arranged clothes, shirts at one end and longer items at the other. Very well trained children for a family that allegedly worked long hours.

He was about to leave the room when a flash of light caught his eye from just beneath the bottom bunk of the bed. He leant down to see that it was a set of keys attached to a plastic student card for a local university. He slipped on a rubber glove then picked it up. The student's name was Amy Sheffield and she certainly wasn't Asian. The photograph showed a young attractive blonde. So who was Amy? She didn't look like the killing type. Was she a family friend, or could she be an accomplice to the murder?

He looked further around the room but there seemed to be no further clues as to who Amy was. He headed for the next room. It was a small bathroom with a shower over the bath. He could see clearly through the glass screen. He opened the cabinet doors and sorted through the contents of the shelves. Nothing unusual.

He moved down the hall to the next room. As he did, his foot hit something and it skidded along the carpet then hit the wall with a sharp bang. He leant down and picked up a mobile phone. He turned it over in his hand realising it was an older type that could not take photographs. He would check it out after his search. He opened the next door quietly and listened in the dark room before reaching for the light switch. Silence. As he flicked the switch there was a sound of a gasp. It was faint, but he was sure he had heard it. He edged toward the closet and removed his gun from its holster. Cautiously opening the door, he stood spread-legged with the gun held out in front of him. Nothing. Moving the long flowing clothing aside with his gun butt, he checked the rest of the space. He turned around slowly and surveyed the rest of the room. Squatting onto his haunches, he lifted the bedcovers and checked under the bed but the space was vacant. There was nobody in the obvious hiding spots. It was then that he noticed the curtain behind the dresser move. He knelt down and could see that there was a rounded bulge behind the curtain in the space under the dresser.

'Police. Don't move. I have a gun.' He heard a whimper. 'Put your hands above your head and come out slowly,' he demanded.

A small hand appeared from behind the curtain, followed by an arm wearing a series of gold bangles. Hunter lowered his gun as an adolescent girl crawled out of the space under the dresser.

'Let me guess. Amy?'

The girl was shaking, but nodded her head. 'Who…who are you?'

'I'm Detective Hunter.'

'Oh thank God!' She fell into his arms sobbing.

Hunter held the young girl uncomfortably for a moment then led her down the hall. He guided her toward the front door, trying as best he could to shield her from the bloody scene in the living room. She was still shaking as he handed her over to the ambulance officer. He went back into the house and checked the other rooms quickly before returning outside. Amy sat on the back floor of the ambulance looking dazed, her feet dangling in the air as the ambulance officer cuffed her arm to check her blood pressure.

'Can you tell me what happened here tonight?' Hunter asked softly.

She started to talk. 'I…I don't know. I heard shouting and screams and I just hid until you came. I tried to phone someone but I dropped my phone and I was too scared to go back for it.'

He held up the phone he had found in the hall. 'Is this yours?'

'Yes.' Her words turned into sobs and her face collapsed into her hands.

He reached out then put a hand on her shoulder. 'Do you remember anything they said?'.

She looked up through tear-streaked eyes. 'No, they had accents. It was hard to understand them.'

It's OK, we'll leave it for now. Is there someone I can call for you?'

'Jade,' she managed then pulled a business card from her pocket with trembling hands.

Hunter took the card from her and read the name. *Jade Sheffield.* He knew of her. She was a junior partner at a prominent legal firm on the strip. He looked back at Amy.

'My sister,' she said in answer to his quizzical look.

The girl was quite visibly distraught so he did not want to press her any further. They could question her at the station after the initial shock had worn off. He took his phone from his pocket and dialled the number on the card, moving away from Amy to explain the situation to her sister.

When Jade arrived at the scene, the ambulance officers were removing the first of the bodies from the house. She raced up to her sister and took her in her arms. Amy crumbled against her sobbing.

Hunter made his way toward them and held out a hand in greeting. 'Hi. Detective Hunter.'

Jade looked up but did not offer a hand in return, her arms clasped firmly around her sister. 'Jade Sheffield,' she said. Their eyes met and flickered briefly before Jade returned her attention to her sister.

Hunter persisted. 'Can you tell me what your sister was doing here tonight?'

'She's the babysitter,' Jade responded in a protective tone. 'She only started working for them a few weeks ago when their older daughter started college.'

'Daughter? We'll have to locate her. Look, I'm going to have to ask you to bring Amy down to the station. What about her parents. Where are they?'

Jade's eyes wandered into the distance. 'They've both passed away. I'm her legal guardian, but she lives on campus most of the time.'

'Sorry,' he said then paused, momentarily lost for words as he thought about the impact of his own father's death. 'I know it's unorthodox, but my partner's left so do you think we could go in your car? I'll have to ask Amy a few more questions but we'll leave it for a bit until she's had a chance to overcome the shock. It was pretty awful, what happened in there.'

Jade extracted herself from her sister's grip and stroked the girl's hair before moving away to speak to the detective more privately. 'What exactly happened in there? I want to know what I'm dealing with.'

'Wish I could tell you. The whole family was blown away, except maybe this daughter. Could be Mafia related. You know the kinds of things they're into here on the Coast. But we don't have any suspects or even a motive as yet.'

'She tried to call me earlier tonight but I missed the call. If only I'd called her back.'

'It's probably a good thing you didn't. She'd dropped her phone and the ring may have alerted them that she was in the house.'

Jade drew a deep breath and held a hand to her chest. 'Oh God! I could have lost her. We only have each other.'

Hunter ran his hands through his hair, feeling a sudden vulnerability in Jade's presence. She was a few years his senior but it wasn't only that. He pointed her toward her car. 'I'll be with you in just a few minutes.' He watched Jade walk her sister away, surprised by his unexpected attraction to the stunning lawyer despite the horrors that had unfolded that night.

As he lit up another cigarette he noticed a slight tremble in his hand. Delayed shock. He looked up at the sky as he drew on the cigarette. A thick cloud cover had moved over blocking out the moon and stars. It looked like the weatherman's prediction for bad weather the next day had been right for once. He shrugged in resignation as he checked out with the other boys then headed toward the car. It was not looking like a morning surf was going to be on the agenda now anyway.

TWO

Since she could remember, Jade had possessed the power to manipulate things to be the way she desired. She never quite understood where that power came from, but when she set her mind on something there was little doubt it would eventuate. It added a certain mystique to her otherwise conventional life.

Jade had unfalteringly followed the path expected of her. After completing high school, she had gone on to university to complete her degree in Law. She was passionate about her profession, having worked relentlessly at establishing her reputation within both her firm and the wider business community. She had risen to the position of junior partner within a prominent criminal law firm on the Gold Coast, Queensland's ultimate tourist destination. People were drawn to the Coast for its long white beaches, its gambling and entertainment scene and some came just for the shopping. Yet others were drawn by the quick cash that could be made in a tourist town from scams and organized crime.

There had been no room in Jade's life for serious relationships, but there had been men. Most intriguing to her was the way men acted in her company. She didn't feel that she was classically beautiful. But her smile seemed to intoxicate people and her eyes, a deep jade like her name, often mesmerized those who dared to look into their depths. She always carried herself with a casual confidence, flicking her thick auburn hair as she walked. She felt her beauty came from somewhere within. She never failed to arouse interest or turn heads when she entered a room.

Tonight was no exception. The firm entertained on a regular basis, mostly in an effort to promote their services to those with the money or power to be beneficial to them. Jade had rehearsed her performance for these functions well. She frequently excelled in bringing new business associations to the firm.

Her target tonight was a local detective who was ardently involved in the development of a juvenile youth program that was of interest to her firm. Jade had caught his eye several times throughout the night. From the corner of her eye, she saw him moving toward her.

'Good evening, Detective Hunter. It's good to see you again.' Her lips formed an infectious smile as she spoke.

'You too. How's your sister doing?'

'She's recovered very well thank you. She's a tough little thing. Like me, I guess. She wouldn't admit it, but that counselor you recommended did her a world of good.'

'Glad to hear it worked out well.'

'Did you ever catch the men that committed that horrible crime?'

Hunter furrowed his brow. 'Yeah, mob hitman by the name of Frank Zuliani. I'm surprised you didn't hear about it.'

'Zuliani? So it wasn't the Russians?'

'No, but they sure tried to make it look that way. Might not have caught him if a witness hadn't come forward at the last minute and identified him. We got the murder weapon but it went missing.'

'Missing? How could that happen?'

Hunter looked embarrassed as he shrugged his shoulders. 'We still haven't found it and he's trying to appeal.'

Jade decided to drop the subject. She skillfully extracted two full glasses from the passing drinks tray, offering one to him. 'Care to partake of our hospitality?'

'I've never been known to turn down a drink, particularly one being offered by a beautiful woman.'

'Oh, but I'm sure there have been numerous opportunities,' she winked.

They both laughed, touching their glasses together in a toast. 'To hospitality', he offered.

'Hospitality, and whatever that may bring,' she said as she took a sip of the French champagne.

From across the room, Charles Ramsey smiled. He had not once regretted the day he had hired Jade Sheffield. She had an uncanny knack of knowing the way things would turn out. She tackled every case relentlessly, always a formidable adversary for the opposing team. He often found himself wishing he had met someone with her spirit earlier in his life. He knew people of her caliber were a rare find and he felt fortunate to have discovered this hot shot.

The senior partner's companion followed his gaze in Jade's direction.

'Is she really as good as they say, Charles?'

'Oh yes, and more, my good Doctor. Why do you ask? Do you find yourself interested, Angelo?'

'Now Charles, you know I'm almost a married man!' The two chuckled at the timeworn innuendo in the joke, Angelo's throaty laugh cutting across the room.

On the other side of the room, Jade was oblivious to the conversation taking place about her. She was surprised to find herself physically attracted to Detective Brent Hunter. She'd barely noticed him last time they'd met as her concern had centred firmly on her sister. As he spoke, she noticed the strong curve of his cheek and the way his tanned skin blended with his thick blonde hair. His eyes were the bluest she had ever seen. She was imagining what it would be like to feel his lips against her skin, when she heard Charles introducing him at the microphone. She blushed slightly, reigning in her emotions.

Charles's commanding voice rang out across the room. 'Detective Hunter has graciously agreed to speak to us tonight about a new youth program called *Time Out*. The aim of the program is to reduce juvenile crime. Brent gives up a great deal of his free time to the rehabilitation of youth offenders, and he has been appointed as the ambassador for the program on the Coast.'

Hunter excused himself then made his way to the podium amidst the respectful applause of the small audience. As his strong, deep voice resonated around the room, Jade found herself moved by his obvious commitment to the youth cause.

'Ladies and Gentlemen, I've seen the most hardened kids' lives altered by this program,' he began, scanning the room and noting the attention he commanded. 'The success of the program rests on exposing high-risk youths to the realities of prison life. We start by placing them in a prison block with real inmates, leaving them to fend for themselves then hear about and experience prison life first hand. The kids placed on this program are just one small step away from doing time, and they know it, so the impact of the program really hits home in their minds. There are few wanting to find themselves back there in a hurry.'

Jade's firm had developed a specialized division in the past year that represented youth offenders. It stood in support of rehabilitation in a bid to raise its community profile. The growing number of youth gangs had brought assault and petty crime to the Coast's once quiet beachside suburbs and it had become a hot issue.

Hunter had the group's undivided attention. His motives were obviously much more sincere. His faith seemed to stem from the successes that he was sharing with his audience. 'You might call it shock therapy. With their eyes opened, the rest of the program becomes easy to administer. We show them what it's like to be a part of a normal family. Something most of them have never known. We ask them to think about what they would like for their children. It's all about breaking the cycle. Then we give them the skills to build a new way of life, with a newfound hope for the future,' he continued, scanning the faces before him. 'So far, the program has been a success in its trial stages. For it to continue, we need the support of people like you. We need recommendations to the program, as an alternative to current sentences. My department and I look forward to your support. Together we can strike forward in the battle against juvenile crime.'

Jade found herself moved by the conviction in Hunter's voice. She clapped loudly, carried away with the emotion of the crowd. He was making his way back toward her. She could not help but notice the strong lean lines of his body echoing in his powerful stride. She smiled to convey to him how impressed she was.

'So what do you do for an encore, Detective Hunter?' Jade's smile widened.

'You may just be lucky enough to find out,' he teased.

Jade felt a schoolgirl blush creeping into her cheeks. 'Another drink?'

Over several more glasses of wine, Jade found herself enjoying the detective's affable manner. She listened intently as he told her about the football team he coached. She detected a great degree of pride as he spoke about how much the boys had grown while taking part in his youth program.

Members of the party wandered over periodically to show their interest in the program, consistently interrupting their conversation.

As another of them walked away, Hunter turned to Jade. 'You want to grab a coffee? Maybe somewhere a little more quiet?'

'Sure, I'd love to. I'm not really needed here any more.'

They slipped out of the room quietly then headed down the hall. They waited for the lift to rise to the sixteenth floor. Jade shifted her weight from one foot to the other, as she watched the numbers on the panel climb. Finally, the doors opened. Hunter stood aside for Jade to enter then followed, pressing the button for the Ground Floor.

She laughed as he took on the formal pretence of a lift operator. 'Third floor – Ladies Underwear,' he said with raised eyebrows. His grin became more mischievous as they sunk to the next level. 'Second floor – culinary delights.' With a twinkle in his eye, he leant behind Jade then pressed the emergency stop button. She braced herself as the lift grinded to a halt.

'Delectable,' he murmured as he reached over to kiss her.

Astonished by his bravado, Jade took a moment to catch her breath. Then she responded hungrily, wanting this younger man with a sudden urgency. Their casual flirtations throughout the night had stirred her emotions. Maybe it was the wine, or maybe her recent thirtieth birthday, that made her suddenly want to experience a slice of her youth again. It had been a long time since she had made love outside the bedroom. She wanted to have him right there. Then the more errant part of her brain took over. She could take him to her office. Did she dare? The idea appealed to her darker side, but she had worked hard to build her professional reputation. What the hell! Who would ever know?

She grabbed him by the collar. 'Let's go up to my office. Level eighteen.'

Hunter was in no mood to argue. He obediently pressed the button for the eighteenth floor. They stifled a giggle as the lift passed the sixteenth floor, thinking of the party members still there oblivious to their shenanigans.

When the doors opened on the eighteenth floor, Hunter already had his shirt unbuttoned with Jade's jacket slung over his shoulder. She took his hand then led him stealthily across the level, shutting her office door behind them. The lights of the Gold Coast's CBD strip cast a starlit backdrop against the fervent scene.

Hunter pressed Jade up against the closed door as his hands started to explore her body. She could feel his hardness as her body responded to his touch. She pulled his shirt down over his forearms then let it drop to the floor, kissing his strong tanned shoulders. He was already working the fastening on her bra. It came free easily. She gasped as his lips greedily followed. They clawed at the rest of their clothing and thrust it around the room in casual misdemeanor.

Both naked now, Hunter lifted Jade then carried her toward her mahogany desk. He swept his arm across the desk and papers and pens fell to the floor with abandon as he placed her on its surface. The leather top felt cool against her bare buttocks, as he leaned over to whisper into her ear. 'I have to have you, now!'

Jade reached up then pulled him down on top of her, moaning as she felt him enter her. Their encounter was urgent and frenzied. Jade cried out as she was overcome by a powerful climax which was closely followed by Hunter's own.

Locked in the afterglow of hard sex, Jade deluded herself into feeling all the excitement of forbidden passion and young love. She felt elated as she glanced around the room at the desk, the chair, the floor. Would she ever feel the same walking into this office? Bathed in perspiration, she stood and faced the window. Looking out beyond the lights, her delusions began to fade.

Hunter placed his arms around her from behind then looked admiringly at their reflection in the glass. 'You really are beautiful.'

As Jade glanced at their reflections, a wave of unease began to work its way up her spine. She wanted to avoid the inevitable questions. She quickly diverted his attention as she moved away and gathered up their clothing. 'How about we take a shower?' Feigning the stealth of an alley cat, she led him still naked down the hall to the bathrooms. Hunter followed with a sly Cheshire cat grin spread across his face.

By the time they had soaped each other down, Hunter was aroused and ready to enter her again. Their second encounter was more controlled and longer lasting as they took the time to explore each other's bodies under the blast of the warm water.

Over an hour had passed by the time they had re-dressed so they decided not to return to the function room. Jade escorted Hunter to the basement car park level of the building.

'Can I call you?' he asked as the lift reached its destination and the doors began to open. Jade had been dreading this moment.

'I really don't know if that's such a good idea.' She tried to keep a note of humour in her voice. 'You wouldn't want to spoil such a perfect memory, would you? And I'm so very busy with these cases at the moment, I don't have a lot of spare time for …' Her voice trailed off as a look of hurt washed across his face.

She felt a slight pang of guilt. As he stepped out of the lift, it struck her just how young he looked. What was he? Mid-twenties? She was forgetting the intensity of experience at that age.

'Thank you,' she mouthed as she pressed the *Close* button. The doors saved her before she had to make any more excuses. She wasn't looking for emotional involvement, particularly with someone with so little life experience. Had she paid attention however, she would have understood the detective was a man of honour, above all else. It was a trait she would later come to regret.

From across the car park, Dr Angelo Morley watched the scene with interest. He had been studying Jade's behaviour throughout the night and had been quite aware she had disappeared somewhere with the strapping young detective over an hour ago. Maybe his task wasn't going to be so hard after all. He had second thoughts as the detective passed him, drawing deeply on a cigarette. Hunter's disheveled appearance gave him away, but the look on his face was far from what the doctor expected to see.

Dr Morley had been watching Jade for long enough to know it was going to be hard to crack that tough exterior. But deep down he knew she had the same needs as every other human being, a base craving for love and affection. He could play the psychological game of love better than anyone could. He was confident of a victory. A tough lawyer was paramount to his eventual success.

He threw his coat into the back seat of his Saab then eased himself behind the wheel. The streetlights reflected off its deep green paintwork as the vehicle sped down the street.

THREE

Dr Angelo Morley, the sign on his door read, *Director of Cardiac Medicine*. He had made it to the top, but the system had not laid out the welcome mat to a person from his background. Background? What did that matter to someone who lay fighting death in the emergency room? He cringed as he recalled the arduous steps it had taken to attain that goal. The path had not been an easy one and he resented bitterly all those who had attempted to block his way. He cast his mind back to the long-ago incident that had determined his future.

Sydney, Australia. December 1970

The young boy crouched beside his mother on the road. His mind spun. Only seconds before his mother had darted toward the pedestrian crossing and then thrown herself into the path of the oncoming vehicle. The scene replayed in slow motion, the thud of the impact echoing through his head. What had gone wrong?

The driver of the vehicle arrived at the same time every day to pick up her daughter from the front gates of the elite private school. As instructed by his conman father, Angelo and his mother had waited for the precise moment as her silver Mercedes passed down the street. The hours of practice they'd endured at his hand had not been of any use. The woman was running late today, so she was traveling faster than usual.

From the pool of blood welling beneath his mother's head, Angelo knew things had gone horribly wrong. There was something he was supposed to do, but he couldn't focus his mind on his part in the sham. Then he spied the phone box out of the corner of his eye. That was it! He was supposed to call an ambulance then his father, who would arrive to gather the witnesses together then collect their details. Staring in distress, he could see that the phone box was now a crumpled mass of steel and glass.

The blood had begun to seep across the scorching asphalt. Wincing as it stained his hands, he tried to remove something from beneath his mother's body. Low moans escaped her lips as she fought through the shock and the pain. Angelo began to tremble. He glared at the object. It was the side mirror from the Mercedes. A guttural cry escaped his throat as he hurled the piece of wreckage across the asphalt. It skidded into a pair of boots. It was only then that he became aware of the crowd surrounding him.

A middle-aged man in shirt and tie was pushing his way through the crowd. 'Excuse me. Excuse me. I'm a doctor,' he said. He reached the side of the boy's mother then felt for a pulse. A look of concern creased his face. 'I think she's trying to say something.'

Angelo put his ear close to his mother's face. Her voice was a low whisper, barely audible as it choked with a strange gurgling sound.

'Promise me…' She labored to breathe as she spoke. 'Do something better with your life…become something…a doctor or a lawyer…don't do this…'

'I promise.' He picked up her bloodstained hand and squeezed it tight. An understanding passed between them as he looked into her eyes. Dark European eyes like his own. He put his arms around her and snuggled into the warmth of her body, now understanding it would be the last time. He did not break eye contact as the tears came, rolling silently down his cheeks. 'I love you, Mum.'

A brief smile crossed her face. 'I love you too, Angelo.' Her eyes became glassy as she left him, sitting on the street, alone.

A siren sounded in the distance. Angelo got up then started running, and he didn't stop running for many years.

Angelo never forgot his promise to his mother. He vowed that one day he would keep it, but for now the swindles he had learnt from his Australian father were enough to keep him alive on the streets. If good for nothing else, at least his lowlife father had given him that.

Angelo knew he had been cast from a mould of strength – streetwise and savvy were the genes that coursed his body. He was determined to keep that promise he made to his mother as she lay dying in the street many years before. He had been prepared to use whatever means and manipulation were available to him no matter who he had to step on to get to the top, but he had not made it without some assistance. There were debts to pay for his success.

In his late teens, Angelo had left Sydney then headed for Queensland's Gold Coast. A tourist Mecca, with its skyscrapers overlooking long sandy beaches, the suburb of Surfers Paradise attracted shoppers and gamblers from all over the world. Many came from nearby Asian countries with fistfuls of cash but only a basic knowledge of the English language. Opportunities abounded for making a quick buck so it wasn't long before he became known to the local crime syndicate; the original Italian mob with their age old codes. Not those Russians that had taken over the Coast lately with their shaky ethics or the bikie gangs that had moved into organized crime. Lured by the easy money into a web of even greater deceit and corruption, he also learnt of the pleasures that money could bring. It was a world far away from the one he had known previously in Sydney.

Taken under their wing, the Italian mob had been happy to cushion his way into the medical profession, and he had been happy to accept their assistance. In the early days, he deluded himself that this was his escape. He had pursued his career in a specialist cardiac hospital in the State's capital, and now headed up the cardiac unit in a one of the Gold Coast's private hospitals. He should have known better. He had become an Associate of the mob and from that there was no escape.

Inevitably, the calls had come. Infrequent at first, they had been simple requests for medical assistance to members of the mob and their families. That was just the warm up for an ongoing demand for medical attention that went unrecorded over the years. He placated himself with the assurance he was still keeping his promise to his mother while his building reputation satisfied his egotistical nature. Who was he to question what a life was worth? When that didn't work, the rewards were more than ample to ease any slight sense of conscience he might feel.

Lately however, there had been talk even *his* liberal conscience found difficult to accept. One of the mob's Associate doctors was of retirement age. Rumour suggested they had chosen Angelo Morley to succeed him. Besides those irregular calls, he had pretty much forged his own career path. If the rumours were true, the choice would not be his to make. It was a risky role to take on. Some of the doctor's patients weren't meant to make it out of the hospital alive. He did not relish being bonded to the mob to such a level.

There was a faint knock on the door. He had mastered this part of the job well.

'Come in, Mrs Dawson. Please, take a seat.'

The elderly woman sighed heavily as she fell into the chair. 'I've just come from the chapel. The pastor is coming over.' All sign of strength she displayed when Angelo saw her the day before seemed drained from her. Her swollen eyes bore witness to her sorrow.

She fixed him with a trusting stare. 'Did he feel anything, Dr Morley?'

'No, Mrs Dawson. Your husband went peacefully in his sleep. I'm afraid the damage to his heart this time was far too great for us to overcome. Sometimes God has his own plans for his beloved children.'

'I'm sure you did everything in your power, Dr Morley, and I shall pray for your soul.' She managed a weak smile.

He returned the smile with a practiced one of his own. He laughed somewhat bitterly to himself. Should he tell her his soul was beyond redemption?

'There are just some formalities, Mrs Dawson then I will take you to see him.'

After she had signed the necessary paperwork, Dr Morley put his arms around the fragile woman then supported her down the hall. Her husband lay in his hospital bed looking as if he were peacefully sleeping. The sheets were crisp and fresh. A nurse had placed a scented red rose beside his head on the pillow. The family pastor already held vigil at the bedside. He held out his hand, guiding Mrs Dawson to join him.

Dr Morley dutifully delivered the widow into her pastor's care then gently closed the door to allow them to say their goodbyes privately.

He ambled back down the hall, closed his own door behind him then let his head fall into his hands on the desk, the woman's grief forgotten as he contemplated his own circumstances.

At only forty-five, Angelo had achieved what many men simply dreamed. He had worked hard to achieve his reputation, so he took pleasure in the nationwide recognition he now received. He enjoyed the satisfaction of saving human lives. It made him feel like he was cheating God himself. That made up for all his misdoings and the inadequacies of his childhood. He was at the top of his profession and well respected by colleagues whom he once would have looked upon as targets. A darker side of his personality co-existed, running just beneath the surface, but he found other releases for it these days. Things best kept private, away from his public life but nonetheless funded by his success. Still, he could not bring himself to acquiesce to the mob's demands.

Angelo ran his fingers through his styled dark hair. His professional reputation was worth a substantial sum, if his insurance premiums were any indication. In moments of idleness, the calculating side of his brain had pieced together a way to cash in on that worth. The idea had risen to the surface as small ripples at first, but as his consciousness put the pieces together, it now crashed against his mind in powerful waves.

His reputation would be worth most to him if it were suddenly destroyed. Destroyed wrongfully. With someone to blame.

There were ways he could possibly achieve that medically but the idea hadn't fully taken shape in his mind until recently, by chance, he had happened upon a copy of an old woman's magazine from the eighties in one of the waiting rooms.

Normally it irked him that waiting rooms provided stale news that was years old but this particular magazine caught his attention. There was a photo of Lindy Chamberlain splashed across the front cover. The woman gained the sympathy of the world when she claimed '*A Dingo Stole My Baby*'. The investigation and subsequent court case had dragged on for years until they finally jailed Lindy for the murder of her child. The evidence was entirely circumstantial. They never found the body of her daughter, Azaria.

It was what transpired later that had set Angelo thinking. After numerous appeals, the courts exonerated Lindy Chamberlain of the crime. She then received a substantial seven-figure payout in compensation for her wrongful conviction and prison term. Her only claim to fame was what the media had made of her. What would the damage to the career of one of the country's top cardiac surgeons be worth? It would certainly be worth a short stint in prison. And he had devised a surefire plan to ensure the term remained as short as was necessary.

On top of the insurance money, there would be compensation. That would surely be enough to see him comfortably into old age. Even if it was not, the benefit was twofold. The destruction of his career meant the syndicate would look elsewhere to groom their Dr Death. The thought of them forcing him into that role made him squeeze his fists into a tight ball. He was not about to let himself be bonded to anyone to that degree.

He had only to bring the pieces together now. He had chosen the 'victim'. It was time to work on the lawyer. He had decided upon a woman, because it would be easier to use his charms to persuade her of his innocence. He would rather go into trial with a lawyer who believed in the cause. A lawyer who believed in her client's innocence would be more able to persuade a jury.

It would help if she were convincing in the first round of his plan. He intended to contrive watertight evidence that would convict him beyond a reasonable doubt. The best lawyers in the land could not win this case. He needed to ensure though, that she continued to believe in his cause. He would lodge at least one appeal, protesting his innocence.

When the time came, she would also need to be willing to fight to achieve the greatest compensation she could obtain for him. He could think of no better means to get a woman to do his bidding, than to make her fall hopelessly in love with him.

Angelo picked up the phone then placed a call to Ramsay & Associates. 'I'd like to make an appointment to see Charles Ramsay please,' he informed the professional-sounding receptionist.

She transferred him through to Charles's secretary. 'Good morning, Dr Morley. I understand you'd like to make an appointment with Charles. Could I ask the nature of your business?'

'I'd like to discuss the business affairs of myself and my future wife, and have wills prepared.'

'How does eleven am tomorrow sound?'

'That would be fine, thank you. Could you please let Charles know I am free for lunch?'

He hoped he would casually bump into Jade during the course of his visit. If he played his cards right, he was sure he could fabricate an excuse to have Charles invite her to lunch.

Phase two of his preparations had begun.

As Angelo drove home that evening, he grinned smugly. He was thinking about the transformation he had been able to make in Jennifer in the two short months since he had found her. The unrefined young girl he had picked up from the streets of Kings Cross was a memory of the past. She would pass very nicely as a Doctor's wife. The large rock on her finger eased her way into social circles she could never have dreamt of before. There weren't many people who could tell the difference between a diamond and the piece of glass his jeweler had masterfully crafted at his request.

Jenny stood on the front balcony of her new home and breathed in the smell of the salt air blowing in off the sea. The coastal apartment was beyond her wildest dreams, overlooking the ocean on one side, and facing toward the hinterland and mountains in the west. The breeze was a bit stiff for her liking so she moved out to the rear balcony. She liked the way the blue-green mountain summits back-dropped the tall buildings. She spread herself out on the balcony sun lounge to watch the sun set over them.

Jenny knew only that Angelo had some scam planned that included her and a lot of money. So far, she had seen more money than she had known in the whole of her life. At her disposal, she had a wardrobe of new clothes and shoes, housed in a room larger than the living room of any house she had ever lived in. Angelo had also afforded her a complete makeover; hair, skin, and even some much-needed dentistry work she just never had the money or courage to have done. The local dentist was a very affable character so Jenny had not feared him in the least.

She held up her hand to admire the sparkling diamond on her left hand. It had surely cost more than she could ever imagine. Why had the Gods decided to smile on her, Jenny Murphy? What had she done to attract such luck?

She had yet to decide what to wear tonight. Angelo had invited two of his colleagues and their wives over for a dinner party in honour of their pending nuptials. The delicious aromas wafting through the door assured her that her meal was coming along nicely while she took a break from the heat of the kitchen. Angelo would be pleased she had followed all of his instructions. She lay back and closed her eyes for a moment, the smile lingering on her face.

Angelo suddenly came through the door, interrupting the serenity. 'I've run you a bath, Jennifer. And I've picked out the black cocktail dress.'

'I thought I might wear the red dress tonight, Angelo.'

'Now Jennifer,' he patronized. 'Don't you understand? These people are very important, not to mention influential. That red dress looks stunning on you for a night out dancing, but it's not really appropriate for playing hostess to a doctor's colleagues.'

Hostess? Jenny focused on the word. She was here because of a business arrangement, but she had easily come to enjoy the lifestyle. If only she could make him feel something for her.

Try as she might, Angelo remained distant and unaffectionate. He was always polite and patient with her, but there had been nothing sexual since their initial encounter, for which he had rewarded her beyond her expectations.

'You're right, Angelo. I'm sorry.' She let him take her hand to help her up from the sun lounge. She smiled for the sake of politeness then headed into the bathroom, alone.

Half an hour later, Jenny emerged from the bedroom glowing and smelling of the expensive perfume Angelo had given her. The black dress hugged her petite frame with graceful elegance. She had pulled her hair back into a stone-studded comb that matched the swirl of diamantes on her dress. She looked like she had dressed this way all her life.

'You look lovely,' Angelo said matter-of-factly as she rejoined him in the kitchen. He had removed her rack of lamb from the oven. He began to dress the bones with paper capping. 'And this meal smells superb.'

His compliments elevated her glow. They were sincere, even if they lacked a degree of warmth. What was this man's story? Why did he lock his heart in a steel fortress, yet still manage to be so liberal in his kindness toward her? Again, she wished she could reach him.

There was a buzz at the intercom. Jenny moved to answer it.

'It's alright, I'll get it,' Angelo said as he pushed her aside.

Angelo escorted his guests onto the front balcony overlooking the ocean then offered them a glass of the vintage cabernet sauvignon he had purchased especially for the occasion.

'Ah, a good drop my man.' His colleague, Daniel Warner, patted him on the back. Angelo had spent many years studying and infiltrating this class of people. He hid his contempt behind a thinly veiled smile as he poured a little of the red wine into a glass then offered it to Daniel for approval.

Daniel swirled the wine around the glass then breathed in the perfume before tasting it. 'Mmm, absolutely superb!' He handed the glass back to Angelo who filled it. Angelo handed another glass to Daniel's wife, Marion.

Marion left the men to their own business and found her way to the kitchen of the expansive apartment, where Jenny was adding the final touches to the meal.

'Could I offer you a hand, my dear?'

Jenny had met the couple only briefly at the hospital. She felt a little inadequate in the presence of this well-refined and obviously wealthy woman. She was careful to hide her insecurity. Angelo had coached her well.

'Thank you for the offer, but everything is under control,' she replied with a warm smile.

Marion set herself down on the bar chair then placed her already empty glass on the bench. She fixed her with a suspicious stare. 'So tell me dear, how did you and Angelo meet? I have to say I never thought a woman would get the better of that man. Try as many have.'

Jenny had rehearsed the answer to this question with Angelo until she had it down to perfection. She almost believed the fabrication herself.

'Well, it's a rather amusing story. I was celebrating a friend's birthday at a restaurant on the strip. Angelo must have pushed his chair back at the precise moment the drinks waiter passed between our tables. As luck would have it, the tray was full and I ended up showered in cold alcohol and ice. Angelo was at my side apologizing and asking me if he could make it up to me by taking me out to dinner some time.'

It was not very original, but effective. She couldn't help adding her own embellishment. 'I looked into those eyes of his and I couldn't refuse. You know what I mean?'

'Of course, my dear,' Marion replied in a knowing tone while nodding her head. Her manner warmed as they chatted over the dinner preparations.

The buzzer sounded a second time. Angelo walked into the kitchen shortly after.

‘Come my darling, I want our new guests to meet you.’

In front of these people, he was a different Angelo. His public persona was much more charismatic than the private man she had come to know. He was graciously charming as he introduced Jenny to the small clique.

‘This is my lovely wife to be, Jennifer. The one lady who was able to steal my heart.’ He pulled her toward him then gently kissed her on the cheek.

‘Well my boy, it had to happen some time.’ Roy Chancellor slapped him playfully on the back. ‘And I can see why.’ He took Jenny’s hand and raised it to his lips, kissing it. ‘Delighted to meet you, Jennifer. I hope you know what you’re getting yourself into. If he ever does you wrong, you just come and see me.’ He winked.

His wife Lilly smacked him across the shoulder. ‘Leave her alone, you old fool,’ she scolded lightheartedly. ‘Can’t you see they can’t keep their eyes off each other?’

Jenny laughed and played along with the charade. She had always prided herself on her ability to blend into her surroundings. She watched Angelo interacting with the group and emulated their actions and speech as he had taught her.

When he had bought her back to the Sydney apartment that first night, she could not believe her good fortune. He had asked her to stay the entire night and paid her three hundred dollars in advance. The place was tasteful yet had a comfortable feeling about it that put her at ease. She had performed the usual services, but he had not been interested in any of the more unusual sexual activities demanded by some clients such as role-playing or S & M. He had moved through the evening with an obvious degree of emotional detachment.

In the morning, she had woken to the smell of eggs and toast. He had cooked enough for the both of them, but also offered her a choice of cereal and fruit.

Jenny was ravenous, having not eaten since lunch the previous day. She accepted the eggs graciously. She was finishing off the second half of a grapefruit, when she looked up into his eyes. She got the distinct impression he was sizing her up.

After pouring her a cup of the aromatic coffee that had been percolating in the kitchen, he began to divulge the real reason he had invited her to stay the night.

Angelo began by describing the years of struggle it had taken to escape his impoverished background to advance to his reputable position. He told her that he had devised a plan that he hinted would allow him to pursue some of his more passionate dreams. This was where Jenny came in. He had a proposition to make to her. He roused her attention even more by mentioning she could live in a waterfront apartment that was even more luxurious than the one they were currently in, and told her that he would share some of the profits with her when the plan was realised.

Jenny wanted to know more about his plan, but he told her he could not yet be sure she was the one for the job. He would reveal the rest when the time was right. What he was willing to reveal was that he would need Jenny to pose as his wife. Because of his very public profile, she needed to be willing to commit herself for possibly a year. Publicly, they needed to develop their relationship in a plausible manner. That way he could carry out his plan with the least suspicion.

Angelo had questioned Jenny at length about her background. She had assured him there was nobody she was acquainted with in Queensland. She had long ago lost touch with her family. Her stepfather had shown more than a fatherly affection toward her. Her mother had chosen to believe him over her own daughter, and then banished her from the house. She had no desire to rekindle any of those troubled relationships. In short, she had nothing to lose so agreed to enter into the deal with little hesitation.

So began a new life for Jennifer Murphy, one in which she became everything she had ever envied and despised. She was street smart due to circumstance, but her true intelligence became evident as Angelo began to initiate her into his world. Jenny learned quickly under his guidance. He became her mentor - a benevolent and patient teacher. There was still something that disturbed Jenny about Dr Angelo Morley, starting with his unsettling laugh. A shadow sometimes passed over those dark eyes hinting of something more sinister. She actually knew very little about his life. Where did the performance end and reality begin?

It was almost two in the morning when Angelo finally shut the door behind the last of their guests. 'Well, that was a very successful evening,' he commended her.

Angelo had been so attentive throughout the night. She decided now was a good time to make her move. She placed her arms around his neck then gently brushed her lips against his. At first, he responded. He had consumed a fair amount of wine that evening. Not much of the expensive stuff, which he reserved for the guests, but later when they were all beyond noticing, a cheaper substitute.

She led him toward the bedroom then together they fell onto the soft divan of the king size bed they pretended to share. She hadn't expected him to give in to her advances but he was a man after all, with physical needs like other men. She was not an unattractive woman and she knew what men wanted. She started to unbutton his shirt, kissing his chest.

He responded with a hunger that she had not known existed in him. He kissed her fiercely, pinning her down to the bed by both wrists with his strong hands. She writhed beneath him and arched herself closer as her body's desire for him grew.

He suddenly sat up then pushed her away. 'Sorry, but this is not part of the plan.' He didn't sound upset but his voice was firm.

Jenny's desire was still raw and she could not hide the annoyance in her voice. 'Have it your way. But when am I going to hear more about this plan of yours?'

He reached over to switch off the light, turning away from her. She heard a low chuckle rise in his throat. 'Soon, my dear. Soon...'

FOUR

Jade tossed and turned under the bed covers. In her nightmare, she was running. A thick fog closed in around her. Its ghostly tendrils clawed at her limbs, which slowed her pace. She could hear the rasp of his breath right behind her as she fought to keep her footing in the haze. Despite the cold, she had broken into a sweat. Adrenaline coursed through her body, urging her on. Held precariously in front of her was the prey he sought. A glass bottle. Inside it, a miniature image of Jade herself, trying in vain to hold on to the glassy walls. The bottle cast a shimmering white glow that Jade struggled fiercely to protect.

Her ankle snapped as it dropped into a crack in the pavement. The bottle flew from her grasp and high into the air. As she crumbled to the ground, Jade looked up in bewilderment and fear. His rancid breath assaulted her nasal passages. She followed his gaze, a look of glee in his contorted red features.

'You will become what you are meant to be,' he chanted.

The miniature Jade screamed, as the bottle began its descent back toward the concrete pavement. The bottle smashed into slivers allowing the white glow to escape, until the consuming darkness swallowed it up.

Jade woke from the nightmare with a scream reverberating inside her head, only to realize it was hers. It exacerbated the pain that suddenly pounded against her forehead. She gingerly opened her eyes then surveyed the room. The numbers on the alarm clock where slightly blurred but she could make out the first number to be an eight. From somewhere beneath the haze, a voice registered that it was Monday morning.

'Shit!' She dragged herself out of bed, showered quickly, threw on some clothes then ran out the door.

When she arrived at her office, Danni, her personal assistant, looked at her with concern.

'Coffee?' was all Jade could manage as she made her way to the bathroom to apply her make up to try to hide some of the signs of her late night.

When she stepped back into her office Danni was waiting with a steaming cup of freshly brewed coffee. Jade sipped it graciously. She suddenly winced, screwing up her face. 'Do we have any aspirin?'

'What's going on with you?' Danni shook her head. She left the room, returning with two aspirin and a glass of water. She sat down opposite Jade and stared at her with pursed lips, still waiting for an answer. Danni was ten years Jade's junior but they had developed a close camaraderie in the years they had worked together. Danni was the mothering type, often scolding her older boss when she acted in a way she deemed inappropriate. But her face held more than a scolding look. Danni seemed to have noticed the recent changes in her boss's behaviour.

Jade looked down, staring at the small white tablets between her fingers. 'Do you know there is no such colour as white? White is actually a combination of all the colours of the spectrum. And black is an absence of all colour…the absence of light.' Jade looked up again, and seeing the confused look on Danni's face said, 'Forget it. Just a strange dream I had last night.'

'No wonder you had strange dreams last night,' Danni chided. 'The amount of alcohol you put away!'

Jade had persuaded Danni to accompany her on a tour of the most popular bars in town. After Danni's insistent urges to end the night had little effect, she had left Jade to her own devices.

'I'm just glad to see you're still alive!' She shook her head cynically. 'Who are you? Where is Jade? And what have you done with her body?'

Jade could see that Danni looked genuinely concerned but she was barely listening to her well-meaning friend. She was still musing over the meaning of her dream. It wasn't always the same, but he was always there. A Hollywood-like image of Satan. And always the same incessant chant. 'You will become what you are meant to be.' What did that mean? What was she meant to be? Bad?

That didn't sound like the woman she thought she was. But was she who she thought she was? She tried to remember a time the feeling had not been there, that underlying attraction for danger and excitement. While her sister was at home playing dolls, she was out on the streets with the local boys carrying out challenging dares and playing practical jokes on the neighbors. She had always felt drawn in part toward the illegal and the illicit. It was strange she had chosen a career leaning toward the upholding of the law.

Her reverie had transported her back to her seventeenth year. She could hear the thunder of the engines. The crowd strained to see past the acrid smoke as the tyres squealed against the bitumen road. A cheer erupted from her throat as the cherry red Monaro burst ahead then crossed the makeshift finish line a quarter of a mile down the road. The piercing sound of sirens cutting the night air sent the crowd scrambling for the nearest car. They tried in vain to make it down the narrow stretch of road before the roadblock was set up.

Sitting in the slow-moving line, empty bottles rattling beneath the seat, Jade felt the thrill escalate until the rhythm of her body was one with the throbbing V8 engine.

The passenger in the back seat hurled a sawn-off shotgun into the bushes, pointing. 'Remember that tree!'

The driver stopped at the roadblock not far down the road. He scowled at the blue-clad arm handing over the ticket as the officer cited him for numerous vehicle safety violations.

Later that night, cries of rapture erupting into the night from the back seat of that same cherry red Monaro. Much later, jumping out in front of her house pumped with the adrenaline of the night. 'See you next weekend!'

Nevertheless, there she was the following Monday morning prim, responsible, with neat uniform and polished shoes. Jade led the discussion on the student representative body gaining the usual admiring looks from her teachers and peers. She played out her role with impeccable responsibility. That was the façade that Jade showed the world then, and had continued to uphold ever since.

Jade partly understood what Danni was trying to say. She could feel that darker part of herself struggling to make it to the surface. It had already begun to pervade her present life. At some recent point in time, she had begun to notice a gradual shift in her perceptions of the world around her and she was questioning her place in it. Could this be some sort of mid-life crisis? She had just reached the milestone of her thirtieth birthday. Maybe that was it, or was this something that had always been there, just waiting for an opportunity to overshadow her carefully constructed life?

There was no way to explain her feelings to Danni when she hardly understood them herself. She changed the subject. 'What's our schedule for this week, Danni?'

Her assistant began to read off the dates and times of the week's forthcoming hearings.

Jade tried to work through the briefs on her desk in preparation for an upcoming trial. She had motions to file and subpoenas to draw. Numerous volumes of relevant case law sat neglected on her desk waiting for her to research them. In its fragile state, her mind refused to concentrate on the tasks so two hours passed without her achieving much. She flicked through her morning telephone messages, thinking she might cope with returning a few of those. One in particular caught her attention:

From: Detective Brent Hunter
Time: 8.30am
Message: Please return call

As she had done several times in the last week, she screwed the message into a tight ball then dropped it into her waste paper basket.

When Charles appeared in the frame of her doorway asking her if she would like to join him and a client for lunch, she did not hesitate to accept.

After his meeting with Charles, Angelo had used the excuse that he had to retrieve his beeper from the car so he could meet them at the nearby restaurant for lunch. Charles was very protective of his protégé. Angelo smirked as he recalled their earlier conversation. Angelo had simply mentioned to Charles he would like to get to know Jade better.

'What about What's Her Name?' Charles had asked, referring to Jennifer and not bothering to hide his disapproval.

'She's no Jade Sheffield, Charles. I think you know that. I can't explain it. From the moment I laid eyes on Jade, I just knew I had to get to know her.'

Angelo knew Charles well enough to know that he felt a fatherly protection toward Jade. He would need to tread carefully. But even Charles would have to admit that she couldn't have asked for more than what he had to offer. Angelo knew that Charles liked and respected him and would speak highly of him to Jade.

'Who knows? Maybe What's Her Name,' Angelo had repeated Charles's phrase mockingly, 'isn't the one after all? You won't tell Jade about Jennifer yet, will you?'

'If that's the way you want it.'

'For now. When the time is right, I will tell her myself,' Angelo promised.

'Well my man, you're playing with fire. If either one of them finds out, I wouldn't want to be in your shoes.'

'Come on Charles. All I'm going to do is meet her. What happens from there is in fate's hands.'

Angelo didn't really believe in fate, but saying it had seemed to satisfy Charles that his intentions were sincere. He intended to make his own fate. Before long, Jade would be under his spell. He would have to try hard to keep his anger in check. He wanted her to see the warm and charming Angelo, the one he knew she would come to love in a very short time. All those scams on the street had certainly honed his acting skills. He had no doubt he could be the man she wanted, or at least the one she thought she did.

Charles and Jade had chosen a table in the open alfresco section on the balcony. The restaurant was not yet busy. It looked out over The Spit, a sand formation separating the Southport Broadwater from the Pacific Ocean. They had a view of the rollercoaster and swinging pirate ship in operation at the Seaworld theme park located at the tip of The Spit. Every so often, a flame shot into the air from the man-made volcano then disappeared leaving a hint of black smoke in the otherwise cloudless blue sky. A yacht sailed leisurely across the Broadwater, reminding Jade of earlier days when her father had taught her to sail out on Moreton Bay. How many years had it been since she had been at the helm of a yacht? She let her mind go blank as it followed the yacht's languid journey across the calm water.

Angelo waited until his two hosts had sat down before making his entrance. He caught Charles's attention from across the room so Charles would point him out to Jade. That way Jade would be watching him on his approach to the table. He was a striking figure in his black Armani suit, which complimented his olive skin perfectly. He wore his hair short and styled with hair product, which highlighted the sharp angles of his Southern European face.

Angelo greeted Charles then smiled warmly at Jade.

'I'd like you to meet our star junior partner, Jade Sheffield.' Charles beamed with pride.

'Oh Charles!' Jade scolded as she rose to shake Angelo's hand. His grasp was warm and firm.

Charles continued the introduction. 'Jade, Dr Angelo Morley.'

'It's a pleasure to meet you, Miss Sheffield. Charles has told me so much about you.'

'Nothing too bad I trust,' Jade laughed.

Angelo winked at her. 'Not that I would care to repeat,'

Jade found it difficult to look directly into Angelo's eyes. They were dark ebony in colour, shining and obsidian. She could feel their intense energy reaching somewhere deep within her, piercing her very soul. It was an unnerving sensation.

The shrill sound of Angelo's beeper interrupted their introductions. He politely excused himself to make a call to the hospital.

Jade couldn't hear what Angelo was saying, but she could tell by his tone he was not happy with the person on the other end of the line. His features were concentrated into an angry frown as he spoke into the phone.

By the time he returned to the table he had regained his composure. 'My sincerest apologies, but there's an emergency back at the hospital.'

Jade raised her eyebrows. 'Occupational hazard?'

'I'm afraid so. It has been so very lovely to meet you, Jade. Next time perhaps.' He looked deeply into her eyes again as he kissed her hand, making a hasty yet gracious exit. She had seen something else in his eyes this time. A boyish eagerness she found oddly appealing.

Jade pondered his departing comment as she watched him leave. Next time? Something about this man intrigued Jade, but there was still something strangely unsettling about him. She suddenly realized she had been holding her breath. She took a gulp of air and turned her attention to Charles.

'So who was that man?'

Charles chuckled. He gave her a brief synopsis of Dr Angelo Morley, neglecting any mention of his upcoming marriage.

She was satisfied. In fact, she was now even impressed. She was looking forward to 'next time'.

'Well I guess it's just us then,' Jade smiled. She was feeling much better now she was out in the fresh air. 'Shall we order?'

Angelo brought the Saab to a screeching halt as the car in front of him stopped at the amber light. *No bloody judgment!* Both cars could have easily made it through the intersection before the light turned red. He'd almost run right into the back of her.

'Fucking idiot!' he screamed out the window, shaking his fist. A nearby pedestrian fixed him with an empathetic stare then looked quickly down and continued on his way.

His mounting anger distracted him. He was irate that someone had seen fit to thwart his plans. He had intended to unveil some of his practiced charm that afternoon on Jade. He wanted her to be totally under his control by the time they discovered his crime. Why did they need *him* in emergency? He mostly consulted these days. He still performed difficult surgical procedures when necessary, but he scheduled those well in advance. Where were the rostered ER doctors? Someone would pay for this interruption. He'd make sure of it!

He put his foot down then swerved around the vehicle in front of him as it took off slowly from the lights. He didn't care about the affront on the elderly woman's face as she took in the meaning of his hand gesture. For good measure, he blew his horn in a long drawn out complaint then sped down the road towards the hospital.

From somewhere underneath his anger, he managed a sly chuckle. The afternoon had not been a complete write-off. He had at least established contact, which gave him an opening to pursue the relationship. He was sure he had caught a flicker of anticipation in Jade's eyes with his departing comment. Perhaps his effort that afternoon had intrigued her enough to get her to accept a dinner invitation. Then he could work on her further, and alone.

Angelo launched the Saab down the car park ramp then angled it into his reserved car space. As he headed for the emergency department, the hospital Director jumped out of a doorway then ushered him into a vacant supply room. Angelo stared at him coldly. The man was a puny weasel with obvious connections in the right places. He'd never liked him.

'Dr Morley, I don't want to alarm you, but I want you to know who we have coming in.'

'Who? The Queen of fucking England?'

There was a grave look on his captor's face. The man was serious.

'Who is it then?'

'It's the Prime Minister. He was opening some new arts building, and he just collapsed. Right there in front of all the TV cameras. The whole bloody nation knows about it. I don't have to tell you how important it is for this hospital that we save this man.' He placed a firm hand on Angelo's shoulder.

The plastic swinging doors slammed open then two ambulance officers steered the trolley into the emergency ward, flanked by heavy-set security guards.

'Get out of my way and let me do my job, Nigel!' Angelo snarled as he shoved the hand away from his shoulder then ran after the trolley.

'Severe chest pain, radiating to the neck and left arm,' shouted one of the ambulance officers as the two men lifted the patient onto the bed. 'Some vomiting, heart rate feeble, CPR performed on the scene.' The nurses honed in, hooking the patient up to the surrounding machinery. The heart monitor began to beep in short rhythmic bursts. Angelo watched the thin line for a moment before turning back to the patient.

Angelo picked up the man's hand to check for a pulse. It was clammy and he was sweating profusely. 'Can you hear me, sir?' He spoke near to the patient's ear.

'Can you tell me where the pain is?' With effort, the man moved his hand to the left side of his chest.

'Anywhere else?'

He nodded. 'Neck, shoulders…' he gasped.

'Is the pain sharp? Dull? Any burning sensations?'

'Crushing pain…burns…' He motioned toward a region just below his sternum.

'Pulse is diminishing,' Angelo warned the team.

'Respiration failing. No recordable BP. We're losing him!' one of the nurses yelled.

The sound from the heart monitor changed to a long piercing beep as the man lost consciousness.

'Defibrillator!' Angelo shouted. 'Two hundred joules!'

He charged the paddles. 'Everybody off!' Angelo positioned them hastily over the patient's heart and sternum.

There was a crashing sound to his right as a young nurse tripped over, dropping a tray of instruments.

‘What the fuck,’ Angelo swore, as she fell into the defibrillator. It tipped toward the floor. He threw the paddles on the bed and up righted the machine just before it hit the floor.

For the second time he ordered everyone away. The man jerked from the bed as the jolts of electricity shook his body.

‘Atropine – one amp,’ Angelo ordered the nurse. She syringed the drug into his intravenous tube, but the line on the machine remained flat.

‘Again! Three sixty joules.’

Everyone moved away before the body jolted from the bed once more.

‘Adrenaline!’

As the new drug worked its way into the man’s bloodstream, the shrill beep of the heart monitor ceased. It returned to its steady rhythmic beep.

‘We have a pulse,’ the nurse reported. ‘BP returning to normal.’

Angelo took a deep breath. He watched the monitor to ensure the patient’s heart maintained its stable rhythm then turned his attention across the bed.

‘You!’ Angelo summoned the young nurse, dragging her by the arm to one side of the room. The air was dense, crackling with hostile energy. ‘Three minutes and he would have been dead!’ He shook a fist at her. ‘Where the hell did you do your training?’

‘I’m s-so sorry. It was my first cardiac…’

‘Sorry isn’t good enough when you are dealing with someone’s life. I’ll be filing a report. If I have anything to do with it, it will be your last!’

The young nurse turned toward her senior as tears formed in her eyes. The older woman nodded toward the door. She ran from the room.

Angelo glared at the remaining people in the room. Nobody dared utter a word. They knew better. They went about their routine in an efficient manner. They had the patient ready for transfer to the Intensive Cardiac Care Unit within a few minutes.

Angelo followed his patient to the ICCU ward to settle him in. The man had still not regained consciousness, but his vital signs were good. They were yet to assess the long-term damage to his heart. He waited while the nurse administered IV fluids and he was sure the medication he'd dispensed was doing its job. It had been a while since he had dealt with an ER patient. The stress of the afternoon had taken its toll. Two security men opened the door for him, nodding their respect as he left the room. He was acutely aware of the firearms resting like sentinels at their hips. The Prime Minister was in safe hands.

The light was fading as Angelo left the building. He was expecting the calmness of dusk as the automatic doors opened. A flashbulb erupted in his face, then another. He closed his eyes to protect them against the onslaught.

A burly male reporter pushed a microphone into his face. 'Dr Morley, can you tell us how the Prime Minister is doing?' The man nudged it so close he could smell the synthetic fibres. Angelo took a moment to adjust. He hadn't expected this, but this sort of publicity was just what he needed. It could only add to his professional worth and the success of his plan.

'I am happy to report the Prime Minister's condition is still critical, but stable. We are hopeful of a full recovery.' That was as much as he was prepared to say to the general press. No doubt the hospital had organised its own press conference to report on the Prime Minister's state of health. He looked through the crowd, eyeing the logos of the various television stations on the microphones. It would be a good idea to give an exclusive interview to the kind of program that would profile him and his achievements. He finally settled upon one, the reporter a young woman whose admiration was evident on her face. He made his way through the crowd towards her.

It was time to set his plan into full steam.

FIVE

The wedding took place in a small timber chapel with beautiful stained glass windows and a traditional bell in the spire. When Angelo had first showed Jenny a photograph of it she was delighted. It was the most romantic thing she had ever seen. It sat nestled into the side of a hill overlooking mountainous rainforest, which extended as far as the eye could see.

Angelo had chosen the church for two reasons. Set in the Gold Coast hinterland, it was well away from the prying eyes of any curious onlookers who might recognize him from the recent publicity. He had managed to keep the details of the wedding away from public eyes and ears. The other was that its size would not accentuate the small number of guests in attendance on Jenny's side. The whole affair would be small and discreet.

Angelo had hired a husband and wife couple to play Jenny's middle-class parents. They were doing a convincing job fussing over her and introducing themselves to the other guests.

Jenny sat in the dressing room, trying to recognize the girl who stared back at her in the mirror. She saw an attractive woman wearing a wedding gown of pure white satin with a myriad of pearlescent beads trailing up the bodice and over each shoulder. It was every girl's fairytale dream. And that was all it was, she had to remind herself. A dream. She tried to imagine ahead to their wedding night but the scenario in her head was blank. They had the honeymoon suite booked in the Sheraton Mirage on the Gold Coast. The hotel sat tucked amongst landscaped gardens, which led to its own private beach where guests could frolic in the sun and sand without the fear of being overrun by other tourists. She supposed that might be the only fun and frolic they would be doing during their stay.

Angelo poked his head into the room. 'Shoo! Shoo!' Jenny's stand-in mother chased him from the room. 'Don't you know its bad luck to see the bride before the wedding?'

Angelo chuckled for the benefit of the few guests milling around the back of the church. The woman was good at her job. He wouldn't begrudge handing over his cash. 'Just wanted to let you know we're all set to go.'

The woman stepped back into the room. 'Are you ready?' she asked Jenny with an empathetic look.

'As ready as I'll ever be!' Jenny was determined to act cheerfully. A girl could find herself easily carried away by the pomp and fluff of her wedding day. Even if this was a dream, she had the lead part, so she was going to enjoy it to the fullest. Who knew? With the money she would gain and the social contacts she had made, one day the dream just might become real.

She winked at her matron of honor, Kirsten, a young woman also hired by Angelo. She seemed nice; the kind of friend Jenny would love to have if she had any friends. Angelo had not allowed her to socialize outside his close circle of associates.

'Let's do it!' she said as Kirsten guided her towards the door.

Kirsten entered the front door of the chapel first. Jenny focused on the small of her back as she walked slowly down the aisle to the traditional wedding march. The faces in the crowd were mostly unknown to her, but even so she was only vaguely aware of them as she took her place beside the man who was soon to become her husband.

Angelo kept his eyes locked on hers during her entire walk down the aisle, his face beaming with happiness. She was sure his smile was not brought on by his future wife or her beauty. He was more likely thinking about how he was going to be a free and wealthy man in just a few short months. This was an integral step in his plan and it was all going as smoothly as he had hoped. Jennifer had become a compliant accomplice. She hoped he would keep his promise to reward her accordingly.

Jenny thought she detected a flicker of interest as Angelo took her hand in his then smiled into her eyes, but she quickly remembered her place when he squeezed her hand tightly enough to make her wince. It was his warning to her not to deviate from the plan, should she happen to get cold feet.

Jenny managed to maintain her smile throughout the ceremony and not stumble on any of her lines. As Angelo placed the plain gold band around her finger, the look in his eyes changed from one of happiness to possession. She was overcome by a sudden feeling that she was now a total prisoner of his will. Had she just sold her soul to the devil?

They left the chapel as Mr and Mrs Angelo Morley, showered by handfuls of rice and the applause of the small crowd. Jennifer's pseudo parents embraced her with the appropriate amount of joy and tears as she joined Angelo in a black limousine to make their way to the small dinner reception.

The speeches, while entirely scripted by Angelo, were heartfelt enough to move the crowd to laughter and tears. The women in the room sighed in awe as the couple took to the dance floor then gracefully waltzed their way around the room. Jenny stepped in time with Angelo just as he had taught her, fearful now of doing anything to gain his disapproval.

She moved through the rest of the night in a detached daze. Not wanting to slip up she had avoided the champagne but her mind felt numb, the build up of stress and nerves clouding her thoughts. There was cake-cutting and present-opening and conversations that she barely remembered. Suddenly, the night was over and she was kissing people, mostly unknown to her, goodbye and hopping back into the limousine.

It deposited them at their hotel and before she realized, they were standing at the door of their suite. The bellboy hovered a respectable distance behind with their bags. Angelo swung the door open then quite unexpectedly picked Jenny up. He carried her over the threshold, throwing a furtive wink back at the bellboy.

Angelo headed straight to the bar. He poured himself a long straight scotch then sat down on the sofa looking admiringly Jenny. She knew she was quite an attractive woman. It was a pity her prior occupation held such contempt for him. She had fitted in quite easily with his friends and colleagues under his careful guidance. Still, he always seemed to have a need to remind her of her place.

He patted his knee for her to join him. Jenny wasn't expecting any amorous advances, so she was sure he was just being appreciative. She sat herself upon Angelo's knee then turned to smile at him.

'Get me another drink,' he demanded as he handed her his empty glass.

Jenny obeyed, fixing him another drink the way he liked it. As she neared him with the glass, she tripped on the edge of the rug. A few drops of the amber liquid splashed across Angelo's white shirt.

'You stupid whore!' He leapt from the chair then struck her across the face with the back of his hand.

She was still reeling from the sting of the blow as he began to kiss her hungrily, tasting the blood on her lips. He bit hard on her swelling lip, then her earlobes and her throat. She cried out in shock but this only spurred him on. He ripped the wedding gown roughly from her shoulders. As the fabric tore, a cruel snicker rose from his throat. No need for sentiment. They would probably throw the gown out with tomorrow's trash. His lips moved to Jenny's breasts, teething her nipples. He bit harder, grazing his teeth brutally over the tender flesh. Again, she cried out in pain but his menacing look silenced her.

The tender and respectful man she had known was gone. In his place was a man she did not recognize. Jenny felt repeatedly violated throughout the long night. His dark desires spoke only of power and submission, as he used her body in ways that made her once again feel like the whore she had been.

Angelo finally fell into a heavy slumber beside her. Jenny slipped out from under the covers. She padded gingerly to the bathroom, closing the door behind her. She looked in the mirror then touched the bruises disfiguring her flesh. Only then did she let go the flood of tears welling inside her.

SIX

It had been a hectic week but Jade had added another coup to her lengthening slate of victories. She had been able to convince a jury to place another of her youth offenders into the 'Time Out' program. It hadn't been an easy task. She had decided not to engage counsel, but to defend him in court herself. The offender had a long history of run-ins with the law, but she had been able to use his story to gain the sympathy of the judge. Brought up in an unstable environment, with an alcoholic mother and an abusive father, he was just the kind of kid that fell through the cracks in the system and could benefit from the program. They had caught him this time in possession of a firearm.

'Why were you carrying a gun, Tim?' she had asked the boy bluntly.

'I'd heard Jimmy was comin' for me.'

'For the sake of the court, who is Jimmy?'

'One a me neighbours. He got some idea in his head I'd moved in on his territory.'

'What do you mean by 'territory'?'

'His girl.'

'And what did you think Jimmy might do to you?'

'Put a fucking bullet in my head!'

He gave his answers with a look of fear and remorse on his face as Jade had coached him to do. He had to gain the sympathy of the judge if they were to convince him to place Tim in the program rather than sentencing him to detention.

'So you only had the gun because you were afraid for your life.'

'Yeah.' His answer was short and definite.

'Would you have used it?'

'I would've threatened him with it if he came near me.'

‘But would you have fired the gun, Tim?’

‘Only if it was the only way I could’ve saved meself.’

Jade looked up at the judge, satisfied with his reaction. ‘OK Tim, thank you,’ she concluded. ‘I have no further questions, your Honour.’

‘You may step down,’ the judge informed the defendant.

Focused as she was on the outcome of her case, when it came time to deliver the closing speech Jade was unaware of the two interested parties watching on.

Detective Brent Hunter stood at the front of the crowd as Jade left the courtroom beaming. He wished he could take her in his arms and congratulate her for her excellent work. He was still completely infatuated with her, and disappointed that she continued to reject his calls.

Dr Angelo Morley lingered more stealthily at the back of the crowd. He did not want Jade to know he had been watching her. He imagined her upbringing. He saw a strong middle class family, parents who pushed her to achieve. He could see her yearning for self-reliance and her growth into the strong independent woman she was today. He congratulated himself on the excellent choice he had made. She would suit his plan perfectly.

Jade headed back to her office and worked solidly for the next few hours, still soaring on the success of her morning. It was Friday and by late afternoon she had let her mind start to wind down from the pressures of the week. She picked up the phone to call a few of her colleagues to see if they wanted to join her for an after-work drink, but placed it back in its cradle as her computer’s speaker signaled she had received email.

Opening her inbox, her heart plunged at the sight of the sender’s name – *Brent Hunter*. Without even opening the message, she hit the delete key then reached back for the phone.

Another message sounded. Jade was tempted to ignore it but it might be the important information she had been waiting for from an interstate research assistant. This time as she glanced over at the screen, she felt her heart palpitate and her mouth became dry. *Dr Angelo Morley*, the sender line read. She took a deep breath as she opened the message then laughed at herself for the irrationality of her nerves. It had been over a week since their brief encounter. In moments of idleness though, she had allowed her mind to wander back to the memory of those dark ebony eyes.

She steeled herself and opened the email, expecting he just had some business matters that needed attending to in Charles's absence. She was surprised at the light-hearted candor of his email.

Dear Miss Sheffield
Please forgive my inadequate attendance when last we met. Had I been allowed the time to consult thoroughly, I would surely have diagnosed a lively dose of conversation, accompanied by a sumptuous meal encompassing the major food groups and plentiful fluids.
I am happy to offer my services without charge to compensate for this slight transgression. I shall be more than happy to schedule an appointment for you at your earliest convenience.
I assure you my recent behavior is no reflection of my impeccable bedside manner.
Your caring physician
Dr Angelo Morley

Jade laughed out loud. His cryptic manner of asking her out was most amusing. How did she accept such an invitation? Should she try to compose something as witty?

Dear Dr Morley
I do feel an initial consultation may be in order. Since treatment may be imperative, I am available for preliminary testing this evening. Only then may we determine the need for me to judge your bedside manner.
Your trusting patient
Jade Sheffield

Jade decided to wait for a response before she asked anyone else to meet with her that evening. It was possible he would be available. Her email alarm sounded before she finished the thought.

Dear Jade
It is most fortunate that I have a spare appointment this evening at 7pm. I shall telephone you now to advise you of your preparations for your tests.
As for judgment of my bedside manner, I shall leave that out for the jury.
I remain,
Firmly yours
Dr Morley

Jade jumped as her telephone shrilled beside her. She picked it up tentatively. 'Jade Sheffield.'

'Hello Miss Sheffield. This is Dr Morley.'

So he wanted to continue the farce? Jade stifled a giggle.

'Hello Dr Morley,' she fawned. 'I am so glad you could see me so soon.'

'These things must be taken care of as quickly as possible. Now where shall I pick you up? These special kinds of tests can't be undertaken at my surgery.'

'I have some things to take care of first, so I'd prefer to meet you somewhere.'

The excuse would enable her to have a quick drink with Danni first. She wouldn't let her assistant know what she was up to, but it would help her to keep her nerves in check when she met Angelo.

'OK, seven it is. Bring along a light jacket and a hearty appetite.' He gave her the address of the restaurant.

Jade held the phone in her hand for several minutes after he rang off. *What was she doing? Well, it was too late to get out of it now. She didn't even know his number.* She dropped the headset back into its cradle as Danni poked her head through the door.

'Let's go down to the bar,' Jade said. 'I'll shout you a drink!'

By the time she was ready to leave the bar, Jade had downed three glasses of wine in quick succession. She stepped precariously into the taxi feeling slightly tipsy since she had not yet eaten. The ride took only ten minutes so the effects of the alcohol had subsided but were still enough to brace her as she stepped out onto the street.

This part of town was once a run down street of strip shopping. The relocation of the money-making property developers toward the coast had brought about a revival of the suburb. Trendy sidewalk cafes had begun to dot the landscape. This section of the street however retained its slightly derelict appearance. The shadows of the night added further to its gloom.

Stepping off the street, Jade found herself transported into another world. The restaurant was dimly lit. Flickering candlelight from each table invaded the crevices of the intricately carved beams, reflecting its warmth from the deep glowing timber. She advised the waitress of the booking. The smartly dressed woman led her through the back door. As she stepped from the room, she felt as if she had left the city altogether. The terraced garden spread over several levels, mature trees overhanging the privately placed tables. Rows of pin lights shone from the branches of the trees like a multitude of distant stars.

Another two steps down then she entered the water garden. It was a fairytale setting. A metal fountain rose from the small pond. Lights shimmered through the cascading water, which highlighted the vivid colours of the bougainvillea canopy. Tropical plants hugged the edges of the pond and a bamboo wall framed the garden separating them from the rest of the guests.

As Angelo stood to greet her, the candlelight cast long shadows that partly obscured his face. Even so, she was awed once again by the strong angle of his jawline and his dark features. A smile lit up his face as he held out his hand. She felt her skin growing warm and her pulse quickening, and blamed it on the alcoholic glow. She could only return the smile as she was once again mesmerized by his deep ebony eyes.

The waitress pulled out Jade's chair and she fell into it a little heavier than she had intended. Angelo did not break eye contact and pretended to ignore her clumsiness. She sat still for a moment, slightly embarrassed.

'I'm glad you agreed to come,' Angelo broke the silence. 'I must say that it's a pleasure to meet a mature and interesting woman. Such a rarity in this world.'

Jade felt a blush moving up her cheek. She was wary, still unsure as to what had enticed her to agree to this meeting. She was uncomfortable with the way he made her feel out of control, but the unfamiliar feeling also intrigued her. She felt the intensity of his dark eyes on her, forcing her to look coyly down at the table. Obviously sensing her discomfort, Angelo motioned for the waitress.

'Care for another drink?' he teased. The accompanying laugh was deep and throaty.

She cast him a crooked smile but still avoided his stare. 'A glass of sauv blanc would be *very* nice, thank you.'

Angelo perused the wine list then selected a wine for her. She was impressed with his choice. It seemed he had taken notice of what she was drinking when they last met. 'And another scotch on the rocks', Angelo added to the waitress as he handed over his empty glass.

In the silence that descended as they waited for their drinks, Angelo reached across the table then took hold of Jade's hands in his. She instinctively pulled away.

'Hey,' he said gently as he reached over then placed his hand on her chin, guiding her face up so he could see into her eyes. 'I really am very glad you agreed to meet me tonight. You know you are an incredibly beautiful woman.'

She tried to hide the flicker of delight in her eyes. Her embarrassment masked it for her within seconds. The waitress approached the table with their drinks and the moment was lost. She took the menu from the waitress and hid behind it on the pretence of selecting a meal. Her nerves had dampened her appetite so she ordered a salad. Angelo ordered a Mediterranean chicken dish.

The waitress returned and placed a basket of bread on the table. Angelo took a piece and waved it under her nose. 'You just have to try this herb bread. It's the most delectable thing I've ever tasted, lightly toasted to perfection...mmm.'

Its aroma was heavenly, but just as Jade went to take a bite, he snatched it away with a chuckle. She laughed too but as Angelo drew closer to her, his manner made it obvious his desire extended beyond just having dinner with her.

Jade gave him a protesting glare. After the drink, she was feeling a little more assertive. 'Would you mind not staring at me like that?'

'I'm sorry, I just can't help myself. There's just something about you.'

Jade was used to this kind of reaction from men but she was struggling to understand the reaction he was engendering in her. Although she really did not have much experience in relationships with men, she frequently stood her ground against powerful male lawyers and generally argued her piece without a qualm. Why did she feel so timid in front of this particular man? Why did she find it so difficult to bring herself to look into his eyes?

Angelo seemed so confidently forward in his intentions. She searched for a response to cover her emotions without encouraging him further. With a veiled hint of sarcasm in her voice, she said, 'You are most charming, Dr Morley.'

Angelo smiled then turned his attention to the meal that the waitress had just placed in front of him. They chatted as they ate. Angelo talked about his love of medicine, which prompted Jade to talk about how she ended up studying law. Gradually her nervous tension eased.

When they had finished the meal and a few more drinks, Angelo signalled for the bill then handed his credit card over to the waitress. She walked away with it to the cash register inside the restaurant.

'Come here,' he whispered as he drew Jade's face gently toward his then tried to kiss her. She turned her head so his kiss landed on her cheek. 'It's OK,' he coaxed as he turned her face then kissed her softly on the lips. 'Wow!' he whistled as he moved his lips away from hers.

Jade was still trying to comprehend her response to the kiss when the waitress returned with the docket and a pen. Angelo signed the chit and handed it back to the waitress, putting his credit card back into his embossed Jag wallet.

He raised his eyebrows. 'What do we do now, beautiful lady?'

She feigned innocence. 'What do you mean?' Suddenly, she found herself not wanting the night to end. She swallowed the last of her wine. 'Do you dance?'

'*Do I dance?* It's my heritage. It's in my blood. What did you have in mind?'

'We could head into the Cavill Mall and see what's happening.'

'Lead the way,' Angelo said as he stood then pulled Jade's chair out for her.

A big Russian bouncer waved them into the club. It was overflowing. The heat of the bodies aroused Jade's senses. Angelo took her hand, clearing a path before her as he led her on to the dance floor. Jade now ached to be close to him so her body gave no argument as he clasped his fingers between hers then pulled her near to him. They moulded into one as they moved slowly to the music in simultaneous rhythm. Angelo's warm breath sent shivers racing up her spine. It increased her desire and she stroked her hands up his strong arms then rested them around the nape of his neck.

In response, Angelo leant down then touched her lips ever so gently with his own. He lingered teasingly for a moment, then moved back to look deeply into her eyes. She pulled him back toward her then their lips touched once more, this time for a long and intense moment. Then he was kissing her with a fervour she had never known, tasting, teasing her with his tongue. It was a kiss that elevated her and held a promise she couldn't even begin to resist.

When he whispered in her ear, 'Let's get out of here,' Jade obediently nodded her head.

They escaped from the noise of the club, Angelo still with his arm protectively around Jade. 'I want to be with you so badly, Jade.'

'I feel the same way.'

'I'm sorry but we can't go back to my place. There is something I have to tell you.' Angelo's expression altered to one of concern and confusion. 'I'm afraid us doctors aren't known for being nice guys. I have to admit something to you. I'm married.' He didn't pause for her reaction, but quickly added, 'But there is just something so intriguing about you that I can't resist. Don't ask me to explain it, but I would really like to continue to see you.'

Angelo's pleading tone strengthened Jade. She felt she was back in power, the way she liked it. Maybe it would be fun to spend some time with this debonair and intelligent man. She wasn't looking for anything too serious anyway. He was probably just after a fling, since he did not seem like the type to commit himself to a life of serial monogamy. It was somewhat flattering to her ego to be the object of his desire. Playing the 'other woman' held a certain appeal for the sinful side of her nature. If he thought he would shock her with his confession, she was not going to give him the satisfaction. For the first time that night, she looked him directly in the eye. 'There's no-one at my place.'

Angelo did not need any further encouragement. He hailed a passing cab then pulled Jade in behind him. All the way home, he lavished compliments on her as he stroked her body and ran his hands through her long hair. Jade felt like the most desirable woman in the universe. As she basked in the warmth of Angelo's tenderness, an ardent glow lit her face. She hated not being in control, but she gave herself permission to let go. It was a new experience for her, being with a man who could stimulate her body and her mind to such a degree. She thought fleetingly of Angelo's wife then pushed the image away completely as the erogenous zones of her mind took over. She was not the one with reason to feel guilt.

As they reached the front door of Jade's apartment, she struggled to place the key in the lock in the darkness. Angelo turned her around then lifted her up against the door. Pressing hard against her, she could feel his need for her. She tried the lock again. As the key turned, the door swung open behind their weight causing them to fall to the floor. They remained there for a while, the moonlight casting a shadowy glow over them as they stripped each other of clothing.

Angelo lifted Jade from the floor then placed her upon the hard wooden dining table. Lifting her legs around his shoulders, he thrust deeply into her. Jade cried out as her perspiring body slid easily against the smooth glossy surface of the table. He carried her, still deeply impaled upon him, towards the sofa. He released her and bent her forwards over the arm of the sofa like a rag doll. She felt his strength as he continued to drive ardently into her from behind. He grabbed hold of Jade's hair then pulled her head toward him, groaning as together they reached a euphoric climax. He collapsed against her, the two of them heaving, sweating and aglow from the experience.

Finally Angelo spoke. 'I'm sorry Jade, I didn't mean for it to be this way. I just wanted you so badly I lost control.'

'I'm not sorry,' she winked.

Angelo smiled with satisfaction. He knew he was making progress. Now he had heightened her desire for him, he could begin his courting routine. He was going to pamper her as she had never known. He stroked her hair. 'Don't get me wrong. I'm not sorry we made love. It was incredible. It's just that I don't normally do this sort of thing. It would have been nice to get to know you first.'

He was certain that was something Jade was not used to hearing. He wanted to differentiate himself from the men she had known. He could already begin to feel his practiced charms taking effect.

He kissed her on the forehead. 'How about we start over? I would love to take you to a wonderful Italian restaurant I know. How would you feel about us spending the night in a luxurious hotel, where I can spoil you to death?'

'Sounds just like what the doctor ordered,' Jade murmured happily.

'Bring an overnight bag with you next Friday then. I'll pick you up from your office.'

SEVEN

The Monday morning alarm woke Jade from a pleasant dream. As she remembered Angelo's dark eyes staring into hers, a smile crossed her face. She stretched her arms over her head then felt the pleasurable sensation move slowly along her extended spine. The glow remained with her while she showered then dressed for work, and had still not left as she entered her office.

Danni sat up straight, seeming to notice the change in her employer's demeanor as Jade flitted past her desk offering a beaming smile with her usual 'Good morning'. She seemed glad to see Jade happy and not the hung over wreck she had been the previous Monday morning.

Her dreamy state lifted as she reluctantly faced the reality of the pending case files on her desk. She turned her mind to work and started to scribble notes on her yellow legal pad. The shrill ring of the phone interrupted her concentration. She picked it up with annoyance. 'Yes!'

'Miss Sheffield, there is a package at reception for you,' the receptionist announced.

'Can't you just have it sent up to me?'

'I think you might want to collect it personally.'

'Oh OK,' Jade replied. 'I'll be down in a while.'

After about fifteen minutes, Jade's curiosity got the better of her so she headed down to the reception area. As she passed one of the assistants in the hall, the girl turned to Jade. 'Wow, where do I find one like that? You lucky thing!'

'One of what?' Jade asked but the girl had already disappeared into one of the meeting rooms.

It was only a few more steps before she understood what the girl had meant. Sitting on the reception desk was a long rectangular shaped box with a huge red bow tied around it.

Through the clear plastic window on the front of the box, she could see rows of perfectly formed rosebuds.

Jade was too stunned to speak.

'They're beautiful,' the receptionist said. 'Is it a special occasion?'

'Umm, no.' Jade picked up the card and opened it discretely. She didn't want to start up the office grapevine. 'It's just a thank you from one of my client's families.'

'Oh, well that's nice.' The receptionist seemed to lose interest once she realized there was no gossip to pass on.

Jade picked up the box then headed back to her office where she could enjoy the pleasure of the gift in private.

The note read: *Dearest Jade, I hope this gift makes your heart skip a beat, as you have made mine. Until Friday, mi amore. Angelo.*

The glow that Jade had felt that morning returned. She took the lid off the box then delighted over the long-stemmed red roses, their buds lined up in four even rows. She counted across the row, one, two, three, four, five, six. Four rows. Not the traditional one dozen long-stemmed red roses, but two dozen! He certainly knew how to make a woman feel special.

Jade realized she still didn't have Angelo's number, so she sent him a brief email of thanks. An auto-reply came back saying he was out of town on business for the week. He hadn't mentioned that. Was his wife accompanying him? She checked the thought before it pitched her into trouble. What she felt was just infatuation! She had to keep her emotions under control.

She set the roses up in a vase on her side credenza then hid the card away in her drawer. Many times over that week she felt a warm glow as she glanced over to watch the delicate petals unfold. As they did, her heart began to unfold too. Her impatience to be with Angelo grew stronger as the week neared its end.

Friday evening finally arrived and Angelo picked her up as promised. She now stood behind him at the check-in desk with an unexpected mix of emotions. They hovered somewhere between anxiety and anticipation: she was anxious because she was fearful of her deepening affections but the accompanying anticipation was being fuelled by her intense desire.

Angelo was true to his word. They dined in a secluded corner of the Italian restaurant then returned to the room. He sat Jade down gently on the side of the bed. She watched him remove a bottle of red wine and two glasses from his overnight bag then carry them into the well-appointed bathroom.

Taking care to ensure the water temperature was just right, Angelo began filling the large spa bath. He dropped a generous amount of bath oil into the water. Its heady aroma quickly filled the room. While the bath filled, he lit tiny candles then placed them around the room, poured the deep coloured wine into the two glasses, then switched off the lights.

Re-entering the bedroom, Angelo held out his hand inviting Jade to join him. As she followed him into the bathroom, he kissed her gently on the lips, his mouth trailing down her throat as he slowly undressed her. She watched him draw in his breath as he took in the image of her standing naked before him, her skin glowing in the candlelight. In his gaze, she suddenly felt more attractive than she could ever remember.

Jade moved her arms around Angelo's shoulders then tried to kiss him back.

'Not yet,' Angelo coaxed as he motioned her toward the waiting tub. I am going to pamper you tonight like you would not believe.' He said it teasingly, drawing out his words. Jade felt once again lured into the depths of those dark eyes. What was it she detected there now that was so alluring? Wickedness?

Angelo held Jade's hand to steady her as she stepped into the inviting bath.

She turned her head back toward him. 'Are you going to join me?'

'Not yet, my sweet.'

Jade enjoyed the possessive sound of those words. The warm water and sumptuous oil combined with the flickering candlelight to soothe her into a state of total relaxation. Angelo handed Jade one of the glasses filled with red wine then set his own on the side of the bath. He reached down into the water to draw out one of Jade's shapely legs. He stroked her leg in a downward motion until he reached the soles of her feet.

Jade took a sip of her wine then lay her head back on a soft towel Angelo had placed on the edge of the bath. She closed her eyes, enjoying the sensation of Angelo's touch. He began to knead the soles of her feet. Whatever tension remained in her body slowly subsided. By the time he reached for the other leg, Jade felt so calm she could have drifted into a peaceful sleep.

How long had she been lying like that? She stole a peek from underneath her eyelids. She was surprised to see that Angelo appeared to be enjoying the sensation as much as she was. He had begun a low satisfied moaning as his fingers slowly worked their way back up her legs then gently along her silken thighs. She gasped as they found their final target.

As Jade yielded to the pleasure of Angelo's touch, she felt a wave of euphoria sweep over her. The hours that followed would remain forever in her mind, haunting her in her darkest moments. He was an artful lover but it was much more than the pleasure he brought to her body that seduced Jade completely. She felt an indefinable connection unlike anything she had known. It surged through her body, welling in her mind until she was sure their very souls entwined. She could no longer sense where her body ended and his began. She felt she had known Angelo for a lifetime, maybe even longer. Was this what it felt like to find your soulmate? She had never really believed in it but for the first time in her life, she had to consider the possibility. It was a feeling she was both unable and unwilling to deny.

Later, as they lay satiated in bed, Angelo stroked Jade's hair and whispered soothingly until her calm breathing told him she had drifted into sleep. He could not take his eyes away from her. He was aware that during the time he had been following Jade he had developed a deep admiration for her, but the realisation dawned slowly as he looked into her serene face.

He was becoming obsessed with her.

He had not planned for this development, but it was a twist that he could build into his plan. After all, he was seeking a more fulfilling existence. He had never really known what love for a woman was, except for the dutiful love he had felt for his mother. Everything Angelo did was a means to an end. Including Jade more permanently in his life may just bring him the fulfilment he ultimately sought.

Angelo drifted into a dream where he and Jade were walking hand in hand along an endless beach. The vividly shining moon slowly disappeared until there was only darkness.

EIGHT

Angelo was enjoying the game and the way he could manipulate people's emotions. It was three weeks since he had set his plan in motion and things were progressing just as he knew they would. It had not been as hard to work Jade out as he had imagined. He often sent her text messages and had set up a few lunchtime rendezvous to maintain her interest, as well as taking her out to dinner on several occasions. He had arranged to meet her the previous day but had cancelled at the last minute citing his wife had unexpectedly turned up at work to surprise him for lunch. There was no lunch with his wife. But there was nothing better to make someone realise how they felt than to introduce a bit of competition. A bit of jealousy would act like a red flag and serve to spice things up a bit. It was a bit of a gamble. Knowing her as he did, standing her up could either piss her off or make her want him more. He suspected the latter would be the case however based on her reactions to date. He had, of course, promised to make it up to her.

In keeping with that promise, he picked up the phone then dialled Jennifer at home. 'I need you to go away for the weekend,' he demanded without even greeting her.

'Go away where?'

His voice softened. 'Where would you like to go? How about Byron Bay? I'll book you into a nice comfortable hotel then you can spend some time relaxing in the sun.'

He knew Jenny was wise enough not to ask questions. She had become accustomed to following his orders.

'Sounds delightful!' She sounded like she meant it. She was probably getting bored hanging around the apartment waiting for him to come home from work. He was keeping her on a short tether since he had decided to set things in motion.

Angelo made the bookings then dialled Jade's office number. He smiled as he spoke, a trick he had learnt made his voice sound more sincere. 'Hi Sweetheart.'

'Hi Angelo.' She sounded very happy to hear his voice. His previous day's endeavour had obviously worked.

'I have some good news for you, Baby.' He paused to build suspense. 'My wife is going to be out of town for the weekend. How would you like to come over and spend the whole weekend with me?'

Jade did not respond immediately but he could hear the change in her breathing.

'Really? I could spend the whole weekend with you at *your* place?'

'I couldn't think of any other way I'd rather spend it than with you snuggled beside me.'

'Oh Angelo, that would be just wonderful!'

Jade woke the next morning in Angelo's bed to the smell of frying omelette. The night had been amazing. She still could not believe he had invited her into his home and his life. Even if it was only for a weekend, she was going to enjoy it to the fullest. She had a contented smile on her face as Angelo popped his head around the door.

'Good morning Sleeping Beauty,' he greeted her with a wide grin.

Her heart glowed warmly in her chest and the glow radiated up to her face. 'Good morning. What smells so delicious?'

'Room service,' he replied as he revealed the tray he had been hiding behind the door laden with freshly squeezed orange juice, toast and jams. He placed it on the bed beside her. 'Help yourself, I'll be right back.'

A few seconds later, he returned with a pot of coffee and two plates with the delicious-smelling omelette that had woken her, topped with sautéed mushrooms and parmesan cheese.

As Jade sat up, Angelo handed her a soft fluffy robe to put on. 'Don't worry,' he said as she looked at him questioningly. 'I bought it especially for you.'

She smiled once again. 'I also got you a toothbrush,' he winked.

Jade thought the omelette was the most delectable thing she had ever tasted, but she was sure her delirious state of mind was contributing to her enjoyment. She still could not believe she was here with Angelo and they still had another two full days ahead of them to spend together. She almost had to pinch herself to believe it was real. She could not let herself be too carried away. The day after, his wife would be here in her place once again. But for now, she felt as if she was walking on air and nothing was going to bring her down from the cloud she was on.

Angelo and Jade spent another few hours together in bed making love and talking then he suddenly jumped up. 'I have an idea! Let's go shopping.'

'Shopping?' She squinted at him as if he was suddenly alien to her.

'I need to get some new business shirts. I'd love you to help me pick them out. You have such incredibly good taste.'

The glow in her chest returned.

It turned out Angelo had very good taste even without her help. They stood in an exclusive men's store in the Cavill Mall. The sales clerk was fussing about trying his hardest to please them. He brought two shirts he had selected then held them up in front of Angelo awaiting his opinion. Angelo pointed in Jade's direction then gestured that he should present them to her instead.

'What do you think, Sweetheart?'

Jade felt herself glow once again under his public endearment. 'I prefer the blue one.'

'I'll take it!' Angelo told the sales clerk.

'Don't you want to try it on Sir?'

'No, I trust the lady's taste.' He smiled lovingly at Jade. She returned the smile, now comfortable looking into his eyes.

Angelo pulled a hideously colourful shirt from another rack. 'What do you think of this one?'

Jade screwed up her nose. 'Well…'

'Come on, tell the truth. You hate it, don't you?'

'Well, I don't think it would be complimentary to your colouring,' she replied trying to be tactful. 'But if you like it, try it on. I could be wrong.'

'I don't think you could ever be wrong my sweet.' He put it back on the rack then tickled her playfully in the ribs.

'You pick one.'

The sales clerk looked on with despondence, seemingly obsolete as Jade selected a grey shirt flecked with black. 'I think this one would set off your eyes.'

'Wow!' Angelo exclaimed. 'You are so perceptive. I love it!'

He held the shirt up against his chest so she could see how it looked. 'How about *we* try them on?' He winked at the sales clerk.

They were the only customers in the shop. The sales clerk moved discretely away and headed towards the checkout as they both entered the fitting room.

The room was fitted with a three-way mirror. Angelo twirled Jade in a circle so he could look at her from every angle. Then he held her in front of him. They both looked at each other in the mirror. 'Looks like a perfect fit to me,' he said as he turned her again. 'You know I just wanted to get you in private so I could do this.' He kissed her slowly at first, then more passionately. He broke away from the kiss suddenly.

'We better get out of here before I get too carried away,' he laughed. 'How about we go have some lunch?'

Jade followed him sheepishly from the fitting rooms, flattening her hair on the way to the sales counter. She avoided eye contact with the sales clerk as Angelo handed over his gold credit card.

'Thank you for your business Sir,' the sales clerk said as he handed back the card with a slighted look.

They wandered down the mall and decided on some take away fish and chips for lunch. They found a shady spot overlooking the glorious white sand beach and spread out the white paper that held their feast. Tourists with colourful towels and beach umbrellas dotted the white strip and surfers bobbed up and down on the waves paying homage to the name of the suburb, Surfers

Paradise. A few pesky seagulls dropped beside them and squawked for food. Jade made the mistake of throwing them a chip and within seconds, a noisy flock had surrounded them. She threw them some more chips and they both laughed as they watched a sea of grey and white feathers scrabbled for the few precious pieces as if they were playing a game akin to musical chairs.

Lunch extended into dinner as they moved on to a beachfront cafe. The surf continued to pound the beach as they sat overlooking the now moonlit waves. They could just make out a dark shape in the distance, a bulk carrier making its way south down the shipping channel. By the time Angelo and Jade arrived back at his apartment, they had consumed several bottles of good wine. They fell into bed laughing then spent the night sleeping in each other's arms.

They spent Sunday lazing in bed with the morning newspapers then relaxing the afternoon away on the balcony with more wine and conversation. Angelo had certainly succeeded in his plan to move things up a notch by asking Jade to accompany him on the shopping trip to help him choose new clothing. He had observed as her feminine instincts took over. He knew he was pressing all the right buttons. That morning Jade had been the one to cook breakfast. As she made herself at home in his kitchen he made sure he played the role of the dutiful husband. Charming the ladies was not a skill Angelo had learnt from his crooked father, but he had helped to lay the foundations. The look in his eyes, his smile, his charming voice; they were all skills he had honed since his childhood.

By the end of the day, Jade found it difficult to pull herself away. She had thoroughly enjoyed the weekend and the time she had spent with Angelo. But she knew that for now, their brief game of playing house was over.

NINE

An article titled *Searching and Examining the Crime Scene* was holding Angelo's interest. He was doing some final research while reflecting on his preparations. Things were still moving along nicely with Jade. He had been handling her with care for the past five weeks and now had her just where he wanted. She seemed completely smitten with him just as he had planned. Although he had not mentioned the *love* word or given her any false hope, he had increased the intensity of their relationship over the last few weeks. He had continued to compliment her on her taste after the shopping trip, which led into his more recent suggestion that she help him with the re-decorating of his apartment. He purposefully dropped a few hints that might lead her to believe he could possibly leave his wife and there could be a future to their relationship. He had, however, continued to ask for her discretion so he was sure nobody knew about their liaisons.

He directed his concentration back to the article. A quote by Paul Kirk had caught his attention. *'This is evidence that does not forget. It is not confused by the excitement of the moment. It is not absent because human witnesses are, it is factual evidence, physical evidence cannot be wrong, it cannot perjure itself...only its interpretation can err.'*

That was exactly what he was counting on! He would stage the apartment to look like he had murdered Jenny there. The evidence had to be convincing enough for the jury to believe 'beyond a reasonable doubt' that he had killed her without the recovery of her body. Since he was a doctor with comprehensive medical knowledge, it would also have to appear that he had at least tried to be clever enough to attempt to cover his tracks.

The article was helping in that respect. It had a comprehensive list of evidence forensics could search for besides the obvious blood and fingerprint tests: lingering smells; signs of activity – food, glasses, ashtrays; signs of struggle; hiding places for weapons; evidence of clean up – damp towels, bloodstains, contents of bins; entry methods; etc. The list provided a veritable feast of possibilities from which to choose.

He looked around for a feasible murder weapon. Something within easy reach but solid enough to strike a fatal blow. He smiled as he remembered a story he once read about a woman who had struck her husband with a frozen leg of lamb then cooked it up and fed it to the unsuspecting police officers.

Ironic as the story was, his weapon must be much more obvious and capable of easy discovery; something people were familiar with seeing in his home. His eyes settled upon his trophy collection leftover from his sailing days. The solid pewter cup, awarded for the prestigious Sydney to Gladstone race, sat atop its heavy wooden base on the sideboard, taking pride of place amongst the crystal glassware. It was perfect, heavy with a few sharp edges that could cause enough damage if struck against the tender parts of the head. Plenty of people could attest to the fact it always sat there, within easy reach.

Jenny had just wandered into the living room from the balcony. She was as ready as she would ever be. He looked over at her with approval.

'It's time,' he said enthusiastically. 'I'm going to share my plan with you. I think you are ready. Sit down.' He motioned to the seat in front of him.

Jenny was a little apprehensive now the moment had arrived. She had begun to appreciate the status quo of her fabricated life. She looked into Angelo's eyes with a mixture of anticipation and disappointment.

'It's simple,' Angelo said, screwing his face into a sinister glare. 'I want to kill you!'

For a moment fear registered on Jenny's face. The wry chuckle that followed Angelo's declaration quashed her doubts. It was just part of the game.

‘Go on,’ she coaxed.

‘Well I’m not really going to kill you,’ Angelo admitted smugly. ‘We are going to fake your death then make it look like I killed you.’

‘You want it to look like you killed me?’ Jenny asked in surprise. ‘Whatever for? Won’t that void the insurance policy?’

Just the previous week, Angelo had taken her to sign a valuable life insurance policy listing him as the beneficiary upon her death. She had imagined the benefit had something to do with his plan.

‘The insurance policy was just part of the damning evidence, my dear.’

‘And what about a body?’

‘I intend there to be convincing evidence that not only were you killed, but at the hands of your insanely jealous husband. A crime of passion as you might have it. There will be no need for anyone to recover the body. I’m sorry I will have to paint you as the harlot, but that shouldn’t be a problem for you.’

It was a low blow but it would serve to remind Jenny of her real place in this charade.

‘Go on,’ she repeated, seeming to check her initial anger.

He had noticed she had been more guarded since their wedding night but he had been cautious about going near her in that way again. He had not apologised but had tried to act as if he was remorseful that the whole incident took place, reverting in the main to his former self. He was careful to keep the abusive man she had discovered hidden away. Nevertheless, Jenny no longer seemed to trust him with the naivety she first had.

She nonetheless listened carefully as he unveiled his plan and the details of how she would suddenly re-appear after her ‘death’, allowing him to make a claim for compensation for false imprisonment and damage to his professional reputation.

‘I’ll give you enough money to set yourself up somewhere up in North Queensland. It’ll have to be somewhere remote from Brisbane so it will seem reasonable that you didn’t see or hear anything about the case. You can just pretend that you moved on and you didn’t want me to know where you’d gone. That will explain why I won't be able to find you to prove my innocence.' He paused, reflective for a moment. 'Maybe somewhere classy, like Port Douglas. A tourist town where they have their own local news and it's all good community related stuff.'

Jenny nodded, caught up in his escalating excitement.

'We'll have to be careful you're not traced. I'll organise you a new name and I.D. to use. I have contacts that can do that easily enough. It will be like you just disappeared.'

'It seems like you've thought it all through pretty carefully,' Jenny said. 'But how will I know when to come back?'

'You can write to me in prison under a pseudonym name then when the time is right we'll plan your reappearance. Can you imagine the publicity something like this will attract? There will probably even be a tidy sum in it for you to tell your own story to the newspapers.'

Angelo was very impressed with his brainchild and he felt that Jenny was intrigued and a little impressed herself. The fact he was prepared to make the sacrifice to spend time in prison proved just how serious he was.

'I'm going to need to take some more blood,' he said.

Angelo had been taking blood from Jenny over the past months to freeze. Until now, Jenny had not seemed game enough to ask why. Now she posed the question.

'We'll need some for the apartment and the car,' Angelo said, 'but I also need to submit some for a little test.'

He needed to establish a plausible motive, one that could conceivably drive a man to commit the crime he intended to stage. Angelo had a vasectomy performed many years back knowing that there were women out there who were only interested in his money and reputation. He would not allow any money-grabbing female to trap him. This now gave him a perfect motive for his crime. If a man were to discover his wife was pregnant, what would be his likely reaction when there was no possible way the child could be his?

He would have the test results faked then placed on her file the morning of the murder. Angelo had befriended a colleague in Pathology who he had persuaded to participate in a few of his midnight S & M and ménage a trios sessions, though on reflection it hadn't taken a lot of persuasion. He had taken photographs that he intended to use if he needed to hold the man over a barrel. With a wife and his first baby on the way however, Angelo was sure the man would be willing to grant him the favour he needed if he merely leant on him a little.

If he timed it right, the police forensics team would then also have a sample of Jenny's blood to compare to the blood they would find in his apartment and car.

'What kind of test?' Jenny asked.

He laughed hoarsely. 'Congratulations, my dear. You're pregnant.'

Jenny was looking down at the appointment card beside her on the passenger seat of the car. *Dr Nicholas Payne, Obstetrician.* It seemed a rather amusing and frightening name for someone in such a profession. Smirking, she tried to recall the details as Angelo had instructed. Her last period was six weeks ago. She had begun to experience bouts of dizziness and nausea. Nothing to it really, the lies had become second nature to her.

She picked up the card then headed into the surgery. The receptionist gave her a warm smile as she checked the details on the card with those on her computer screen.

'Do we have a wee specimen today?' she asked in a voice that sounded as if she were speaking to a small child.

Jenny gave her a bemused look and shook her head. The receptionist handed her a small clear specimen jar.

She pointed down the hall. 'The ladies room is that way. We just need a sample from the middle of your stream.'

Jenny took the bottle then self-consciously made her way to the bathroom. She felt all eyes in the waiting room watching her. She had heard there was little dignity in pregnancy.

On her return, she handed the jar to the receptionist then took a seat among the group of women in varying stages of pregnancy. She watched a small toddler playing in the corner, rushing back and forth to show his mother each new discovery from the toy box. What would it feel like if this were real?

Eventually the receptionist called her name. She had been waiting almost an hour. It was lucky the woman had requested that 'specimen'.

'Mrs Morley,' Dr Payne welcomed her. 'I'm so happy to finally meet you. Angelo has spoken so often of you.'

Jenny smiled back then answered the doctor's questions precisely as Angelo had instructed. The doctor moved to the cabinet above the sink then removed a bottle of tape strips. He unscrewed the jar, placed one into the urine sample then came back to his seat.

'Won't be long now.'

Jenny knew what the result would show. When the doctor lifted the tape out of the jar, he flashed it toward Jenny. 'Negative, but given it's still early days this is inconclusive. I'll organise a blood test then we'll know for sure.'

This was exactly what Angelo had wanted. Jenny had not even had to make the request.

'Have you been immunised for Rubella?' the doctor queried as he typed out the pathology request.

Jade nodded her head in the affirmative. 'I think they did that one at school.'

'Have you ever had a test for HIV?' He saw the concerned look on Jenny's face then added, 'Don't worry, it's just a routine test we perform for all pregnant women these days.' He paused to let the information sink in, but when she still had not answered he continued. 'Well, I'll order those while we're at it. No point in having to go back again. They will show us your immunity to the Rubella, which can have harmful effects on the baby if you contract it while pregnant. The pathology is just next door,' he said as he typed information into the computer. A request slip printed out next to him and he handed it to her. 'If you are able to do this now, then the test results should be available by tomorrow or the day after. Just give me a call and I'm happy to let you know over the phone. Then if the result is positive, we can schedule some more appointments from there.'

'Thank you Dr Payne.' Jenny feigned a smile of happiness as she stood to shake his hand. 'I'll be in touch. One more thing, could you not mention this to Angelo? We haven't been married long so I'm not sure how he'll react. I'd like to break the news to him in my own time.'

'Of course,' Doctor Payne replied showing her to the door.

Jenny walked next door to the pathology where thankfully there was no line up. Her patience was wearing thin after the time she had spent waiting in the surgery. Thank God she wasn't really pregnant so she didn't have to go through that again!

Jenny was no stranger to needles, but by the time the kindly nurse had taken three vials of her blood for testing, she was feeling a little faint. The nurse gave her a couple of jelly beans and told her she could sit in the reception area for a little while until she felt better, but Jenny was eager to get out of the place as quickly as possible. She headed directly for her car.

She was reversing out of her car park when she was startled by a loud crunch of metal. A large black car had suddenly appeared, travelling at high speed for the small car park, and then run directly into the rear of her car. Cursing her bad luck, Jenny opened the door with the intention of giving the careless driver a piece of her mind.

She stepped out of her car then tried to peer through the dark glass windows of the black car. She rapped on the window. A menacing face appeared behind the glass. It sneered at her then the car abruptly powered away leaving her shocked and a little shaken. As the car sped out of the driveway, she caught the beginning of the licence plate – 101 C... Then she fainted.

When Jenny came to, she was lying on a hard bed with stiff white sheets. As her mind struggled back to consciousness, her eyes slowly opened. She remembered the face through the dark window and shuddered.

'It's OK, love.' The nurse gently helped her into a seated position adding, 'Slowly does it. How does your head feel? You fainted out in the car park, but you'll be fine. No bumps.' The nurse handed her a drink. 'Here have some of this.'

Jenny took a sip of the drink then recoiled in disgust. 'Yuck!'

'It's just a little glucose drink to restore you energy. Have you eaten today?'

'No, I've just had a coffee.'

'Well that'll explain why you fainted, after giving us all that blood. Just sit there as long as you need to. We've contacted your husband to come down to get you.'

'Oh that's not necessary, really,' Jenny pleaded. 'I'm fine now.'

She tried to stand up but had to grab for the bed, feeling a bit unsteady on her feet. It took a few moments to regain her balance, but as soon as she felt normal again she headed for the door. With her head down, she walked right into Angelo's arms he came through the automatic doors.

'Jennifer, are you OK?'

'I'm fine, let's just get out of here.' She continued out to the car park with Angelo following her closely.

'What a great performance!' Angelo congratulated her as he caught up with her.

'What performance?' Jenny shrieked. 'Look at my car!'

A frown creased Angelo's brow. 'What happened?'

'Someone drove straight into me. I swear, I think he did it on purpose!'

'What makes you think that?'

'Because he sneered at me! Some guy sneered at me through the tinted window of his fucking black car like he was some kind of mafia gangster!'

Angelo's face registered the dread that he had been fighting all day. Did someone have a hint of his plan? How could they? The only people who knew about it were he and Jenny. She did not know anyone from his past and he was sure she wouldn't have mentioned it to anyone else. Yet this afternoon when he had come out to get in his car, there it was; a perfectly burned black circle in the grass beside his Saab.

He knew what that meant. It was a mafia warning. That, combined with a small unexplained car accident involving a family member. Someone from within the organisation must have discovered his plan to get out. Anxiety gripped at his chest.

‘I only got part of the bastard’s number plate,’ Jenny snarled. ‘It was 101 C-something. Is that good enough to report them to the police?’

Angelo felt the blood drain from his face. He knew the rest of the number plate well. ‘It’s OK Jenny. Let me take care of it.’

There was a code in the organisation that could not be broken without consequence, and the warning was just to remind him of that. He couldn’t be certain how far they would go. ‘I think we better just leave the car here. I’ll drop you home then come back.’ He tried to think of a plausible excuse. ‘The police might want to have a look at it.’ He was more concerned about how serious they were, and if the car could be wired.

With some urgent work still to do that afternoon, Angelo decided to come back later and check the car out properly. He would also have to thoroughly search his home and office as they had almost certainly been tapped. One thing he was certain of, he was *not* going to inform the police.

Angelo was sitting in his office trying to comprehend the reports in front of him. He was distracted by the earlier events of the day. His pager suddenly interrupted with a message from the emergency department. He fumbled the phone out of its cradle then called the ER.

‘Dr Morley, we could use you down here,’ a breathless voice answered. ‘Gunshot wound. We’re afraid he could arrest at any moment.’

‘I’ll be right down.’

As he placed the handset back down, it sprang to life with another shrill ring. He contemplated ignoring it in his rush to get downstairs to the patient, but decided to answer in case it was the emergency department phoning back.

‘Angelo.’ He froze at the sound of the gravely Italian voice that he had listened to and respected for most of his life.

‘Hello,’ he answered cautiously.

‘We find ourselves in a spot of bother.’

He had been dreading this moment all day but he was determined not to let his apprehension show in his voice. 'What kind of bother would that be?'

'You know I have always looked upon you as a son. I have nurtured you and-a watched your career take off. But it is you, Angelo, who has made-a yourself the success you are today. I want you to know, like-a any father, I am very proud of your achievements.'

'Thank you, sir,' Angelo responded, holding his breath. He was waiting for the 'but' to come. He had convinced himself they had somehow found out about his intentions and they would not be happy about his plans to leave the mob.

'The time has come for you to step up-a in our organisation, Angelo.'

Angelo swallowed hard. He had been expecting to hear these words for some time now but after the events of that day, he was confused.

'Sometimes things do not-a go according to plan, even though we think-a we are in control. Do you agree, Angelo?'

'Well…yes.' He winced, waiting for the inevitable blow.

'There is a patient that has just-a been admitted to your ER with rather serious gunshot wounds. This man was not-a meant to survive.'

Angelo had an inkling where this was heading. They were not going to confront him directly at all. Instead, they were going to test his loyalty by drawing him in even more deeply.

'I'm sure you can see-a to it that our plans are carried through to completion.'

Angelo was silent as he contemplated his dilemma.

'Do you understand-a what I am saying, Angelo?'

'Yes Sir, I do.'

'Then we will speak again soon.' The line went dead.

Angelo slammed the phone back into its cradle. He did not like to be told what to do, but he had not been left with much choice. If he went ahead with this, they may think he had given up his foolish ideas then leave him alone for a bit. He did not need much more time to put his plan into action. He pushed back his chair then headed down to the emergency ward.

After stepping out of the lift, he quickly gowned up then entered the cubicle where a resident doctor and a number of nurses were working on the patient. The first thing that struck him was how young the boy looked. He could not have been more than sixteen. It was likely that the intended hit was some form of retribution aimed at somebody else.

Angelo evaluated the patient's vital signs on the overhead machines. They were not strong but under normal circumstances, he was sure he could have saved the boy's life. The line on the heart monitor suddenly went flat then the code blue alert sounded. The patient had gone into arrest. The younger doctor began to administer CPR as he called for the crash cart.

'I'll get it,' Angelo offered.

He took the longest time he could to get the cart without looking suspicious. As he feigned his rush back into the cubicle, the patient's condition had become even more critical. It would be far too risky to attempt anything in front of these trained medical staff. He did not want an evident mistake to impact on his excellent record either. He ordered everyone aside then went to work on re-starting the young boy's heart.

Everyone in the room breathed a collective sigh of relief as the line on the machine started to blip again. 'Let's get him into theatre before we lose him again,' the younger doctor ordered. 'Dr Morley, are you able to attend?'

'Certainly.' He might find himself with another chance in there to follow through with his orders.

'Are the parents here?' The doctor nodded in the direction of the waiting room. 'I'll inform them,' Angelo offered then walked out of the cubicle before anyone could argue. They might find it strange that he did not follow them directly to theatre but he was interested in finding out who the boy's parents were.

He found the mother in the waiting room crying on the shoulder of a younger woman who he presumed was the boy's sister. They looked like a normal middle-class family. The mother could once have been rather attractive but now looked like an average suburban housewife in her forties. The daughter was blonde, in her early twenties and fashionably dressed. She appeared to be trying to maintain some strength for the older woman, but kept glancing in anticipation down the hall. A look of relief suddenly filled her face. Angelo followed her gaze to see a tall dark-haired man in a business suit approaching from the other end of the hall. He looked almost annoyed, as if this event had dragged him away from an important business negotiation. As he reached the two women, he embraced them both in his large arms. While he wore a look of concern, Angelo could detect that his underlying emotion was anger. This man knew why his son was in the hospital.

Angelo did not recognise him. He walked quickly toward the family then explained their son's condition and the procedure that was about to take place. The mother could not contain the sobs that racked her body. Her husband moved to console her but she turned away from him. Instead, she allowed her daughter to put her arms around her. It seemed she knew why her son was in hospital too and she was laying the blame squarely on her husband's shoulders. Angelo could guess what kind of business he was in.

The boy's mother lifted her head from her daughter's shoulder then looked at Angelo imploringly. 'Please save him.'

'We'll do everything we can,' Angelo promised. In reality, his intentions could not be further from his promise. His experience as a doctor would have been enough to learn to detach from the sentiment of these situations, but he also had an emotional disposition that lacked empathy. It was going to come in handy in this instance. Angelo left the family in the waiting room then headed quickly toward the theatre.

The bullet had done extensive injury to the young boy's chest. The surgeon was already trying to assess the damage among the carnage of his blood-filled organs and respiratory system. Blood was seeping from crevices in his chest wall as quickly as they pumped it into him, but piece by piece, the surgeon closed the leaks and put him back together. Angelo was really just in the theatre on stand-by in case they needed his expertise, but the boy's young and otherwise healthy heart withstood the procedure. After several hours, the operation was complete and an orderly was called in to wheel him up to the intensive care unit.

Angelo again volunteered to speak to the family. Although he was careful to inform them things were still touch and go, he could see the wave of relief passing over them as he told them their son had survived the surgery. The boy was not yet breathing unaided but he explained that he was in a stable but critical condition. He encouraged them to go home for the night. They could do nothing more to help him, and they were not permitted in his room yet. Angelo promised he would keep an eye on the boy. He intended to stay around for a while longer until things at the hospital quietened down.

In the wee hours of the night, Angelo ventured back down to the intensive care ward. He checked on the nurses. They were gossiping at the nurse's station so they did not even glance his way as he passed them. He entered the boy's room then switched off the heart monitor. He picked up the boy's limp hand then felt for his pulse as he switched off the respirator. Within seconds, the boy stopped breathing. Angelo held onto his hand until he could no longer feel a pulse. Then he switched the heart monitor back on. A long steady beep rang out as the flat line passed across the screen.

Within moments, two of the nurses had appeared at the door. Angelo already had the paddles in his hand to attempt to defibrillate the patient, but his efforts were futile. He called time of death at 2.46am. He signed the appropriate paperwork then left the room before anyone could think to question what he had been doing there. It was plausible for him to be doing an overnight round in intensive care given he had worked with the patient, but he was still slightly paranoid given the circumstances.

He headed toward the car park as quickly as he could. Someone else could inform the parents. He had done what he had to do and did not intend to give it much further thought.

TEN

The following day had been long and extremely busy, but Angelo had finally finished the last of his consultations. He stabbed at the *Close Door* button in the lift as he saw Daniel Warner racing towards it. He did not have the time or the patience right now to put up with the irksome man. When the doors opened again, he hurried to his car. He wanted to make it to the hardware store before it closed for the evening.

He walked through the doorway of his apartment an hour later, laden with bags of electronic gadgetry and other items he would need to set his plan in motion. His first task was to find out if someone had been monitoring his apartment. He pulled out the electronic equipment and rigged it the way he had been taught. He then did a sweeping search of the apartment, under the furniture and around all the fittings. Nothing.

Think! It had to be somewhere less obvious. Looking up, he surveyed the light fittings. A perfect hiding place. How often did you look up at the ceiling? He pulled a dining chair over to the living room light then swept the fitting.

The machine responded with a shrill beep. Angelo cursed. Standing on tiptoes, he unscrewed the light shade then removed the small device. Dragging the chair into the dining room, he discovered another one in the light shade there. He found the final bug hidden in the bedroom. How long had they been there and how much did they know? Was it possible they had listened in to every word when he revealed his plan to Jennifer? He had to get things underway as quickly as possible, beginning to feel he would be safer in the custody of the police now than out in the open. He did a second sweep of the apartment until he was sure he had thwarted all of their surveillance efforts.

Angelo then took the blood from the freezer that he had taken from Jenny over the past few months. He put it in the refrigerator to thaw so it would not begin to clot. Opening the other bags, he took out the heavy black plastic sheeting and tape he had purchased from the hardware store. He folded the hardware bag neatly, with the docket clearly visible inside, then placed it in the kitchen drawer on top of the plastic shopping bags they kept to line the rubbish bin. Then he pulled out the vacuum cleaner and scattered some fine dust from the full bag over the cabinet where his trophy stood. When he picked up the trophy there was a clean square left beneath it, indicating that something was missing from the arrangement. Next, he propped up a store mannequin he had purchased, that stood about the same height as Jenny, in the middle of the living room.

While he waited for Jenny to come home, he packed her a suitcase with new clothes and the toiletries she would need for her trip. He did not want her to take any of her things from the apartment so it would look like she had disappeared unexpectedly. He took the suitcase down to the garage and put it in the boot of her car. Moving the car out of the garage, he parked it under the streetlights where it was easily visible to prying eyes from the neighbouring windows. By the time Jenny walked in the door a few hours later, everything would be ready to go. He was in a fervent mood.

Jade had become completely infatuated with Angelo. She found her day frequently interrupted by thoughts of him. She pulled up his emails, reading them several times a day, then Googled his name just to find pictures of him she could pore over, while inventing scenarios in her head in which they were together. She found herself dreaming about a future with him. She knew this was not how she was meant to be thinking. She had become involved with him knowing he was married and there was no future to their relationship, but the way he had been lavishing his attention on her, surely there were problems at home. She could still feel the strength and warmth of his arms around her after their last stormy encounter that day at lunch.

Angelo had seemed rather anxious about something, though still very passionate towards her. Could he be having the same feelings as she was about their relationship?

It was not the ideal way she expected it to happen, but perhaps this was it. That elusive thing called…love. There, she had said it. Put it right out there in the open, where she could not take it back. She could no longer deny that she was hopelessly in love with him.

Despite her numerous Google searches, she had not been able to find any information about Angelo's personal life. Her curiosity was piqued. At the very least, she wanted to get a glimpse of the woman he had married. Now she had made this admission to herself, she saw Angelo's wife as the competition. She needed to assess whether the odds were in her favour.

Curiosity finally won out. Impulsively, she picked up her keys then headed for the car. He had told her many things about himself, one of which included his residential address. Perhaps if she waited in the hall of his apartment block she could at least get a glance of Angelo's wife without anybody being the wiser. It was a bit irrational, but maybe that was why there were so many clichés about love based on madness. She was feeling far from rational today.

When Jade reached the secure building, she found it was inaccessible unless you had a key or one of the tenants buzzed you in. She stood fishing through her bag as if she were looking for her keys, waiting for someone to head toward the entrance of the building. A man appeared then opened the door for her, smiling her through. As she headed for the lift, a tall strikingly dressed young woman entered the building. She looked relieved as Jade held the lift doors open for her. 'Thank you,' she said then turned her head away.

Jade had already pressed the button for the top floor. The woman seemed satisfied with her choice. Could this be her adversary? From her position behind her, Jade had the opportunity to spy at her in the mirrored wall of the lift. She was young and pretty, not at all the cold-hearted woman she had imagined. This couldn't be her. There were two apartments on the top floor. She had to be one of the other tenants.

As the two women exited the lift, the other one headed for the first door. Jade was shocked that it was indeed Angelo's apartment number. She stopped for a moment at the end of the hall. Her breaths were short and sharp and she began to feel disorientated. She leant against the wall to steady herself. Fearful someone might see her, she made her way back to the lift then hurried out of the building.

As Jenny entered the apartment, Angelo jumped from the couch. 'I've been waiting for you. It's time!' A strange grin played across his face that Jenny did not dare challenge.

'What do you need me to do?' she asked cautiously.

'My dear, I need you to act like you're dying!' He moved toward her with a menacing look.

They had been over this part of the plan. Angelo wanted to leave signs of a struggle, so he and Jenny tousled around the coffee table, knocking it off centre. He pushed her knee into the sharp corner causing her to cry out in pain. 'Sorry, didn't mean that,' he feigned in apology, although he had done it purposely to leave traces of her skin and blood. He pushed her into the bookshelf with a crash, knocking a few of the books to the carpet. All the while Jenny was screaming as loudly as she could, just as Angelo had instructed her, in the hope that the nosey stuck up neighbours might hear.

Angelo took the container of thawed blood from the refrigerator. He took a thick sponge then soaked up a generous amount. He taped this to the side of the mannequins head then picked up the heavy trophy. He swung it as hard as he could into the sponge area several times in an attempt to replicate a frenzied attack. The blood splattered across the furniture and up the walls. A small amount ascended onto the light shade above.

He poured more blood onto Jennifer's head and down her clothing. He asked her to lie down then dragged her across the floor into the kitchen, leaving a trail of bloodied drag marks. Once there, he poured the rest of the blood onto the floor, enough to indicate that she had bled to death. He wrapped her in the black plastic then bound the tape around the bundle a few times, using a knife from the kitchen block to cut the tape. Ensuring ample air was making its way into the sheath, he instructed her not to make any further noise. He thrust the leftover tape and the trophy, still tarnished with Jenny's blood, into the back of the kitchen cupboard to deal with later as further evidence of his crime. Lifting the bundle over his shoulder, he jagged it on the doorframe as he went through to leave a small piece of the plastic there then headed for Jenny's car. The screams may have alerted the neighbours enough to make them look out the window but just for good measure, he leant on the car horn to rouse their curiosity. The horn blared into the still night. Taking advantage of his possible audience, he lifted the bundle into the boot of the car. 'I'll get you out soon,' he promised as he slammed the boot lid and Jenny descended into darkness.

Jade had been sitting in her car, which she had parked across the street, deliberating over the situation. She wanted Angelo but she could not quite have him for herself. She was not used to this feeling. She was used to getting what she wanted. The uncertainty of her emotions unhinged her slightly. Did this young woman deserve to lose her husband? Should she allow herself to be responsible for that? Should she continue to see Angelo, or walk away now? She tossed the questions over in her head but still could not make sense of her feelings. Unaware of how long she had sat there mulling things over, the darkness had crept up on her. She put the keys in the ignition. She was about to start the engine when she caught sight of Angelo with a large bundle over his shoulder. As she watched, he opened the car door then the shrill horn sounded across the street. He moved to the boot then placed the bundle inside before getting into the car.

Intrigued, Jade started her car, deciding to follow him. Maybe things had come to a head and he was moving out? Did she dare to hope?

Angelo drove a short distance down the road, pulling in behind the clubhouse of the local soccer field. He knew the public facilities had a shower. Lifting Jenny out of the boot, he carried her into the shower block. He ripped the tape from the black plastic, releasing her, and then went back to the car to get her some fresh clothes while she washed away the traces of blood from her body and hair. He bundled her bloody clothes and the black plastic into a large garbage bag then put it back into the boot, making sure some of the blood smeared across the carpet.

'Don't take too long,' he chided when he came back to find Jenny still in the shower. 'You have a flight to catch.'

Clean of her blood, Jenny finally emerged from the shower block then jumped back into the car eagerly, ready to play out her role in the scam.

Not wanting Angelo to know she was following him, Jade had held the car back, parking under the shadows of the trees when he pulled into the car park at the soccer field. The darkness made it difficult to see what he was doing, but it was possible he may have needed to use the facilities if his wife had thrown him out of his apartment unexpectedly. She decided to sit and wait.

Not long after, she watched him emerge from the shower block. He opened the boot of the car but she could not see what he was doing from her position. He walked back to the shower block and returned a short while later. He had been sitting in his car for about five minutes when another person came out from the shower block then jumped into the passenger side of the car. It was the woman from the lift. Jade was sure there had been nobody else in the car when Angelo had left his apartment. Unless the person had been hiding. But why? What the hell was going on? She was intrigued, but a touch of annoyance was now creeping in. Perhaps this woman was not Angelo's wife after all.

She was determined to find out what was going on. As the car moved slowly past her, she ducked out of sight. She started her car's engine then resumed her pursuit.

Angelo was heading west out of town. There were not as many cars on the road here. Although he did not know what kind of car Jade drove, she was cautious to hang back where he would not be able to recognise her in his rear view mirror. When he pulled off the road into one of the reserves alongside the river, she drove past unsure what she should do next. There was another entrance a little further up that allowed her to park the car just out of view, but still have a vantage point that allowed her to see his car if he came back out. Several minutes passed. How long should she wait? What was he doing in the darkness with that woman in the car? It did not take too much imagination to figure it out. He was cheating on her! It didn't matter to her that she was doing the very same thing to Angelo's wife. She was in love with him. He was hers! Her anger had started as a slow simmer but as the minutes ticked by and she stewed on the possibilities, it grew to boiling point and jealousy began to set in. Another fifteen minutes went by. Who did this other woman think she was! Her emotions were quickly getting to a point where they threatened to overpower her usually rational mind.

Angelo had driven out of town until he reached the secluded reserve alongside the river. It was a popular picnic spot during the day, but at this time of night it was deserted and would serve his purpose. The dirt track that led off the road was a little muddy so after driving its length, he stopped the car then stepped out to get some of the same mud on his shoes as was in the treads of the car tyres. He hoisted the bag of clothes and plastic well into the bushes then headed back out to the main road. Here he handed Jenny a pre-paid mobile phone and her bag he had packed, which already included new I.D. cards he had illegally obtained for her, along with cards to access a bank account he had set up in that name. He had set up all the accounts with online statements and direct debit payments so that there would be no paper trail back to her.

'Call yourself a taxi then head straight to the airport. Here's your ticket for Cairns, you should easily make this flight but if you don't just call and have it re-scheduled. I'll be in touch on this phone in the next few days.'

Jenny nodded.

‘Now remember, don’t call me! Stick to the plan and everything will be all right.’ With that, he sped off into the night.

As Jade had continued to watch, the car emerged from the bushes then stopped on the shoulder of the road. The woman alighted from the car then stood for a while stooped in the window speaking to Angelo. They exchanged something but there didn’t seem to be any disharmony between them. Then he just drove off leaving her there in the dark on the side of the road. Jade’s suspicions grew stronger. Had he just paid her? Was this woman a hooker? She squeezed the steering wheel with both hands as her anger turned to fury. She saw the woman place a mobile phone to her ear. She was going to find out the truth right now before the woman went anywhere! She started the car then headed toward her. After pulling the car onto the shoulder of the road, Jade got out then walked toward the woman.

After Angelo had driven off, Jenny dialled the taxi company. She was put on hold and was waiting for an operator to answer when a car pulled onto the shoulder of the road. Someone got out then approached her. Had Angelo forgotten something? She strained her eyes to see the person in the glare of the headlights. The silhouette did not appear menacing, so she stepped toward it.

As Jade walked toward the woman, she noticed a look of surprise on her face which turned to relief. Jade pointed at her, shaking her finger. Her wrath gathered full momentum. ‘I want to know who the hell you are, and I want to know what you were just doing with Angelo,’ she shrieked then let loose with a barrage of abuse. She heard the words coming from her mouth, but it was as if she was not there. She felt a strange sense of detachment from the scene.

Jenny stared into Jade’s bulging eyes then started to back away.

‘You’re not going anywhere until you answer my questions!’ Jade screeched as she lunged for her.

Jenny started to run back down the trail toward the cover of the bushes, but Jade chased after her, all the while screaming senselessly. The dark rage consumed her from within, her actions now feeling beyond her control. Although Jenny was taller, the women were of similar build. Jade easily pulled her to the ground then pinned her down with all the strength she could muster, aided by the adrenaline coursing through her system. Jenny struggled, managing to hurl Jade aside and get up but making it only a few steps before a hard blow connected with the side of her head. Once again that night her own blood streamed down the side of her face as the second blow found its mark. She slumped toward the ground.

The sight of blood gushing from the woman's head was enough to draw Jade back to reality. The woman was lying still on the ground. Jade stared in horror at the bloody rock in her hand as if she was not aware of how it got there. She let go of it and watched it fall to the ground as if in slow motion. She felt a sudden weakness in her legs and fell leadenly to her knees. The woman did not appear to be breathing. Her rage subsided, turning quickly to panic. What had she done? How could she have lost total control of her emotions like that? How could she have let a man do this to her?

She felt for a pulse but could not find one. She put her face close to the woman's mouth but could not feel any breath. Oh God, she had killed her! What should she do now? She staggered away from the body, trying to gather her frayed thoughts. Should she call the police and explain that it was all a terrible accident? She had not meant to kill her. She just didn't want her to get away before she got the answers she needed. Would they believe her? How would she explain what she was doing out here on the side of the road in the middle of nowhere? She didn't even know who this woman was.

She paused at the thought. Maybe nobody knew or cared where this woman was tonight. That gave her an advantage. She tried to put herself into the minds of the many criminals she had defended. What would they do now?

She was a protector of the law. She had to call the police. Or did she? Who was she kidding with her misplaced idealism? The law was not about justice. She, of all people, knew how a clever defence lawyer could manipulate it. She had represented clients she believed were guilty and many of them had walked. She flinched. She wasn't a cold-blooded murderer like them. This was just a tragic mishap. She had acted in a fit of passion. She had simply made a mistake.

In the distance, she saw a set of headlights approaching so she knew she had to make a decision fast. She grabbed the woman's lifeless arms then dragged her a little way down the dirt trail. She rolled her body into the bushes then ran back to her car. Breathing heavily from the exertion, she picked up the small overnight bag the woman had been carrying then tossed it on to the floor of the car before starting the engine. She planted her foot on the accelerator, her tyres spraying gravel as she hurriedly drove off.

She did not notice the black car, which had been camouflaged in the shadows, emerge from the reserve minutes after.

PART TWO

TOTAL ECLIPSE…

For a long time there was only the light…impenetrable white light, shining like a beacon through the surrounding darkness.

It was but another moment in time…

The blur began to widen. The edges shimmered, as the shadow continued on its evasive path. Unable to resist its fate, parts of the light became blocked in entirety…and it began to give its purity over to the darkness…

ELEVEN

Hate is like acid. It can damage the vessel in which it is stored as well as destroy the object on which it is poured.
- *Ann Landers*

Jade had hardly slept. Images of the woman's lifeless face had haunted her all night. When she did finally achieve sleep, the dream came again. She woke in the dark in a cold sweat with the words of the satanic figure again echoing in her head. *You will become what you are meant to be.*

By the time she got to work, she was functioning by instinct only and barely remembered the drive in. She had been unable to eat a thing all morning, her churning stomach lurching if she even thought of food. She flinched as Danni entered the room but accepted her offer of coffee. She asked her assistant to hold her calls then sat catatonically behind her desk, immobilised by a state of panic.

Danni returned with the coffee and placed it in front of Jade without a word before leaving the office and closing the door behind her. Jade stared at it for timeless moments, then lifted it to her lips and began to sip the warm brown liquid. She felt trapped by the consequences of her decision to run from the scene last night. It had affirmed her guilt. There was no way to turn back now. She forced herself to pick up a file and began working.

As the day progressed, slowly the bewilderment subsided as the defender in her took over. Her focus turned to self-preservation. She had her career to protect, as well as the rest of her life. She was also responsible for her sister's wellbeing, now that her parents had passed on. What were her options? Should she argue diminished capacity due to uncontrollable rage? It was a defence that had proved successful before. There had certainly been a lack of premeditation or malice. She had simply been seeking information but had lost control of her emotions. But could she prove that? She would need to reveal the relationship between her and Angelo. He would not like that one bit. At any rate, the best she could expect was to have the charges reduced to voluntary manslaughter. That still carried a hefty prison term that signalled the end of her career. She couldn't look out for her sister from prison. No, she had made the right choice. She just had to block it from her mind and act as if it had never happened. She had maintained discretion in her relationship with Angelo. Nobody could connect the two of them, even if it were somehow established that he was the last person to be seen with the woman alive.

There was a certain power in knowing she could get away with murder. She felt a new sense of indestructibility. For years, she had fought for her place in what was still perceived to be a man's world, knowing when and how to be strong, yet still relying on her feminine charms when necessary. It was a delicate balance she had to achieve to be taken seriously, but she had never failed to measure up. She could feel the steady thump of her heart as her confidence grew.

After leaving Jenny that night, Angelo had driven her car to the Marriott hotel. He had followed another car through the security gates and parked it in the corner of the car park. For good measure, he had slashed the back tyres and left one of the doors slightly ajar to encourage someone to investigate and report the car to the police as quickly as possible. He then looked around for potential witnesses. There was a young couple heading for the lift. He walked briskly to catch them then entered the lift, striking up a conversation and bidding them a good night so they had a good opportunity to identify him if such an occasion arose. He then left the hotel and walked the few blocks back to his apartment.

When Angelo had got back to the apartment, the blood had already begun to congeal on the walls and dry where it had seeped into the carpet. Leaving his muddied shoes by the door, he had taken out the sponges and cleaning agents he had purchased then began the cleanup process. When he had finished, the bloodstains were no longer as obvious, but there were still some marks on the walls and white carpet. The pungent odour of the cleaning agents filled the room. Although he hoped they would not remove all the evidence that forensics would be able to detect, at least it looked like he had made a good effort to clean up. He had taken care to leave the blood on the corner of the coffee table and the light fitting as evidence for the police to find. If he wanted it to appear that he was trying to hide the crime, he had to dispose of the murder weapon. He had wrapped the trophy in a plastic bag, still with Jenny's blood and his fingerprints on it, then took it down to the industrial bin in the car park, sure that they would search the bin while looking for a murder weapon. When he returned to the apartment, he had rinsed the sponges haphazardly in the sink then stuffed them in the kitchen tidy, intending to leave them there as further evidence. The night had exhausted and mentally drained him. After a quick shower, he had gone to bed then fallen into a dreamless sleep.

Angelo awoke the next morning feeling refreshed after his restful night's sleep. He had been deciding how long into the day he should wait to file a missing person's report on his wife, when the phone beside the bed let out a shrill ring. He picked it up in annoyance thinking it might be the hospital calling his home number. He had forgotten to turn his beeper back on last night in his exhausted state.

'Hello,' he answered gruffly.

'Mr Morley?' a deep voice asked.

Angelo did not recognise the voice. 'Doctor Morley,' he corrected guardedly.

'My apologies, Dr Morley. This is Senior Sergeant Tom Harris. I'm sorry to interrupt you at home but it's a matter of some urgency. The hospital gave us this number to contact you.'

'What is it?' Angelo asked.

'Dr Morley, do you know where your wife is?'

'No,' Angelo replied trying to sound concerned. 'Has something happened to her? I was very worried when she didn't come home last night, and her mobile phone isn't answering. I thought you might be her calling now.'

'Where was your wife last night?'

'She told me she was visiting a friend. I thought she might've had a little too much to drink and just decided to stay over.'

'Was she driving last night?'

Angelo feigned anguish. 'Yes. Has she been in a car accident? Oh God!'

'I don't want to alarm you just yet, Dr Morley, but we've received a report of a car registered in your wife's name being found abandoned in a hotel car park. There are some suspicious circumstances surrounding it and we'd like to ask you some questions. I'm sending an officer over to collect you in about fifteen minutes and bring you to the police station.'

Harris did not give Angelo a chance to argue. He had rung off.

Angelo got up then threw some clothes on. He was thankful his good planning was already paying off. Catching a glimpse of his dishevelled appearance in the hall mirror, he decided to leave himself that way. He wanted to look like he had slept fitfully worrying at the whereabouts of his wife.

The buzzer sounded indicating someone had arrived at the downstairs security door. Angelo pushed the button then spoke into the microphone.

'Dr Morley, Detective Brent Hunter. I believe Senior Sergeant Harris has spoken to you about assisting us with our investigations?'

'Detective Hunter. I'll be right down.' Now this was an interesting turn of events. Angelo still remembered the confused look on the young detective's face as he unknowingly passed him in the car park that night after the function in Jade's building. Jade had mentioned to him that the detective had continued to pursue her since but that she had ignored his calls. If he was the investigating officer, and Angelo knew Jade as well as he thought he did, it would make her even more determined to defend him, just to prove Hunter wrong.

When they arrived at the station, Hunter escorted Angelo to an interrogation room. He offered him a coffee that he gratefully accepted, having not had time to partake of his usual morning caffeine fix. After that, Hunter left him there for almost half an hour. Angelo figured it was an attempt to make him nervous. They were probably watching his behaviour on screen, recorded by the camera protruding from the far corner of the ceiling. He tried to look agitated by fidgeting in his seat. He got up several times to pace back and forth across the room. By the time Hunter returned with the steaming brew, Angelo's body had started to suffer from caffeine withdrawal so his agitation was becoming real.

Hunter had actually been looking for his partner. Andrews had conveniently disappeared on a routine assignment when the Senior Sergeant was looking for someone to bring in the suspect. When they could not locate him, Harris instructed Hunter to go ahead with the investigation on his own and offered to act as a witness for the interview.

Hunter pulled out the chair directly across from Angelo and took a seat. He pulled a soft pack of Marlboro Lights from his pocket and offered them to Angelo. Angelo shook his head. Hunter dropped the pack onto the table then sat there eyeing him with a tenacious stare.

Angelo presumed this was another tactic meant to rattle him so he looked down at the table staring anxiously at his hands, willing them to shake. A few minutes later, the Senior Sergeant entered the room and stood behind the detective. He switched on the recording device to capture the interview.

'Dr Morley,' Hunter began. 'We've just been having a very interesting chat with one of your neighbours. Can you tell me your whereabouts and what you were doing last night?'

Angelo shifted in his seat. 'I was at home, watching TV.'

'Can anyone vouch for that?'

‘As I told you, my wife was over at a friend’s house so I just stayed in and waited for her.’

‘What time did your wife leave to go to her friend’s house?’

‘She went over during the day while I was at work. I haven’t seen her since breakfast yesterday morning.’

Hunter leaned forward, closing the distance between himself and Angelo. ‘And you can give us the contact details for this ‘friend’?’

Angelo leant back, as if threatened by Hunter’s close proximity. ‘Well, no. I can’t actually. She didn’t tell me which friend it was. Just that she was going.’

‘You didn’t find that strange?’

‘Why would I? I trust my wife Detective.’

Hunter stared at him then shrugged. He paused before asking, ‘Did you leave the house at any point during the night, Dr Morley?’

Angelo replied feebly, ‘Yes. I took out the garbage.’

‘And what time was that?’

His eyes moved sideways, as if he was trying to recall the events of the evening. ‘Let me see, it was just after the news, so it must have been around six thirty.’ He met Hunter’s eyes again and asked in an imploring voice, ‘Why is this relevant? Can you tell me what’s happened to my wife?’

‘The question is: Can you tell me what’s happened to your wife, Dr Morley?’ Hunter’s voice was level yet commanding. For a young detective, he was doing a good job at intimidation. Angelo respected him for that.

Angelo feigned indignation. ‘Look, I don’t know what you’re insinuating but I demand you tell me what this is all about! I haven’t seen my wife since yesterday and you’re really starting to worry me.’

‘When we found your wife’s car this morning, it contained a large amount of blood. That in itself is suspicious, but your wife now appears to be missing and we have reports from your neighbour about a domestic dispute that took place in your apartment last night.’

Angelo’s posture stiffened. ‘What does that prove?’

'Well for one thing, it means your story doesn't check out. You told us your wife wasn't home at all last night but a resident of your building reports she saw her entering the building around five that afternoon.'

Angelo was silent.

'Even more interesting, Dr Morley, is the fact that we have an eye witness account of you loading a bundle about the size of a body into the boot of Mrs Morley's car, which you allege she had driven to her friend's house last night.' Hunter's scowl exuded menace as his voice rose. 'It was *you*, in fact, who drove that car last night, wasn't it Dr Morley? And that bundle you put into the boot of the car was your dead wife!'

Angelo blinked hard but held his gaze. He looked defiantly into the detective's eyes for a long moment saying nothing. When he spoke, his voice was calm. 'I'd like to have my lawyer, Jade Sheffield, present before I answer any more of your questions.'

Hunter may have been quick, but he was not quick enough to disguise his reaction to the mention of Jade's name as a crushed look came over his face. Angelo smirked. So, the stalwart detective had a weakness after all. He would bear that in mind on the chance that he could use it to his advantage at some future time.

A knock sounded on the door then a young officer entered the room, handing a sheet of paper to Hunter. He leaned back in his chair, having recovered his composure. 'We have a warrant to search your apartment, Dr Morley.' He looked thoughtful. Turning back to the officer, he said, 'Get his lawyer, Jade Sheffield, on the phone. I'll ask her to meet us there.'

Hunter picked up the cigarette packet still sitting on the table and flicked one from the pack. He lit it up and blew the smoke in the direction of Angelo's face as he leered into his eyes.

Danni knocked then entered her boss's office tentatively, handing Jade a phone message. 'I'm sorry, I know you said you didn't want to take any calls but he said it was urgent.'

Jade looked at the message, determined to get back into the swing of things. She stared at the name on the piece of paper. *Detective Brent Hunter.* It had been weeks since she had given any thought to the night she had spent with the young detective. At first, the calls had come frequently. Once, maybe twice, he could have been prone to think her busy schedule prevented her from returning his calls. He must have worked out that his pursuit was in vain. Finally, he had stopped calling. A feeling of dread gripped Jade's stomach as she looked at the message. Surely, nobody could have known what had happened last night. She needed to be certain.

She picked up the phone then cautiously tapped out the number, not knowing what to expect. When Brent answered, his tone was professional. It did not betray any of the emotion she had anticipated.

'Jade, thanks for returning my call. We have a suspect in custody. He's asking for you to represent him.'

'Yes. And the client's name?' Jade asked trying to maintain a business-like manner.

'Dr Angelo Morley.'

Jade gasped audibly. She quickly recovered her composure. 'What's the allegation?'

'Murder!'

She did not hear the rest of his words. They had discovered the body already! A vision of the woman's bloodied face flashed through Jade's mind. What had she done? Now she had implicated Angelo in a crime she had committed. Someone must have seen him with that woman last night. She tried to bring her mind back to the present. What was Brent saying?

'Jade?'

'Oh. Sorry. Yes?'

'We're about to conduct a search of the assailant's apartment,' Hunter continued, 'and he's asked for you be present. The apartment is in the Q1 building. Do you know it?'

Jade flinched at his accusatory tone and asked hesitantly, 'His apartment or the building?'

After a moment, Hunter said, 'The building.'

‘Yes. Of course I do. But you’ll have to give me the apartment number.’

‘We’re heading there now. We’ll meet you outside.’

‘OK. I’ll be right over. Who do I ask for at the scene?’ Jade bit her lip to try to keep the tremor out of her voice.

‘Ask for me,’ said Brent, a slight taunt in his voice.

It seemed he was going to make this difficult for her after all.

When Jade pulled up outside the building, she could not recall much of the drive there. Her mind had been going over the events of the previous night, trying to work its way out of all this mess. Guilt clawed at her heart when she saw two armed police officers flanking Angelo as they led him through the door. She fell in line with them then followed the group to the lift.

‘Dr Morley, please don’t say a word unless I instruct you to,’ she called out as she caught up with them.

He turned then looked at her with pleading eyes. She wanted to reach out to comfort him, to tell him it would all be OK, that she knew he had not done this terrible thing. But she knew she couldn’t do that. For now, she had to keep her wits about her and remain as professional as possible.

Angelo’s manner changed as they rode to the top floor in the lift. He was shifting from one foot to the other, looking more and more anxious as the numbers ascended on the red panel. What did he have to be anxious about? She was the one who should be a nervous wreck. She was amazed that she was maintaining such composure under the circumstances.

Upon reaching the apartment, Hunter requested that Angelo unlock the door. Angelo entered the room flanked by the two officers, followed by Hunter, with Jade bringing up the rear. One of the officers pushed Angelo into a dining room chair then set off to commence his search. Hunter sat down opposite Angelo. Jade took a chair on the other side of the table.

‘Just what exactly do you expect to find here, Detective Hunter?’ she asked.

‘Something to corroborate our witness’s story, who heard screams before she saw Dr Morley place a body-sized bundle into the boot of his car then drive off,' he answered without making eye contact with her. He was glaring at Angelo as he spoke.

One of the officers, noticing the coffee table was askew, leant down to take a better look. He moved the rug aside to discover brownish stains in the white carpet. 'Looks like we have blood here,' he called out.

'Care to explain that, Dr Morley?' Hunter asked.

'Don't say a word,' Jade retorted.

Angelo sat back and smilingly obeyed. He seemed to be a bit more relaxed now, almost smug in his demeanour, and happy to let Jade be in control.

'Get forensics down here now,' Hunter shouted to the other officer who was working his way meticulously through the kitchen.

'More traces of blood in here,' he replied before following Hunter's orders and radioing for a forensic investigator.

Hunter stood then removed the handcuffs from his belt. 'Dr Morley, please stand. You are under arrest for the murder of your wife, Jennifer Morley. You have the right to remain silent.' As he placed the cuffs on Angelo's wrists, he continued to read him his rights.

Jade looked on in disbelief. She remembered Angelo loading the bundle into his car. Her mind swam with confusion. Angelo's wife was dead? Could it have been his wife after all that she had killed? How would that explain the blood just found in the apartment and the 'bundle' he put in his car. It *had* been about the size of a body. So why had he paid that woman? Had she somehow been a party to this crime, or had she been a witness to it? Was he paying her off? She forced herself to stifle her confusion and instead concentrate on what was going on around her.

Hunter was asking something about a weapon. One of the officers stood beside him carefully holding a knife in his gloved hand. Another officer walked in with what appeared to be some kind of large trophy. 'Found this in the industrial bin,' he reported with a conceited grin. 'Awarded to Angelo Morley.' It glistened in the sunlight streaming through the door. When she saw the reddish marks on the side of it, her heart sank.

'Detective Hunter, my client will answer no further questions until we are in an official interview situation with myself present to represent him.' She tried to sound authoritative so the shakiness she felt was not evident in her voice.

'As you wish, Miss Sheffield.' Hunter turned to one of the officers. 'Take him away. I'll wait here for forensics.'

As they led Angelo past Jade, he looked into her eyes in the same way he had lovingly looked into them for the past few weeks. 'I didn't do it,' he whispered. She let her hand fall lightly on his shoulder as she followed them out of the apartment.

Although it was obvious to everyone that a crime had been committed in the apartment, without a body it was going to be hard to link the blood samples to Jennifer Morley. Hunter didn't want to wait around while they searched for the body on the chance they were forced to release Angelo. If he could at least match the blood type, they may have probable cause to hold him in custody. The most logical place to begin was the hospital where her husband worked. After securing the crime scene and making what notes he needed to, he left the forensics team to what they did best. He headed back to the station to arrange a subpoena to access the medical records of Jennifer Morley.

A few hours later Hunter arrived at the hospital with the paperwork in hand. A grim-looking woman greeted him at the desk. Her hair was pulled tightly back into a bun and the buttons on her uniform strained to hold in her burgeoning figure. When he flashed his badge then advised that he wished to obtain a copy of Jennifer Morley's medical records, she looked at him with disdain.

The nurse took down the details then pointed to the over-full waiting room. 'Might take a while. There are sick people here.' She waved him away with a look of annoyance. 'Take a seat.'

After what seemed like hours of enduring the room full of sick and injured people, Hunter finally heard someone call his name.

He moved toward the older man who ushered him into a small consulting cubicle alongside the waiting room.

'Dr Daniel Warner,' the man introduced himself. 'Now what is this about? Dr Morley is a very close friend of mine so I want to make sure everything is above board.'

'I'm afraid I'm not at liberty to say, Dr Warner. I would just like to secure Mrs Morley's medical records in accordance with the conditions of the subpoena then be on my way.'

'Whoa up my boy,' Warner goaded as he opened the file in front of him. He flicked through the pages then suddenly wrinkled his brow. 'Hmm.'

'What is it, Dr Warner?'

'There's a request here from two days ago for a full set of bloods.'

Hunter bolted upright up at the news, his voice hopeful. 'Does that mean the hospital has a sample of Mrs Morley's blood on hand?'

'Why yes. The results have been confirmed with Mrs Morley, but the blood will still be in the process of disposal…' Warner's voice trailed off as his eyes narrowed.

Hunter sat forward in his chair. 'What is it?'

'Hmm. Very odd.'

'What is?'

'The results show Mrs Morley is pregnant.'

'Why is that so odd, Dr Warner?'

'Because Angelo cannot father children. He's had a vasectomy. I performed it myself five years ago.'

'Do you think Mrs Morley knew that?'

'Well, it would seem not.'

Hunter could not believe his luck. Not only was he going to be able to prove the blood in the apartment was Jennifer Morley's, but the doctor had just unwittingly dropped a motive right into his eagerly awaiting hands.

'I'm going to need to get my hands on that blood,' Hunter told the doctor as he scooped up the medical records from the table and tidied them back into the folder.

'You still haven't told me what this is all about,' Warner said.

'We have reason to believe Mrs Morley may have been murdered.'

The older man clapped a hand to his chest. 'Murdered? Oh dear! Does Angelo know?'

'I can't discuss the matters of the case with you Dr Warner, but I would appreciate your full co-operation.'

'Of course, yes. Whatever I can do to help. I'll order the samples be recovered and transported to your forensics lab at once.' It seemed his initial shock had dissipated and he was feeling as if he was an important part of the investigation.

'Thank you so much for your assistance, Dr Warner. I promise you once we get to the bottom of this matter you will be the first to be informed.' It was a lie, but he felt the encouragement would hurry the old bugger along.

Hunter was on his phone before he exited the hospital doors. 'Sarge, we have a break. I reckon we pull the team and be ready to brief them in an hour.'

Hunter flicked through his notes while he waited for the team to assemble around him. Senior Sergeant Harris headed up the table, with Hunter to his right. The two officers who had attended the scene filed into the room then took their places.

'OK', Harris directed, 'What do we have?'

Hunter consulted his notes. 'There were no visible signs of break in. Whoever carried out the attack either had access to the apartment or someone let them in.'

'So it was likely the person was known the victim?' Harris deduced.

Hunter nodded his head. 'Precisely. Since the building is secured they would've had to buzz if they didn't have a key.'

Constable Ian Davies spoke next. 'I've interviewed the neighbours directly on the floor of the apartment and the one below. I don't think the sound would've carried much further than that. The neighbour immediately next door reported hearing sounds like screams coming out of the apartment around sixish that evening when she went out to water her plants, but she admits she didn't take much notice. Thought they were just watching a movie. The other neighbours didn't seem too interested in speaking to me.'

'What about our witness?' Harris asked.

Senior Constable Nick Schodell joined the discussion. 'She lives in one of the lower floor apartments facing the street. Chair of the body corporate, so knows most of the residents in the building and makes it her business to keep an eye on what's going on around there. Good for us but I bet the other residents hate her! She reports that about 6.30pm on the night in question she saw Dr Morley carrying a dark coloured bundle which she has described as…' He paused as he consulted his notes. 'Heavy and slumping over his shoulder like a body. He came out from the car park entrance and she says he was acting quite suspiciously as he put the bundle into the boot of the car.'

Hunter's eyebrows lifted. 'Suspiciously?'

'Yeah, she said he was looking around a lot and at one point he accidentally leant on the car horn then appeared anxious to get the bundle into the boot as quick as possible.'

'Good work, Nick. I assume she'll be willing to testify?'

He gave Hunter a sly grin. 'She seemed delighted at the prospect.'

'It's a wonder nobody else reported it,' Hunter said.

'It's that kind of demographic,' Davies piped in. 'Keep to your own business.'

They all shook their heads and grunted in acknowledgement. The Gold Coast supported residents in even higher density than it ever had but even so, people these days were lucky if they even knew their immediate neighbours. Communication had become something that took place over the telephone or internet lines more frequently than face to face.

'Everything's been sent off to the lab for testing,' he continued. 'The knife seemed to have some sort of sticky residue on it, like the glue on tape. We found a hardware receipt for plastic sheeting and tape, so that might explain it. We also found a fragment of plastic snagged on the door. They've been sent in for comparison.'

'So we're looking at a stabbing?' Harris asked.

Davies shook his head. 'No Senior, according to forensics, it was likely the offender struck the victim with a blunt instrument. Looks like he used a heavy sailing trophy we found with blood on it. Seems he made an attempt to clean up but forensics have also come up with traces of blood splatters up the walls and ceiling and drag marks across the kitchen floor. We found damp sponges in the bin so they suspect they'll also show traces of the same blood. The forensics boys want to carry out a reconstruction of the crime once they've run the analysis through the computer. They'll let us know when they have it all arranged.'

'Excellent work,' Hunter said. He had saved his trump card for last. 'But I have even better news. I have here the medical records of Mrs Morley and as we speak, a sample of her blood is on its way to our forensics lab. According to the records, the alleged victim had a positive pregnancy test the day before she was killed. Lucky for us, the hospital still had the blood so we can use it to match the blood in the apartment and the car.'

Davies fixed him with a look of disgust. 'So we can nail him with a double murder?'

'Better than that. Morley was unable to father children. He'd had a vasectomy performed five years ago. If we can prove he knew about the pregnancy then Gentleman, we have ourselves a motive!'

Hunter let the news sink in for a moment then said with a satisfying smile, 'Let's keep this one to ourselves for the moment.'

TWELVE

Jade sat across from Angelo in the interview room. It was a small box of a room with a bare white table in the centre of it and no windows. A camera jutted from one corner of the ceiling, the constant red blink reminding them that they were not alone. She felt as if they were caged animals on display at a zoo. Except she knew, unlike Angelo, that she could leave at any time.

She had taken notes as Angelo described the events of the previous night. She was reading them back to him to make sure he had not missed anything important. According to him, he'd had a heated argument with his wife so she had thrown him out. The 'bundle' was what clothing and personal items he could grab in the heat of the moment, wrapped in a sheet. He did not know what happened to his wife after he left the apartment. He had come back later but she was gone, so he went to bed thinking she would return the next day. He had lied to the police about his wife's whereabouts to save himself from the embarrassment of having to reveal the reason for the fight. He winked at Jade. Was he insinuating the fight was about her? Obviously, he was not going to say it aloud while the police were monitoring their conversation.

Jade was not sure what to believe. The man sitting across from her had held her tenderly in his arms the day before – but he had also withheld the truth from her. She was hopelessly in love with him, but he was hiding a large part of this story from her. As much as she itched to ask, Jade could not question him about the other woman. How would she explain why she had been following him? And the last thing she wanted to do was to incriminate herself by placing herself at the scene. It would only be a matter of time before someone found the body. She had not gone to too much effort to conceal it in her haste to get away from there.

She needed to get away from Angelo's imploring stare for a while. 'I'll just go see if I can rustle us up a coffee. Be back in a tic.'

She returned a little while later, handing him a coffee in a polystyrene cup as she sipped her own. 'OK, what they have on you is all circumstantial.'

'So they haven't actually found Jennifer?' He moved his hand toward the coffee, looking suddenly hopeful.

'No. They don't have a body. That's in our favour. They're basing their case on the account of the eyewitness and forensic evidence. We'll have to wait until they have all the tests completed but at this stage there's no way they can prove the blood is in fact your wife's.'

Angelo looked at her over the rim of the cup as he blew on the hot coffee. 'Even if it was, how would they prove she's dead?' There was a sudden coldness in his eyes, which took her by surprise.

She sat back in her chair, unconsciously edging away from him. 'They're able to use the blood patterns to establish the severity of the attack. At this stage, they're only working on assumptions. I'll be in a better position to advise you once we've got all the evidence in hand.'

If he noticed her change in demeanour, he did not show it. 'When will that be?'

'The investigative team have invited me to attend a reconstruction at the crime scene. I think it's important I do that so I can make sure they depict the evidence accurately if this makes it to court.'

'And then what happens?' Angelo sat back in his chair too, suddenly assuming a relaxed pose. She was confused. Did he have that much reliance on her expertise?

'They want to interview you after that, so I want you to tell them exactly what you've told me. I'll be right beside you during the interview, so if you're unsure of whether or not to answer a question just look at me, and I'll nod yes or no.'

Angelo nodded his understanding as Jade stood for a moment with her hand on his shoulder to show her support, despite her tumultuous emotions. She wanted to believe in him. She was unable to show anything more personal in case someone was watching them. She hated to leave him alone in the room but made her way to the door.

It had been a long day but it was far from over yet. The team had scheduled the reconstruction for five pm, so Jade headed back to her office to catch up on her messages and anything else that required her urgent attention.

She settled herself behind her desk, trying to keep her mind in the present. Danni poked her head into the office. 'Tough day, hey?'

'You bet,' Jade sighed.

'I'll get you a coffee. You look like you could use one.'

'Thanks,' Jade said with an appreciative smile. She had not even had time to stop for lunch.

'By the way, this package arrived for you while you were out.' Danni handed Jade a cardboard CD mailer addressed to her. She turned it over but there was no indication of who the sender was. She shook the package out of habit but it made no sound. She cut through the tape then extracted the CD. There was still no indication of who had sent it to her or what the contents were. She looked at the box again. It was definitely addressed to her. She inserted it into her PC then turned up the speakers. At first, there was a faint crackling sound but then she was surprised to hear a familiar voice. It was Angelo, and there was a second voice – a woman's voice. Jade hit pause on her media player, walked over then closed her office door. She sat back then listened while Angelo gave an entire account of his carefully schemed plan. The woman interrupted with a question here and there, but was mostly silent. Jade's mouth hung open.

'I already have the lawyer eating out of my hands,' Angelo had boasted on the tape. His guttural laugh rang in her ears as tears began to sting her eyes. She could not believe it. He had been playing her all along.

When Danni walked back in with her coffee, Jade wiped the tears from her eyes then pushed past her. 'I'm sorry, I have to go,' she said as she ran out of the office with the CD in her hand.

When Jade got to the car park, she lowered herself into her car then put the CD into the player. She still could not comprehend what she had just heard. Her mind was blank with shock so she had to listen to the whole conversation twice before it started to make sense. There was no murder in the apartment. He had staged the whole thing to look like there had been one. She was just a pawn in his get rich quick scheme. The man she loved had betrayed her. The tears started to stream down her face as she let the enormity of the truth sink in. He had never loved her. He had used her.

Through her tears, Jade spied something on the passenger-side floor of her car. In her confused emotional state since the night of the woman's death, she had totally forgotten about the overnight bag. She picked it up then opened the zipper, rifling through the clothing in search of some form of ID. Her hand fell onto the smooth leather of the woman's purse. She pulled it out of the bag, along with a travel agent wallet with the Flight Centre logo on the front. She opened the purse first then extracted a drivers' licence. The woman's smiling face stared up into her eyes making her flinch. It was her! And the name on the licence was Jennifer Morley.

It seemed that the person she had killed really was Angelo's wife, not his real wife, but the woman legally married to him and purporting to be his wife. The woman had been a pawn in his little game too, as she had learnt on the tape. She had killed the woman he had allegedly murdered.

As far as Angelo knew, the woman was still alive. Jade had listened to him tell her he would send her to far north Queensland, and how they would keep in contact for as long as was necessary until he could bring her back to finish his now ill-fated scheme. She opened up the travel wallet then pulled out an airline itinerary. The ticket to Cairns had been booked in the name Julianne McGuire. Who the hell was she? She shook the wallet and two cards fell out into her lap. She picked up the first one - a credit card for the ANZ Bank in the same name – Julianne McGuire. She turned it over. It looked new, devoid of the scratches that usually developed after repeated swipes through EFTPOS terminals. The other card lay face down. She picked it up then again stared into the face of the woman she had killed. This licence belonged to Julianne McGuire. It was all true. The ticket to Cairns, the fake ID and credit cards, they all corroborated what she had heard in the recording.

Suddenly the words from her dream flashed through her mind. *You will become what you are meant to be.*

She felt the anger seethe through her body, every nerve ending raw and on edge. By the time she turned the key in the ignition, she was gritting her teeth. If he wanted to play the game of betrayal, she held the ultimate hand. The police would discover the body at some point. She felt a malevolent chuckle rise up in her throat. Angelo had just incriminated himself 'beyond a reasonable doubt'. He would pay for this!

Swallowing down her tears, she started the engine then planted her foot on the accelerator. She let the speed empower her as she drove over to meet the forensics team.

Jade stood with Hunter and the other officers in the Morleys's apartment trying to give her attention to the members of the forensic team as they detailed the physical evidence they had uncovered at the scene. They began in the living room. 'The arterial spray indicates the victim was standing here when the offender struck the first blow.' He pointed downward. 'She falls to the floor here as the offender inflicts subsequent blows. By measuring the location and dimensions of each bloodstain, and the path of each drop we've been able to establish that she received several blows to the head in quick succession.'

A second officer took over. 'The evidence points to a frenzied attack with a heavy instrument,' he explained. 'Such an attack is usually spurred by some form of anger or rage'.

Hunter smiled to himself. It tied in perfectly with his motive.

'She was dragged across the floor here to the kitchen.' Jade shuddered as she followed the men into the kitchen, imagining the scene. It conjured up images of the body she had dragged across the gravel into the bushes that night.

'Looks like there was a bleed out here.' She could not see any blood but a wide stain glowed when they shone a bluish light on it. 'There's a very high probability the attack would have resulted in the death of the victim.'

'What about time of death,' Hunter asked. 'Does that tie in with our witness accounts?'

'The coagulation of the blood suggests the crime happened in the twenty-four hour period prior to its discovery.'

Satisfied he had enough evidence to bring an indictment against Angelo Morley, Hunter decided to head back to the station to interrogate his suspect.

'You coming?' he asked Jade.

She followed him out the door with a mixture of emotions. She was still irate that Angelo had played her for a fool, but she also held a strange sense of admiration for his success in deceiving the law enforcement agencies. If she were going to get away with her own crime, then she too would have to give herself over to her darker side and take on some of his treacherous ways. Either way, she intended to make him pay for his betrayal.

When they were all present in the interview room, Hunter stood at the head of the table then slammed his palms down on its surface, leaning toward Angelo. 'Now Dr Morley, let's start again and this time I want the truth!'

Angelo deferred to Jade. She nodded her head to indicate he could tell the story as he had told it to her earlier that day.

'Dr Morley, where were you last night at approximately 6pm?' Hunter boomed.

'I was at home with my wife.'

'Then why did you tell us earlier that your wife was not at home?'

Jade watched as Angelo feigned humiliation. 'I was too embarrassed to say she'd thrown me out of my own apartment.'

'Was there a fight between you and your wife?'

'Yes.' Angelo did not elaborate.

'And what was the fight about Dr Morley?'

'Umm, she, umm...I'd rather not say.' He looked at Jade for approval.

'Let me make a suggestion Dr Morley,' Hunter continued. 'Did your wife inform you she was pregnant?'

Angelo's surprised expression looked real. It mirrored Jade's own. He avoided her eyes, seemingly aware in his peripheral vision that she was glaring at him. 'Why yes, she did. How did you know about that?'

'I know a lot of things Dr Morley, including the fact that the child could not possibly have been yours.'

Angelo turned toward Jade, giving her a quick look of apology. She had not said a word as she sat listening to the unanticipated events unfolding in front of her. More lies.

'How did you feel about that news?'

'Well of course, I was more than a little angry. We got into a fight about it and she became hysterical. She told me to get out. In hindsight, I should have thrown her out!'

'And you left?'

'Yes. I was so shocked I just bundled up what belongings I could in a hurry then left. That was the bundle I was seen putting into the boot of my car.'

'Did you get physical with your wife that night?'

'Of course not! We just argued. It may have been heated but I didn't touch her. When I left Jennifer, she was alive. I don't know what happened to her after that. When I came back later the apartment was in darkness and she was gone.'

A sudden look of guilt played across his face. 'Oh no, you don't think she could have done this to herself?'

'*No*. I don't think that at all, Dr Morley. According to the forensics report someone beat your wife to death with a heavy object.' He paused for effect. 'Do you own a trophy won in the Sydney to Gladstone yacht classic, Dr Morley?'

'Why, yes I do,' he stated with a small glimmer of pride.

'And where do you keep this trophy?'

'It is always on the sideboard in the living room.'

'Can you explain what it was doing in the back of your kitchen cupboard covered in your wife's blood?'

'The bastards!' Angelo retorted. He looked up at Hunter who was staring at him menacingly. 'No, I do *not* know what it was doing there, Detective.'

Jade knew that Hunter had no solid evidence. He was stretching the truth until he had the results of the forensics tests to prove the blood belonged to Jennifer Morley. He probably wanted to unhinge Angelo enough so he would spend a restless night mulling over his predicament, hoping he would be more compliant in the morning.

As if he had read her mind, Hunter said, 'OK, Dr Morley. We'll be accommodating you tonight, compliments of the Queensland Police Force. We'll be speaking to you again tomorrow when we have the results of the forensic tests.'

Angelo turned to Jade. 'Can they do that?'

'I'm afraid so.' She was not in any mood to argue his cause after he had once again withheld the truth from her.

An officer entered the room to escort Angelo to the holding cells. Jade did not think Hunter would realise his hopes. It looked like Angelo was going to sleep very well that night. As far as he knew, his plan was right on track.

Jade felt suddenly drained. There were still a lot of loose ends but she was not even going to attempt to connect them tonight. She packed up her files, avoiding even looking at Hunter then headed home to try to get a night's reprieve from her thoughts.

Hunter sat reflecting on the evidence in the case so far. He was sure that the blood results would come in as a positive match for Jennifer Morley. Angelo's story about the 'bundle' didn't gel. He sat staring at the crime scene photos of the traces of blood found in the boot of the car. If they matched them to Jennifer Morley then there was no doubt that the bundle seen by their eyewitness had been her body. Now if he could just place Angelo at the secondary crime scene, where they had found the car, it would be an open and shut case. It would not even matter that they had not recovered the body.

His night was not over yet. He picked up his notebook then headed over to the hotel where they had found the car.

Luckily for him, he discovered that most of the guests staying in the hotel the night before had not yet checked out. He narrowed the guest list down to those who had a car parked on the same level as Jennifer Morley's car. Carrying a copy of Angelo's mugshot, he started knocking on the door numbers on his list. At the third door, a young man answered. He had a towel around his hips. Hunter apologised, realising from the man's flushed face that he had interrupted a private moment. 'I'm sorry to bother you, Sir. Detective Hunter, Gold Coast Police. I'd just like to ask you if you'd seen this man on the premises last night.'

The young man took the photograph from him, staring at it intently. 'Yeah, I think I did.' He turned into the room. 'Suzie, come here for a minute.'

An attractive blonde woman peeked out from behind him. She wore a fluffy bathrobe and her hair was in disarray. He thrust the photo at her. 'Isn't this the guy we were talking to in the lift last night? Remember he noticed the yacht club insignia on my shirt and told us he'd placed in the Sydney to Gladstone?'

'Umm, yep I think that's him,' she agreed.

Hunter hiked his shoulders. 'You think? Can either of you be more precise?'

She stared at the photo again. 'Yep, I'm fairly certain this is the man that was in the lift with us.' Her partner nodded his head.

Got him! Hunter tried to contain his glee. 'Would that be the lift to the car park?'

The young man answered. 'Yeah, we had just got back from Jupiters Casino. Had quite a win on the roulette wheel and…'

'Mr?' Hunter queried cutting him off.

'Rawlings,' the young man offered. 'James Rawlings the Third.' He gestured toward the woman. 'And this is my lovely bride, Suzanne Rawlings.'

Honeymooners? That would explain the glow on their faces. 'Mr and Mrs Rawlings, I'm sorry to have to interrupt your evening, but I would really appreciate it if you could come down to the station to make a statement that you saw this man in the car park last night?'

Rawlings puffed out his chest. 'Well, if it's important, of course. We could do that.' He turned to his wife for her approval. She nodded sheepishly. Turning back to the detective, he asked, 'What's he supposed to have done?'

'We believe he may have murdered his wife.'

Suzanne gasped. The young couple looked at each other in bewilderment. 'We'll just get dressed,' they echoed in unison.

THIRTEEN

Jade had a trial scheduled the following morning so she had focussed on that case to avoid having to give too much of her mind over to thinking about Angelo or her situation.

As she walked from the court building feeling triumphant from her latest victory, a heavyset man in dark clothing approached her. His bulk gave the impression that he had no neck and his head was balancing squarely on his shoulders. 'Miss Sheffield.' It was a statement rather than a question.

'Yes,' she said cautiously on the chance this frightening looking man was a disgruntled friend or relative of the complainant in the case. The judge had just pronounced her client not guilty on a charge of rape. For a change, she believed this one was innocent.

The man handed her an envelope. A snarl suddenly contorted his features. 'Do what it says and you'll remain safe.'

She looked down at the envelope, turning it over in her hands. It was a plain white envelope with no external markings. When she looked up all she could see was the man's broad back as he strode away from her. 'Wait,' she called but his steps quickened and she had no desire to chase him. Now intrigued more than frightened, Jade slipped the envelope into her briefcase as she hurried down the street in the opposite direction. She was running late for her client meeting with Angelo at the police station.

Hunter held the floor in the conference room at the station with the Senior Sergeant and the rest of the team surrounding him. He read from the comprehensive forensics report. As suspected, the blood at both the primary and secondary crime scenes was a DNA match to the blood sample taken from Jennifer Morley at the hospital.

Forensics had also matched the mud they found on a set of shoes in the apartment to the mud in the tyre treads of the car found in the hotel car park. The soil analysis indicated it was from an area forested by eucalypts, which may assist them in the search for the body. Angelo's fingerprints were present on the knife and trophy, and in Jennifer Morley's car. These things on their own may not have stood up as evidence given Angelo's ready access to the items and his wife's car, but considered in the context of the offence they reinforced the case and could help sway a jury toward a guilty verdict.

He read in detail the results of the bloodstain analysis then showed the charts and computer simulations the forensics team had produced to support their conclusion that the victim would have sustained injuries occasioning death. Hunter then summarised the other evidence they had collected including the statements from the eyewitness from the apartment building and the couple from the hotel.

Harris seemed satisfied. 'It looks like we have enough to indict him on. Let's try to get a date for a committal hearing.'

'I'll give Dr Morley the good news,' Hunter grinned as he left the room.

Jade was sitting with her client as Hunter entered the room. Her former feelings for Angelo replaced by a sense of loathing, she had to be careful to keep the emotion from outwardly showing. She hated having to keep up the charade that she still cared about him. It helped that they had agreed it was best to refrain from any public displays of affection. They had been conversing for the last hour, going over the details of Angelo's account of the events and covering off the eventuality of committal proceedings. He'd had the opportunity to tell her the truth in private but he had stuck to his story. It seemed he was going to go through with this con. She was nothing more than a tool to him, employed to get the job done right. She could not believe his gall. Her sub-conscience began plotting its own little game of betrayal as she vowed to maintain her professional facade to hide her anger.

Hunter dropped a copy of Angelo's statement in front of him. They had typed it up as an official-looking document and he said in an even more official voice, 'Please read this statement then advise if you wish to make any changes. Otherwise sign at the bottom here.' He tapped his finger on the line several times.

Angelo read the document then nodded his head in agreement that the contents were accurate. He picked up the pen then signed it with feigned despondency. 'What happens next?'

'We've applied to have the case heard by a magistrate at committal proceedings. It's a formality really, to determine whether there's enough evidence to go to trial before a jury. Your lawyer can explain the details but we're pretty sure the evidence we have is going to convince a jury you murdered your wife *beyond a reasonable doubt.*' He emphasised the last words.

Jade suspected that Hunter always enjoyed this moment. The moment when he looked into an assailant's eyes and could see they knew they had been outsmarted by the law. But Angelo's eyes told a different story. If she didn't know better, she would have suspected he was some kind of psychopath without any real emotion. But she knew the reason for the look of glee in his eyes. He was getting exactly what he wanted.

'Given the nature of the charges, you'll be remanded in custody until such time as the committal hearing takes place. An officer and transport vehicle will be here soon to transfer you to the correctional facility.'

'I'd like to be informed the moment you find my wife,' Angelo spat defiantly at the detective. 'You've made a grave mistake and you're going to pay for it.'

'Is that a threat, Dr Morley?'

'No. It's simply the truth.'

The truth? Jade's gut twisted bitterly. *You wouldn't know the truth if it jumped up and bit you on the arse, Angelo Morley. You want truth? Let's give them the real truth. That you are a deceitful, cheating liar!* She realised she had been glaring at him and consciously softened her face. If Angelo thought she was going to represent him to the best of her abilities to get him off this charge he was sorely mistaken. She intended to see to it that he spent as long as possible in prison. The game had just begun.

She sat with Angelo, begrudgingly answering his questions until the correctional officer arrived. She watched with silent satisfaction as the burly man shackled his wrists and ankles then began to lead him away. Angelo stopped for a moment then took her fingers with his handcuffed hands. He moved them to his lips then kissed her on the back of her knuckles as he looked intently into her eyes. 'Arrivederci Bella.'

Jade sighed with relief as they walked out the door. She could finally stop pretending she gave a damn.

The man pushed Angelo into the back of the waiting prison van. Another officer stood as the door opened, his gun conspicuously flaunted on his hip.

'Ciao,' a thick Italian accent suddenly boomed from the shadows of the interior. 'If it isn't-a Dr Angelo Morley?' Angelo recognised the man. He glared at him, impugning him to shut up. The man took the hint.

The officer stared enquiringly at Angelo. 'Friend of yours?'

'I'm a doctor. Treated him once,' he offered in explanation. He did not add that it was for an unreported knife wound. For the rest of the journey he sat in sombre silence, not taking his eyes away from the floor so he could avoid conversation.

When they reached their destination, the guards escorted Angelo and the other man to a holding area where they awaited processing through the prison system. Angelo signed the register then handed over his personal belongings, which the guard put into a box with his name and number on them then placed on a shelf for later storage. The unsmiling man handed him a clear plastic carry bag with some basic toiletry items – toothpaste, toothbrush, soap, and a comb – and plain grey prison issue clothing. Another guard then herded him and the other men into a long shower cubicle where he watched while they stripped down then experienced their first group shower. One by one, they filed into another room where they were subjected to an external search then an internal cavity search before the guards allowed them to dress in their prison uniforms. Stripped of all dignity, the guard then marched them to the remand section of the prison. Angelo found himself placed into a cell with the man who had travelled with him in the prison van.

'Hey-a, remember me? I'm-a Frank Zuliani.' He offered his hand. 'What you in-a for?'

Angelo took the man's hand then shook it firmly. It may pay to have allies inside. He was not sure how long he was going to be there. 'Murder,' he answered.

'Śi, me too,' Frank grinned.

FOURTEEN

The story had been splashed across the headlines of the national newspapers. *Prominent heart surgeon arrested in wife's disappearance.* Angelo's photo made front page. Jade glowered knowingly he would be pleased with himself.

It had been a long week, but as the days passed she felt more and more confident that she would go unpunished for her crime. The crime itself would not go unpunished however. Natural justice would see to it that Angelo would pay for what he had set in motion. There was a slight easing of her conscience in the notion. As her humiliation intensified, she had easily been able to reassign her feelings of guilt to him.

While these thoughts occupied her mind, her hand had been absentmindedly doodling on her desk pad. When she looked down, she was astonished that she had made an exact replica of the logo from top of the newspaper. She smiled sarcastically. Maybe she should have taken up forgery rather than law.

A sudden idea struck her. She walked over to the locked filing cabinet where she had hidden the credit cards belonging to both Jennifer Morley and the imposter, Julianne McGuire. She took them out, looking at the signatures on the back. A cinch! She ripped the page off the desk pad to reveal a fresh sheet then began practicing the signatures until she had perfected them. She was in the mood for vengeance. 'How about I have a little fun at your expense, Angelo?' she said aloud. It was the very least she deserved. Maybe a nice diamond pendant, some new designer clothes…

As she tucked the cards out of view in the zippered lining of her briefcase, she noticed the white envelope she had placed there a few days before. Jade had entirely forgotten the incident outside the courthouse. She tore open the envelope then removed its contents. There was a single sheet of paper with a post office box number typed on it for the local post office. She tipped the envelope up. A key fell out. First the CD, and now this! Could the same person have sent it? She dropped the items back into her briefcase then headed out of her office, having abandoned her plans for the vengeful shopping spree in light of this new mission

'Just ducking out to grab some lunch, Danni. I won't be long.'

Danni looked up to see Jade's back as she disappeared out of the office. Jade missed the look of concern on her face. Her assistant was worried about her boss and how distant she had seemed that week. She had tried to talk to her on numerous occasions but Jade had been oblivious to her attempts, wrapped up as she was in her dilemma.

When Jade got to the post office, she scanned her eye along the numbers on the black post office boxes until she found the number typed on the sheet of paper she held tightly in her hand. It was one of the larger sized boxes. She fumbled with the key as she inserted it. The lock turned then she opened the door to reveal a thick package wedged sideways in the box. It was the only item there. She carefully removed it, noticing with apprehension that it had her name on it.

Jade slipped the package into her already bulging briefcase then headed back to the privacy of her office. Her growing anxiety had suppressed her hunger. Almost as an afterthought, she stopped to purchase a sandwich from the deli so Danni would not be suspicious at her arriving back empty-handed. It would also give her an excuse to block any interruptions for a while.

She smiled at Danni as she walked through the door but did not have time to address the girl's concerned look. Seated behind her desk, door closed, Jade opened the package spilling its contents onto her desk. There were two other thick envelopes in it but a CD case captured Jade's attention. She opened the case with shaking hands then looked at the disc. It was a DVD this time but again there were no markings to indicate its subject matter. She placed it into her CD drive. The box began to whir as her computer read the disc. The media player automatically leapt up on the screen. Jade picked up her sandwich then took a bite while she waited for the picture to load.

As it did, she dropped her sandwich, oblivious to the salad falling into her lap and onto the floor, and stared open-mouthed at the screen. She watched in horror as the scene played out before her: the argument between her and Jennifer Morley, the frenzied attack then dragging the lifeless form into the bushes. Jade closed her eyes as she relived the night. She could feel the bile rising in her throat as her heart began to pound mercilessly against her chest wall. When she opened her eyes, the clip had stopped and she began to tremble uncontrollably as she sat staring at a still image of herself on the screen standing over the body.

A gravely Italian voice sounded through the speakers. 'Ciao Miss Sheffield. Don't-a be concerned. We have removed the body. You won't be implicated if-a you follow our instructions carefully. We will-a be in touch.'

Jade pushed aside the scattered ingredients of her sandwich, steeling herself against the nausea that bubbled up from the pit of her stomach. Who were *we,* and what did they want with her? Were these people on Angelo's side? Did he know about this? If he did he was a good actor, but then he *had* duped her all along. Had someone been following him too? They must have had quite sophisticated equipment to get those shots in the dark. What would they 'be in touch' for? Could someone be planning to extort her?

She picked up one of the envelopes then tore it open. It contained news clippings of the case, and a report on the upcoming trial, which named her as the defence lawyer. They had wasted no time in scheduling the committal hearing for the high profile case. A magistrate had already ruled there was enough evidence to take the case to trial. The Director of Public Prosecutions was in the process of preparing the indictment so the trial date would soon be set. She would not be engaging counsel as Angelo had insisted she represent him personally in court. It was not common practice but it was allowable. She had argued at first, having only acted in that capacity in minor cases, but

Angelo had begged her to do it. She finally conceded on the basis that it gave her further opportunity to ensure his downfall. She had easily been able to convince her superiors she was up to the task.

Jade opened the second envelope. It too was full of news clippings, but these went back over several years. They were reports on organised crime, mostly on the Gold Coast and in South East Queensland. What was the purpose of this? Was this some sort of clue as to who had sent the package? One in particular suddenly jumped out at her. It was a report of the murder of the Asian family that her sister Amy had been babysitting for at the time. Someone had clearly circled her sister's name in red pen. The colour drained from her face. She dropped her head into her hands on the desk, trying to think what it could all mean. Was it some kind of threat? Could her sister be in danger too because of her mistakes?

Jade hit the play button then ran the clip again. Her courtroom instincts took over as she analysed the scene. Although she knew who the people in the film were, it would be difficult for anyone else to make a positive ID. It was dark and the camera angle meant most of the shots were of the backs of their heads. Her car had appeared in part of one of the shots. There was certainly equipment around these days that could enhance the images enough to pick out her number plate.

Jade pulled out the credit cards for Jennifer Morley and Julianne McGuire then mulled over what she should do. She still had Jennifer Morley's purse with the ID's as well. Had anyone notified the bank to cancel the cards? It was unlikely since the police had not yet established she was officially dead. Nobody could convict her of murder if there was no victim. It was time to prove Mrs Jennifer Morley was still very much alive.

She opened up her internet browser then typed in the website for Qantas airlines. You did not even have to show ID these days for domestic flights. You could just check in online and print your own boarding pass. She checked the available flights to Cairns the following morning. She could make the six am one. It was an easy two and a half hour flight to tropical north

Queensland. She entered the passenger name, Jennifer Morley, followed by the numbers on the credit card. The system accepted the card details so she hit the print button to obtain a copy of the flight itinerary then proceeded to the check in page to print her boarding pass. Putting everything discreetly into her briefcase, she headed for the door. She needed to pick up a few things and pack.

'I'll see you on Monday, Danni. Have a lovely weekend.'

She was gone before Danni could reply. Once again, her assistant had not had the chance to have that talk with her boss and friend.

FIFTEEN

As the plane touched down in Cairns, Jade found herself in awe of the tree-shrouded mountains that loomed over the town. She had not been to the far north since she was a teenager but it seemed that not much had changed. It was a different world up here where things travelled at a slower pace. The rainforest flanked the surrounding mountains, still standing as it had for millions of years. Much of the land remained in pristine condition, the Government having now returned much of it to its native tribal owners. The Daintree rainforest, just a few hours to the north gave claim to some of the oldest species of flora on Earth, dating back to the dinosaur era. The region was also well known for its modern dinosaurs, the crocodiles.

The airport was modern yet provincial. The humidity hit her at full force as she stepped out of the aircraft onto the steamy tarmac then made her way across to the space frame building. She was here. Jade Sheffield. Jennifer Morley. Julianne McGuire. She could be any or all of them this weekend. It was probably wise to leave Jade out of the little group, so she had brought ample cash with her in case either of the credit cards unexpectedly exceeded their limits. She did not want to leave any trace that she had been in Cairns. She had bought herself a dark wig to cover her own auburn locks and look more like the woman in the licence photo. She picked up her bag from the carousel then headed out to the taxi rank.

Jade had booked into the popular Rydges Hotel in the centre of town under the name of Jennifer Morley. She intended to use the credit card around town all weekend so the police could trace it to this location. The desk clerk took a scan of the card then handed her the room key with a smile. So far, so good. By the time she had to sign the account she would have perfected the signature. She waved the bellboy away as he eagerly offered to help with her bag. It was best not to have too many people remembering her since she did not really resemble the tall dark-featured woman despite her attempt at a disguise.

Jade did not have a set plan for her weekend in Cairns but she could certainly do with some rest and relaxation after her hellish week. She filled the spa bath in the luxurious bathroom then slipped into the soothing water. For a moment, her mind wandered to the night in the hotel with Angelo. A sudden feeling of emptiness threatened to overwhelm her but she pushed the memories aside. It had been a lie. All lies. She lay back letting her mind go blank as the bubbles rushed around her and soothed her tense muscles.

Later, wrapped in the soft bathrobe supplied by the hotel, Jade sat at the table and continued to practice Jennifer's signature. It was not one of those undecipherable scribbles. It was simply her full name written in what was likely her normal cursive writing. It gave Jade another idea. In the recording she had listened to, Angelo explained to Jennifer that he would have her write to him from North Queensland under a pseudonym name. Obviously, that name was Julianne McGuire. One of Jade's high school hobbies had been calligraphy, so she was very adept at reproducing written script. She picked up a sheet of paper from the hotel's stationery supply and started to develop the letters in the way Jennifer had written them in her signature.

When she was confident with her work, she began the letter. *Dear Angelo...* She wrote three more letters dated over a period of several weeks, giving news of life in sunny north Queensland then signed them with Julianne McGuire's signature. Putting them into separate envelopes, she slipped them into her handbag leaving the first letter unsealed.

The next morning Jade went to the post office to open a post office box in the name of Julianne McGuire, paying the annual fee with the credit card in that name to establish that the woman had been there and seemingly taken up residence in the town. She added the post office box address into the body of the letter so Angelo could reply, then sealed the envelope and posted it to him at the prison. Let him think his plan was going smoothly and Jennifer was still alive. If the details of his plan were ever to become known, then he could attest to the fact that Jennifer had still been very much alive and abiding by the instructions he had given her. She dropped the key into her handbag then looked around at the staff in the store. A pimple-faced young boy of about sixteen was advising an elderly woman at the Postpak shelves. Jade walked toward him then waited until he had helped the woman select the appropriate sized box for her parcel.

'Can I help you?' he asked. Jade gave him a wink then told him what a helpful young man he was. She noticed his blush at the compliment.

She treated him to a flirtatious smile. 'I was just wondering if you would be able to help me out.' She dropped her voice then explained conspiratorially, 'My father is a guard in a prison down in Brisbane. I'm twenty-five years old and he thinks I'm fifteen and he can still tell me what to do! You know how it is?'

Jade had shaved five years off her age but she knew she could get away with it. The boy nodded his head in empathy. Jade had picked her mark well. 'You see I met these people and they've asked me to go backpacking with them. I don't want my Dad to find out about it, he'll just totally freak out. If I don't write to him from here every few weeks like I promised he'll send the police out looking for me and I'll have no fun before I have to go back to uni!'

The boy looked genuinely concerned for her. 'What can I do to help?'

'I'd just like you to post these letters for me. I've dated them a few weeks apart. I'll be back in a few months and he will be none the wiser. I'm happy to pay you for your trouble.' She reached into her handbag to pull out her purse in a gesture of goodwill.

'Don't worry about it. My old man's a bit of a pig too. I'd be happy to do it for you.'

'Thank you, you're a lifesaver!' Jade kissed him on the cheek. 'I've just put the date in the corner here. See? So you know when to send them. Here are the stamps. You can just stick them over the top of the date when you send them.'

'You can trust me with your life,' he promised.

'It might come to that.' She scowled then let her smile return. 'You really are a lifesaver. I don't know how to thank you. Can I get your number so I can call you when I get back into town?'

He scribbled it down for Jade on a scrap of paper. She wanted to be able to check up to make sure he kept his word. She kissed him once more on the cheek then threw another smile back in his direction as she left the post office.

Directly next door to the post office was a real estate agency. Jade picked up a rental property list from the display stand outside the door. The dark-skinned receptionist was startled by the alert bell as Jade walked in the door. She looked up from her typing. 'How can I help you?' she enquired in a manner more professional than her presentation suggested.

'Hi. I'm looking for a place to rent. Is this all you have at the moment?'

'Yeah,' the girl replied in a thick native accent. 'We suggest you take a drive by the properties first to see if you're interested. If you'd like to inspect any of them I can make an appointment for you with the property manager.' Her speech was grammar perfect as if she had rehearsed it many times.

Jade thanked the girl then turned to head for the door. She was thinking about how she could apply for one of the properties in the name of Jennifer Morley. She turned back to the girl. 'Do you think I could get an application form from you? I'm only in town for the weekend and I'm a bit pressed for time. Would it be OK for me to fax my application in to you from my hotel if I find something I like?'

'Certainly. Just fax it back to us with photocopies of your licence and the other identification listed on the form and it will be fine.'

These regional folk were so trusting. Nothing like what she would have to go through in the city with the 100 point ID system and showing her photo identification in person. It was too easy.

Jade thanked her again then headed out the door. It was time for Jennifer Morley to have some fun in Cairns!

Jade spent a few hours shopping, using Julianne McGuire's credit card to make purchases of personal items and clothing she may need when she arrived. She made some more expensive purchases at the Pier with Jennifer Morley's credit card. Things a girl might purchase if she was looking for some serious retail therapy to get over a traumatic relationship break up.

All that shopping had given her a healthy appetite. Wandering down the café strip along the foreshore, Jade perused the menu boards of the various cafes and restaurants famed for their fresh seafood. She sat at a table facing the ocean then ordered a feast of the local fare: succulent oysters and scallops as a starter, the popular fish barramundi, topped with the delicious giant claws of a mud crab. The chef had colourfully presented the seafood amongst tropical fruits and salad. Jade raised her glass of wine then toasted toward the horizon with contempt. *To you Angelo.* She savoured the meal in a leisurely manner while completing the rental application form for the first property on the real estate list. After finishing her meal, she signed for the bill using Jennifer's credit card, adding a sizeable tip. The total bill came to seventy-five dollars. Not bad for a lunch for one. A doctor's wife would be used to such extravagance.

Jade headed back to her hotel laden with her purchases. By the time she had walked the few blocks in the humid weather she was glowing with perspiration. She could feel the internal heat forcing its way out through her skin. She upended one of the shopping bags onto the bed then donned the expensive new bikini she had splashed out on in the surf shop. Throwing the fluffy hotel towel over her shoulder, she headed for the swimming pool.

The water refreshed her so she swam five laps of the pool before settling herself on one of the sun lounges to take advantage of the north Queensland rays. A couple, obviously honeymooners, were splashing playfully in one end of the pool. Jade eyed them enviously from underneath her new three hundred dollar sunglasses. Under normal circumstances she would have been happy to see them frolicking lovingly in the sun. She lay back then let the now familiar feelings take over. Angelo's actions had left a gaping void where her heart had once been. Anger was the only emotion that could fill it right now. At first, the anger had been like a new woollen jumper, scratchy and irritating. But in the way that wool eventually wears, her anger had come to be almost comforting.

That night, Jade's sleep was restless as she dreamt of plots of revenge. She woke early then pounded out some of her anger on the treadmill in the hotel gym. The hotel business lounge was on the same floor as the gym. After she had showered, she made use of the facilities to photocopy the licence and credit card of Jennifer Morley then fax them and the rental application form back to the real estate. Later in the day she would phone to withdraw the application, advising her plans had changed and she would be back in a few weeks. She would ask them to keep the documentation on file so she would not have to fill it in again in case they had another suitable property at the time. She knew how hungry real estate agents could be. They were eager to keep everyone's contact details they could get their hands on, especially someone new to the town. She would check online to apply for another property in a few weeks.

Back in her room, Jade contemplated what to do with the rest of her Sunday. Perhaps she should hire a car in the name of Jennifer Morley. She flicked through the guest information book. Cairns itself was set on the bay so at low tide it offered only a view of the unattractive mud flats. An easy drive north, according to the brochures, Palm Cove sported beaches with beautiful white sand. It was the wrong season to be able to wade in the surf, the coastal waters hostage to the deadly box jellyfish for the next few months, but the scene looked beautiful nonetheless. She set off in the direction of the car hire office she had seen on her travels yesterday, credit card in hand.

When Jade finally handed over Jennifer Morley's credit card that afternoon to check out of the hotel, she crossed her fingers it had sufficient credit left on it to cover the charges. She breathed a sigh of relief as the machine flashed *Transaction Approved,* then she signed the signature on the slip.

'I hope you enjoyed your stay with us Mrs Morley,' the desk clerk said with a wide friendly smile as Jade picked up her bag, now bulging with her purchases.

'Oh very much so, thank you.' Jade was very satisfied with her accomplishments that weekend. Along with her new wardrobe she had felt entitled to at Angelo's expense, a new sense of control pervaded her. The pitiful feelings of vulnerability were gone. What had taken over was a colossal surge of power and invincibility. She headed for the airport full of self-admiration, marvelling at the strength that she had managed to summon up over the last week.

SIXTEEN

'Wow,' whistled Danni as Jade breezed into the office on Monday morning. 'Someone's spent the weekend at the beach. Look at your tan!'

Jade hesitated, caught a little off guard. 'Err, yeah.'

'So where did you go, Tahiti?'

'Umm, just down to Burleigh,' Jade laughed trying to make light of it.

'The sun must have been awfully hot for you to get a fantastic tan like that in a couple of days.'

Jade avoided any further questions from Danni as she scuttled into her office then shut the door. Danni cocked her head sideways then went back to her typing.

Jade lifted the new sheets of paper out of her tray, ignoring the small pile of 'too hard' items that inevitably built up in the bottom of the tray. There was a notice in relation to Angelo's trial. It had been set down for twelve weeks time. Good. He deserved to spend some time in prison paying for what he did to her. It also gave her some time to establish that Jennifer was still alive. With a bit of luck the inmates in the prison were giving him a hard time already.

Except for Frank Zuliani, Angelo had not attempted to make any other connections since his incarceration. It was gratifying to be in a place where he no longer had to put on false pretences. To the contrary, he had made it known there was a mean streak in his nature. It was an advantage to him here as it encouraged the other inmates to keep their distance. His one concern was that the mob might have someone on the inside that they could use to relay their message to him. Now he was of no further use to them, he stood the risk of them bringing down their own sentence. The fact that the death penalty was not law in Australia meant nothing to them. They had their own code and ways of dealing with things.

Because of this concern, Angelo was on guard most of the time. As he went about his daily prison routine, he kept a vigilant watch on everyone within his vicinity. Detecting even the slightest movement in his peripheral vision became instinctive, which proved to be more than prudent.

As he saw the switchblade coming toward him, he dropped his meal tray down to block its path. It clattered along with its contents to the floor making the surrounding inmates look up from their meals. Twisting the young man's arm until he weakened, Angelo forced him to drop the knife and fall to the ground in pain. He was about to take a swing when guards on both sides lifted him then pulled him away. Another guard dragged the man to his feet. Angelo watched him wince as a blow landed in the soft part of his stomach. The guard led the man away holding his injured arm.

'Bastard!' the young man spat at him. 'You'll get what's coming to ya.'

It was all over in a matter of minutes. The guard let Angelo go then beckoned him toward the queue. 'Line up and get another plate mate.'

Everyone went back to eating as if nothing had happened. This was how prison life was: a battle for supremacy. Angelo re-joined the queue then let a deep guttural laugh escape his throat and project across the room. He could not show any fear in here. They were like dogs. They could smell it.

He doubted the young man had any connection with the organisation. He was just a weaselly punk who had a huge chip on his shoulder and did not like people from Angelo's status in life. Still, it had unnerved him. He didn't know what kind of stunts *they* might pull so he started to ask around the exercise yard later that day. It appeared his mafia connections were quite well publicised throughout the inmate community. Frank Zuliani had a big mouth. He made a mental note to have a word with him about that. On the positive side, nobody was about to mess with him in a hurry. They had the impression that the big burly Italian was his minder. The incident in the mess hall that day also served to add to his reputation as a tough guy in his own right.

It looked like the next three months of prison life were going to be a snap. He would just do his time and keep out of trouble, while he waited for his trial date to approach. Three months of his life was a small price to pay for the rewards he would gain when it was over.

At the end of the day, the guards herded the prisoners from the exercise yard into their small cells. They had a few hours to entertain themselves before they called 'lights out'.

Angelo had collected his mail from the administration office earlier that afternoon. 'Got yourself a girlfriend waiting out there for you cobber?' the officer had asked with a sly wink.

He had handed Angelo one small envelope. It had the crest of the Rydges Hotel on the front. He looked more closely at the postmark. Cairns. The administration staff had already opened and perused it. He now sat down to read it eagerly. He had only had the chance to attempt one call to Jennifer so far on the mobile phone he had given her, but he had a recorded message. It was paramount to his plan that they keep in contact. *Dear Angelo*, the letter began.

When he had finished reading about the sun and the sand, he began his reply. He assured her he was fine then advised her of the date set for the trial. He wrote that he would let her know when he felt ready for a 'visit' but the time was not yet right then thanked her for her support. Mindful the staff would read the letter before sending it, he wrote nothing that gave anything away other than that they were old friends. He addressed it to Julianne McGuire at the post office box address in Cairns she had supplied. He would deliver it back to the office the next day. A satisfied smile played across his dark features. Things were travelling along exactly as planned.

Angelo slipped the letter into the bible in the top drawer of his small desk. He was not religious but God was probably the only one who would be looking out for him now. No, that was not true. Jade still appeared to be on his side, despite the revelation about the pregnancy coming as a bit of a shock to her. Maybe he should have told her about it, but he had managed to smooth that one over. She was still obviously infatuated with him and continued to have faith in his innocence. He was confident she would put up a good fight to clear his name. When they had succeeded and he was a wealthy man, then he could plan his future with her.

Maybe they could leave the country to re-discover his European roots. He might even be able to become a family man. He would certainly give his own son more than his mongrel father had given him. Angelo had tried to track him down once, mostly to give him a piece of his mind. The bum had drunk himself to death years before, probably without a second thought toward the welfare of his young son.

He remembered his promise to his mother as she lay dying on the street. *This one's for you Mum.*

He fell asleep dreaming his mother's protective arms were around him.

SEVENTEEN

The three months passed without too much event. Jade's sister Amy had come to stay with her for a break from university life and they had spent an enjoyable week together. After that, she had settled back into her normal working routine and the night she had accidentally killed Jennifer Morley seemed like a distant dream. She continued to play out her counsel role in Angelo's case, visiting him on a weekly basis to go over the evidence and plans for his defence. She was glad she did not have to over-play her feelings for him, but she let him continue to believe they existed.

Nobody had 'been in touch', as promised on the DVD she had hidden securely away at home. Could it have just been a ploy Angelo had instigated to test her loyalty? Surely he would have said something by now if he knew of Jennifer's death. Although she was feeling very much in control of the situation and believed that she was in the clear, a niggling doubt remained that someone could reveal her crime at any moment. To guarantee her insurance policy remained in place, she continued to carry out the plans she had made in Cairns. Posing as Jennifer Morley, she kept in contact with the real estate agency checking from time to time what properties they had available. She advised them she was in a probationary period in her job, so she would be looking to rent as soon as they had confirmed her permanency. She also phoned the young boy from the post office a few days after the first letter was due to be posted to thank him again for helping her out. He had not failed her and told her he looked forward to her return to Cairns. She had kept all the credit card receipts should they somehow be required to find their way into the hands of the law.

Jade had spent some time working in close proximity with Brent Hunter. As she observed him in action on the case, the respect she'd had for the young detective when they first met had grown. His investigation was thorough and his motives were pure. Emotionally though, his immaturity still showed in his dealings with her. In his efforts to impress her he probably shared too many of the details of the forensic report with her, particularly given she was working for the other side. She was intrigued that he still seemed to have a very strong ardour for her.

There is a common saying that goes, *Keep your friends close, and your enemies closer*. Thinking it might be to her later benefit to cultivate the relationship, she began flirting with him at every possible opportunity. It was only a matter of time before they ended up in bed together again. There was no way Jade was going to let herself trust another man, so she maintained control of the relationship and kept things on a casual and discreet basis.

Although she was enjoying the lull her life had fallen into, the trial date persistently loomed in her calendar. Finally, the day arrived. She and the Crown Prosecutor spent the first day selecting the jury. Jade checked over their personal details as the men and women, who had been selected randomly from the electoral role, came to the stand. At the end of the process, seven men and five women made up the jury. Two of the jurors Jade had been adamant in selecting were divorced women. Their embittered faces indicated they would have little sympathy for any man, let alone a man like Angelo.

The next day Angelo sat beside Jade in the Supreme Court. As she read her notes, he brushed his hand gently against hers. She looked up then smiled encouragingly at him, using all her effort not to recoil in disgust.

Nathan Riley, a recently appointed Crown Prosecutor, occupied the seat to Jade's right. His greenness suggested the DPP were confident of winning the case.

The bailiff began by announcing, 'All rise for the Honourable Justice Barlow.'

After the judge and the rest of the court seated themselves, the indictment against Angelo was read out.

‘Would the accused please stand,’ Justice Barlow instructed.

Angelo rose from his seat. Jade noticed his chiselled features had become a little gaunter over the past three months, but he still cut an imposing figure in his charcoal pinstriped suit.

‘How do you plead?’

‘Not guilty, your Honour.’

The judge turned to the Crown Prosecutor. ‘You may call your first witness.’

‘The Crown calls Mrs Colleen Privett.’

The small podgy woman shuffled toward the stand. She had dressed for the event in an impeccably tailored navy suit, but the outdated crochet collared blouse belied her fashion sense. Her face was lit up with an enthusiastic grin.

Nathan Riley guided her through her account of the events on the night Jennifer Morley was allegedly killed. Jade knew she should probably object to some of the witness’s biased judgements, but she held her tongue. Colleen was doing a good job of gaining the jury’s empathy. She looked over to see the two divorced women nodding their heads in disapproval.

Jade considered her cross-examination. She could have found ample ways to discredit the witness and cause doubt in the jury’s mind. Probably many a resident in the building would attest to her nature. She seemed like a busybody who would have no qualms in falsifying a story for the sake of gossip. However, she did not want to discredit the witness. She wanted the jury to believe her. She had to find something that would make it appear she was doing her job without actually damaging the witness’s testimony.

Jade could tell from the way the woman squinted her eyesight was not 20/20. Surely, she must wear glasses. She spied the chain around the woman’s neck. Her glasses were hanging beneath her blouse. Her vanity may have forced her to leave them there today. Jade stepped toward the woman.

‘Mrs Privett, can you read the sign at the back of the room for me.’

As the woman looked toward the back wall, her squinting became more evident. ‘No, I’m afraid I can’t, I’m sorry.’

‘Mrs Privett, how far away from you was the man in question when you saw him load this bundle into the car,’ she asked pointing toward Angelo.

‘Well, he was at the curb,’ she answered uneasily, seeming to realise that Jade was up to something. ‘It was about the same distance as that wall.’

Jade moved closer to the woman and bellowed, ‘Then how, Mrs Privett, can you be sure the man you saw was in fact the accused, Angelo Morley?’ She pointed again in the direction of her client.

Colleen Privett looked at Angelo then back at Jade in dismay. ‘I…I...was wearing my glasses,’ she stammered.

Jade feigned defeat. ‘Do you have your glasses here with you today, Mrs Privett?’

She moved her hands toward her blouse then lifted her glasses to her eyes.

Jade pointed toward the sign she had previously asked the witness to read.

Colleen Privett stated in a clear voice, ‘It says, *Please ensure mobile phones remain switched off at all times*.’

Jade stole a quick glance at the jury. They all looked convinced. Perfect! She turned to Angelo and gave him a look of apology. He was beaming at her. She had fooled him too.

‘No further questions, your Honour.’

‘The witness may stand down,’ directed Justice Barlow.

Over the next few days, the vast array of forensic evidence was examined and the testimonies of expert witnesses were heard. When he could spare the time, Hunter would slip in quietly to sit in on the proceedings. Jade could feel the warmth of his admiration as he smiled down on her, despite the fact he had already given evidence *against* her client. He had just slipped in the door as the judge pulled her up on one of her questions. She was in the middle of her cross-examination of a forensics expert.

‘Let me re-phrase the question.’ Jade drew out her words. ‘Can you say one hundred percent, emphatically, that the injuries the alleged victim sustained would have led to her death?’

'Not with one hundred percent certainty, not without a body, no.'

She should have stopped him there but she let him continue. 'Had the victim obtained medical attention then the chances of survival may have increased. But without replacement of the blood loss...' He shrugged his shoulders.

The jury already knew from Hunter's testimony there was no record of any such medical treatment on the night in question. The looks on their faces seemed already to seal Angelo's fate.

Jade brought Dr Daniel Warner to the stand to act as a character witness for Angelo, knowing he was the one who had given up the information about the pregnancy and Angelo's vasectomy. The Crown Prosecutor would tear him apart. Under Jade's questioning, he painted a glowing picture of Dr Angelo Morley and his achievements, making particular mention of how he had saved the Prime Minister's life. After Nathan Riley brought up the information about the vasectomy that Daniel had unwittingly given to the police, the witness continued with an air of uncertainty. Jade could sense the shadow of doubt that this cast in the jurors' minds as they shifted in their seats.

The final witness brought to the stand was Angelo Morley. Although Jade wanted the jury to fully share the strength of her loathing for him, she had to be careful not to let them see it.

'Dr Morley, can you explain in your own words what happened on the night your wife disappeared?' Jade began. Angelo recited his version of the night's events as he and Jade had rehearsed it many times. He attempted to gain the sympathy of the jury by speaking of his heartbreak at his wife's obvious infidelity. He certainly knew how to put on a good act. Fortunately, it seemed the jury were not as duped by his charms as she had been.

On the last day of the trial, when both Jade and Nathan summed up their respective cases, the weight of the evidence lay in the Crown Prosecutor's favour. The jury retired to consider their verdict so Jade headed back to her office to await their decision. In her experience, if a jury were to return a guilty verdict they would decide upon it more quickly than not.

Jade checked her voicemail messages, which had mounted during the day while she was in court. When she heard the gravely Italian voice, she felt a chill work its way up her spine. 'Ciao, Miss Sheffield. We have-a followed your trial with-a great interest. We are-a very impressed and are-a sure to be engaging your services in the near future.'

Who were *we?* Who had sent the CD and the DVD, and now wanted to engage her services? She didn't really want to contemplate the idea. Whoever they were, she was at their mercy while they had that tape and she did not think there was any way she could ever get it back. What was done was done. She had already resigned herself to that fact. Her experiences over the past few months had de-sensitised the degree to which her emotions controlled her. All she could do was wait until they made their demands, while she continued to cover her tracks. At least it didn't sound like they were going to extort her for money as she had first thought.

The following afternoon Jade received a call to say the jury had reached a verdict. She hurried down to the Supreme Court then took her place beside Angelo. He wrung his hands anxiously. She suspected it was an act but played her part to reassure him.

The jury spokesperson, one of the divorced women chosen by Jade, stood then faced Justice Barlow with a satisfied grin.

He called, 'Would the defendant please rise. Has the jury reached a decision?'

'We have, your Honour.'

'And how say you?'

The juror cast Angelo a spiteful glare. 'On the count of murder, we, the members of the jury, find the defendant *guilty!*'

Angelo sunk to his chair, acting like a defeated man. In reality, Jade knew he must have been feeling triumphant. Everything had gone according to plan, including her apparent eagerness to fight for his innocence. He would be silently patting himself on the back at the brilliant ally he had gained in her and what an asset she would be when the time came to mount his case against the Crown. How wrong he was.

Jade looked into Angelo's eyes, mustering as much sympathy as she could feign. 'I'm truly sorry Angelo.'

'Don't worry. I know you did your best but the evidence was against us. We can start working on the appeal. I'll be getting out of prison sooner than you think, and then we can get things back to where they were. I promise you.'

Huh! That's what you think. Angelo could rot in prison, or hell, or wherever else he ended up for all she cared. The only reason she had remained involved in this charade was to ensure her own safety and see him pay for what he had done to her.

If only the body been discovered. She wanted Angelo to see he had committed an act from which there was no escape. But somebody with another agenda had thwarted that plan by removing the body. Her skin went cold at the thought.

She would have to consider her next move very carefully.

EIGHTEEN

Jade sat at her desk the next day listening to the voicemail messages left while she was in court. The previous call had been a hang up. The pen she had been scribbling with tore through the paper as she exerted additional pressure on it. Why did people fear speaking to a machine? She was a busy woman and they couldn't expect her to be there to take every call. It was a private number too, which equally annoyed her that she did not even know who the caller was.

When she heard the gravely Italian voice in the next message say, 'Buongiorno, Miss Sheffield,' she dropped her pencil and instantly forgot her annoyance at the previous caller. 'I'm-a sorry to have missed you again,' the voice continued. 'We were-a very impressed with your efforts yesterday. We have a very important case we would-a like to engage you on. I'll be in touch again very soon.' The caller rang off without saying goodbye or leaving a return number.

She felt her body stiffen. Had this man with the gravely voice been in her courtroom yesterday? Could she have stared right into his eyes but not known he was there? She tried to bring to mind a mental picture of the courtroom but she had been so focussed on the case she had failed to take notice of the people who had been sitting in the room that day.

The call launched her into action. She picked up the phone then dialled the real estate agency to advise that her employer had confirmed her role as permanent so she would like to apply to rent one of the furnished properties they had listed. She gave the real estate her own name, Jade Sheffield, as the employer reference and her direct office number. She had become quite chatty with the property manager over the past three months so she doubted the woman would do too much checking into Jennifer Morley's history.

Later that day Jade received a call from the real estate agency on her work line. She recognised the number. Putting on a different voice, she gave Jennifer Morley a glowing reference. Sure enough, not much later she received a call on her mobile phone, which she answered as Jennifer Morley, to say they had accepted her application. She thanked the woman then advised she was in Brisbane for work. The woman agreed to fax the documentation so she could sign and return it by express post that day. She had taken enough cash from the Morley's account using Jennifer's card to cover the transaction. She wanted to be prepared in the event that the bank froze the account upon the pronouncement of Jennifer's death. Rather than pay the rent online as they had suggested, she took the cash to the bank then deposited the bond money and the first two weeks rent to the real estate's trust account. They would not be able to trace whom it had come from that way. Then she dialled the number of the boy she had met at the post office in Cairns.

'Hi, it's Julianne. Remember me?' After a bit of chitchat and a few made up stories about her trip, Jade's tone turned more serious. 'Look, I know I've already asked you to do so much for me, but I was wondering if I could ask just one more favour?'

'Sure, anything,' he eagerly responded.

'Well I've decided I'm not going home to uni. I'm coming back. I rented a house in Cairns.'

'Hey, that's fantastic!'

'I know, but I just know when my father finds out he's going to come up here and try to drag me home. I've used a different name, Jennifer Morley, but I just bet he'll go around every real estate agent with my photo to ask if they've seen me.'

'He sounds like a right prick, this old man of yours.'

'Well I know it's just because he loves me, but there comes a time when you have to do things on your own. Right?'

'You betcha,' he agreed.

'So I was wondering if maybe you could pick up the keys for me. It's just from the real estate next door to you. I'll ring them to tell them I'm sending someone over because I'm so flat out at work. I've already paid all the money, so I think they'll buy it.'

'Yeah, no worries. I'll give it a go.'

'Thanks. I know I've said this before, but you're a lifesaver! I'll call you back in a minute.'

Jade hung up then made the call to the real estate, thanking the property manager for her understanding.

She phoned the boy back. He answered on the first ring. Confirming the arrangements, she reminded him to ask for the keys for Jennifer Morley. He seemed eager to do her bidding. She felt a little guilty playing on his naivety but she had come too far now to turn back. She had to cover her tracks as best she could.

'I'm not sure exactly when I'll be back so could you hang on to the keys for a few days and I'll let you know when I can pick them up from you.' Jade was toying with the idea of whether she should go back to Cairns or whether she should just get him to put the keys in the post office box.

It would probably be beneficial to use the cards around town again but she was not sure if the bank would have cancelled them now Angelo had been charged with Jennifer's murder.

She would sleep on it and make the decision in the morning.

NINETEEN

It was Saturday and Jade and Brent were lying in bed. The early morning sun streaming through the window had just woken them. While Jade still maintained her emotional distance, she had come to find comfort in the physical intimacy of the relationship. The only thing that bothered her was his smoking habit. She turned away from him. 'Argh, your breath reeks! Why do you have to smoke before bed?'

Brent turned toward her and propped himself up on one elbow. 'I always like to smoke after sex,' he grinned. He hesitated for a moment. 'Jade, I probably shouldn't be telling you this, but now Jennifer Morley has been declared officially dead, the executors of her estate have contacted us.'

Jade sat up, her posture stiffening. 'Go on.'

'Well, it appears Angelo arranged a very large life insurance policy for his wife just before he killed her, naming himself as the sole beneficiary. That just goes to show we got the right man, but that's not the most interesting thing.' He stared a long moment into her eyes.

'Stop acting like a damn cop all the time and just spit it out.' Jade whacked him over the head with her pillow, partly in mock annoyance but mostly because she was eager to hear what he had to say.

'There have been some substantial purchases made using Jennifer Morley's credit card after her death. The executors would obviously like to recover the funds and have asked us to investigate.'

'So why are you telling me this?'

'I have to go away for a few days. We've traced the purchases to Cairns. Someone has been living the high life up there at the Morley's expense. The card is linked to Angelo Morley's bank account.'

Good! Jade was happy she had received *some* compensation for the time she had wasted on him, but kept her face impassive.

Brent continued. 'It's just possible, if we find this person, that they may be able to lead us to the location of Jennifer's body. I know Morley is planning to appeal so if we have a body then our case is much more concrete than it is now.' He looked over at Jade waiting for her reaction. 'I really shouldn't be telling you this.'

She tried to appear as if she were deep in concentration. 'You don't think it could mean Jennifer Morley is still alive, do you?' Planting the seed couldn't hurt. 'Maybe the whole thing was a setup to cash in on the insurance money.'

'That angle hadn't even occurred to me.' Brent admitted. 'You have a brilliant mind, Jade Sheffield.' He planted a kiss on the top of her head.

Jade's brilliantly scheming mind took another step forward. She remembered the overnight bag and other personal belongings of Jennifer Morley's. If she could somehow plant these to provide evidence Jennifer had been alive and living in Cairns, they may be convinced she was still alive now. It meant Angelo would probably win his appeal on the grounds they could establish reasonable doubt, but he would not get his hands on any of the insurance money or compensation as he had planned. His career was already in tatters. He would still pay for what he had done *and* it would help keep her in the clear.

Jade's thoughts transferred into words. 'How would you feel if I came to Cairns with you?'

He looked at her sternly. 'It's not going to be a holiday, Jade.'

'I know that. But it would be in the interests of my case to find out if Jennifer is alive. Even if there is some suspicion of her being alive, it would help me to establish reasonable doubt and give me a case for appeal against the murder charge.' She gave him a longing stare and battered her eyes. She knew he would be unable to resist it.

'Oh, OK,' he caved.

‘Oh thank you, thank you, thank you!’ Jade squealed as she straddled him then started planting kisses down his chest. He felt himself rise in anticipation of her reward as she reached down and guided his waiting hardness into her mouth.

After they had showered together and Jade had left, Hunter picked up the file sent from Cairns then leafed through its contents. Everything in the folder indicated Jennifer Morley had been in Cairns and that she was the woman who had rented the property there. He tried to phone the mobile number from the real estate records but a recorded message told him it was no longer connected. That didn’t really prove anything. She could have given them a false number. He looked at the rental application form, scrutinising it for anything he may have missed. It was a faxed copy, which she had completed many months earlier. Someone had crossed out the section completed for employment references in blue pen then written another number there. The handwriting was different.

Hunter picked up his mobile phone then dialled the number. The voice that answered the call was very familiar to him. It was Jade’s voice asking him to leave a message on her office voicemail system. It shocked him as much as it had when the Senior Sergeant had alerted him to it the previous day. He had not really wanted to contemplate her involvement, but the oaths he had made were to justice and upholding the law. He had no choice.

That Friday morning, the Senior Sergeant had called an impromptu meeting. As was often the case, his partner Andrews was off doing his own thing and was not in attendance. Harris let him in on the information about the rental property and advised there was speculation of something going on between Angelo Morley and his lawyer, Jade Sheffield. Hunter had reviewed the interview tapes with him and had to agree that the body language between Angelo and Jade indicated there was more going on than just a lawyer/client relationship. Her attempt to be professional seemed to be forced. Nobody could have missed the smouldering looks that passed between them. Hunter just wasn’t convinced whether they stemmed from passion or anger. No matter how he felt about her, it was his job to find out what Jade's connection was to all this. Harris ordered him to investigate the anomalies they had uncovered. He was not aware of the relationship between Hunter and Jade.

He had convinced Harris to keep his suspicions between the two of them until he could establish whether they held any weight. When Hunter mentioned later to his partner that he had to travel to Cairns as part of the investigation, Andrews was happy to let him go alone.

'Bloody stinkin' hot hole in summer,' Andrews complained. 'You can have that one all to yourself!'

It would make things much easier for Hunter. Agreeing to allow Jade to accompany him to Cairns had been a setup so he could establish if and how she was involved in the whole affair.

Back at her apartment, Jade packed her things for the tropical monsoonal weather in Cairns alongside the contents of Jennifer Morley's overnight bag and some of the items she had purchased on the credit card on her previous visit. She folded the bag itself into a tight square then hid it beneath her clothing. Even if they searched her bag at the airport, none of the items would look out of place. She had hidden the credit cards and ID's in the zippered side of her handbag, which she intended to carry on the plane and not let out of her sight.

It was with mixed emotions that Jade boarded the flight two days later. She had already checked in online, choosing a window seat that already had occupants in the neighbouring seats. She did not wish to spend the two-hour flight in idle chitchat with Brent, preferring to use the time to formulate a plan.

'I'll see you in Cairns,' she winked at Brent as he passed her then headed toward the back of the aircraft.

The monsoon season had started in the tropics so as the plane began its descent into Cairns, Jade was disappointed that the thick clouds hid her much adored mountains from view. It was very different to her flight just a few months earlier. Still, there was a mystical quality to the white clouds that held them in the air like a wizard's glove. Eventually they broke through the cloudbank. She caught sight of the luscious tropical landscape, the bay edged by palm trees with the mountains rising around them. Jade decided in that moment that Cairns was her second most favourite place in the world.

As she waited for her luggage to appear on the carousel, Brent crept up behind her then planted a kiss on her shoulder. 'Welcome to Cairns, Miss Sheffield. Can I get your luggage for you?'

Jade smiled back at him. 'No thank you, kind Sir.' She was trying not to show her paranoia, but there was no way she was going to let anyone touch that bag.

Jade remained in the car while Brent checked into the four star motel in the CBD she was unofficially sharing with him. The police department were certainly not putting him up in any fancy hotel. She could have arranged her own room elsewhere but it might look a bit suspicious to Brent. She would just have to be careful. He was a detective by nature, but he had no reason to distrust her. She felt sure she was safe. The room was at least comfortable, with a double bed, and not far from the Esplanade.

'I'm sorry Jade but I have to go and check in with the local boys,' Brent apologised once they had settled into the room.

'No problem. I might just take a bit of a look around town.' Jade was flicking through the hotel compendium, feigning interest as if she had never been to Cairns before. 'It looks like a beautiful place.'

'Great, well you do that and I'll give you a call in a few hours to let you know where we're at.' He kissed her and headed for the door.

As soon as Brent had left the motel, Jade took out Jennifer's overnight bag then began to pack the things into it she wanted to leave at the house. She picked up her mobile then called the boy from the post office.

'Hi, it's Julianne,' she said cheerfully. 'I'm back in town so I'd like to get my keys for the house. Would you like to catch up for a coffee?' He seemed eager to do so and agreed to meet with her right away. Jade picked up the bag then headed off in the direction of the post office.

Jade spent about half an hour faking animated stories about her travels over a coffee, then thanked him profusely and paid the bill. 'I'm really busy with this new job I've started, but I'll try to give you a call over the next few weeks so we can catch up again.'

He looked disappointed that she was leaving, but replied, 'That would be rad. Good luck and let me know if there's anything else you need.'

'Thanks so much for your help. If anyone comes looking for me, promise me you won't tell them you ever saw me. It could be my father or his goons.'

'I promise.'

Jade stood up then kissed him on the cheek, brushing her lips against his as she moved her face away. She smiled and waved goodbye as he stood blushing.

Walking a little further into town, she entered the supermarket where she purchased grocery items, cleaning products and toiletries as well as a set of rubber gloves. Then she caught a taxi to Jennifer Morley's new house, paying cash for the fare.

Jade slipped on the rubber gloves before unlocking the front door. The house was modestly furnished but had a homey feel about it. She set about packing away the grocery items. She had purchased tinned and packaged food that would not spoil. She placed these in the pantry and refrigerator so it looked like somebody was living in the house. She also put the toiletry items in the bathroom, squeezing half of the toothpaste down the sink then leaving it on the basin with the toothbrush and rolling some of the toilet paper off the roll then flushing it down the toilet. Doing the same with the cleaning products, she part emptied the bottles down the sink so it looked like they had been used.

Taking out the linen the property owner had supplied, she made the beds then hung towels haphazardly around the bathroom and kitchen. She placed sponges in the kitchen sink then left some dishes in the dishwasher. Hanging the clothing she had brought in the closet, she placed the overnight bag on the top shelf. She had saved the flight tags from her earlier flight in the name of Jennifer Morley then attached these to the bag. She left the boarding passes in the bedside table drawer, along with some other personal items from the bag.

Jade had also collected the junk mail from the letterbox so she scattered this across the kitchen bench. She wrote some notes to herself, including a shopping list, in Jennifer's handwriting then stuck them onto the fridge with a magnetised calendar left as a courtesy by the real estate. As an afterthought, she went to the bedroom for one of the pillows then tossed it onto the couch, patting an impression into it where a head may have rested.

When she was satisfied the house looked lived in, Jade locked the door behind her, stripped off the gloves and put them in her pocket then headed back to the motel.

When Brent entered the motel room about six that evening, Jade had settled herself on the bed with a cup of coffee and was watching the local news. He looked excited.

She jumped up from the bed. 'So, what did you find out?'

'You know what Jade, the more I think about it, the more I think you could be right. Maybe Jennifer Morley is still alive and we've all been taken for a ride.'

'Why do you think that?'

'How about we go out and I'll tell you all about it over dinner. I'm starved!'

'Sounds fantastic. I found these wonderful seafood restaurants down along the Esplanade while I was wandering around today. You do like seafood, don't you?' Jade asked realising how very little she knew about Brent despite the time they had spent together.

'Is the Pope Catholic? Let's go!'

Brent had borrowed an unmarked police vehicle from the station. He opened the door for Jade and closed it behind her. It reminded her of the night Angelo had taken her to dinner and treated her like a princess. The memory cut like a sharp blade into her chest. She winced and pushed it aside. There was no time for wallowing or misery. There was work to do.

A strong breeze had kept the clouds and rain at bay for the day, and was now cooling the Esplanade with its salty breath. Brent and Jade decided to be daring and ordered a dish called 'Tastes of Australia', which included the native flavours of barramundi, crocodile and kangaroo. To Jade, the crocodile didn't taste much different to chicken, but the kangaroo, cooked rare, was a delight to her tastebuds.

Brent had ordered a bottle of red wine with dinner and they had already finished it. He ordered a second. Jade was careful not to drink too much, wanting to keep her wits about her. She had been nursing her glass and had only drunk a little from the first bottle. As Brent began on the second bottle, he seemed more and more willing to share what he had learnt that day.

The Cairns detectives had conducted a thorough investigation. It didn't surprise Jade that they had been able to trace all of her credit card purchases. Anyone could have stolen and used the card. What did surprise Jade is that they had already found out about the house Jennifer Morley had rented. The real estate must have been very efficient in lodging her bond with the Rental Bond Authority as soon as they received the paperwork.

'I mentioned your theory about the insurance money to the team, and they think you might be on to something.'

'You told them it was my theory?'

'Of course I did. I'm not into taking credit I don't deserve. But don't worry, I didn't tell them about us or that you were here with me.'

Jade placed a hand over his. He really was one of the few principled men she knew.

She sat up in her chair, removing her hand. 'So what happens now?'

'As much as any of us hate to admit it, we may have convicted Angelo wrongly of murder. As far as your case goes, if we find Jennifer Morley alive then the conviction will be overturned and your case will be won.'

'What about the insurance fraud?'

'We'll charge him for that if we can, but we'll have to go back over the evidence to prove he was involved.'

She lowered her voice. 'So have you checked out the house yet?'

'We sent a couple of the boys over there this arvo but nobody answered the door. We've arranged to get a search warrant, but we have to wait until some time tomorrow morning for it. They don't do things in a hurry up here.'

Brent drained the glass he held in his hand then excused himself to head out to the footpath for a cigarette. When he was out of earshot, he called the Senior Sergeant at the station to check in and advised that so far he had not uncovered anything to indicate that Jade Sheffield had been in Cairns. 'Either she's very good at covering her tracks or she really didn't have anything to do with the rental.' His voice indicated he wanted the latter to be true but his cop instincts would not let her fool him. He hung up the phone then lit up the cigarette he had been turning between his fingers. He took a long drag then blew out, watching the plumes of smoke thin then dissipate into the humid air. Thankfully, their case against Jade was just as thin.

As Jade waited for Brent's return, the waitress came over and refilled his glass. Jade waved her away as she tried to do the same with hers. She needed to be able to think clearly. Tomorrow, the police would go to the house and conclude that Jennifer was alive. How could she make sure they tied Angelo to Cairns? She was still mulling it over as Brent sat himself heavily back down at the table. He had become quite intoxicated.

He drank the last glass of wine down quickly. 'Let's go home,' he winked at her.

'OK, but I'm driving.' She took the keys from his shaky hand.

After a few minutes of drunken fumbling back in their room, Brent fell into a deep alcohol-induced sleep and began to snore. Jade was too distracted to mind much. It was a long time before she fell asleep beside him, still thinking about how she could link Angelo and Jennifer together in Cairns.

Jade woke with a start and looked at the numbers on the alarm clock. Five am. The dream had woken her again, but she suddenly had a brainwave that pushed the vague memory of the demon-like figure out of her mind. The letters! That was it. Angelo may have written back to Julianne. She still had the key to the post office box.

Brent was still snoring solidly beside her, sleeping off the effects of the two bottles of red wine. He was not usually a big drinker and she wondered what had led him to indulge the night before. She lifted herself gently out of the bed and padded over to the table where she had dropped his car keys after driving him home. She quickly threw on some clothes, picked up the keys then let herself quietly out the door.

It was still dim outside. The heavy grey cloud cover blocked the morning sun and threatened rain for the rest of the day. Jade felt safe under its cover of semi-darkness. Most sensible people would still be at home, tucked under the sheets.

When she got to the post office there was not a soul in view. She cleared the box, finding three letters in reply to the three she had sent to Angelo. They were clearly marked from the prison and addressed to the post office box in Cairns. She opened them using a tissue, being careful not to get her fingerprints on them, and read the contents. Nothing to give away his plan there, but they were all signed Angelo Morley. At least they would tie him to Jennifer and a Cairns address. She drove over to the house, and parked a little down the street. Checking carefully that nobody was surveying the house, she slipped down the side and entered through the rear door. She placed the letters in the bedside table drawer amongst the boarding passes and other personal items, dropped the post office box key in there as well, and then left the house as quickly and quietly as she could.

As Jade tried to walk inconspicuously up the street toward the car, a sudden deluge of rain showered forth from the sky and she was drenched in a matter of seconds. She ran for the car and drove back to the motel as quickly as she could through the teaming rain, aware that Brent could wake up at any moment and discover she had taken the car. It was easier not to have to come up with an excuse.

It was still pouring as she dashed from the car and let herself into the motel room. She had just removed her clothes and towelled herself dry as Brent began to stir. She picked up her wet clothes and threw them out of sight as he walked into the bathroom.

'Shit! Why didn't you wake me up?' he moaned looking at the clock. Her eyes followed the direction of his. It was seven-thirty am.

'How long have you been up?' he asked looking at her wet hair then screwing his eyes shut.

'I'm sorry, I just got up and had a shower,' she answered as calmly as she could. 'I thought I'd let you sleep it off a while longer. I didn't realise you had to be up early.'

Brent winced. 'That's OK. I'm sorry. I shouldn't have drunk all that red wine. My head is killing me. I have no right to take it out on you. I'll just jump in the shower myself and maybe I'll feel a bit better.'

Brent turned on the taps and stepped under the sharp needles of water. He let it run over his head for a while until it felt slightly better, then reached out for the soap. Strange? There was no soap in the shower. He stepped out dripping and picked up the cake of soap on the washbasin. Maybe Jade had used it out there after her shower. But it was dry. There was something else nagging at him too, but he could not quite put his finger on it. He looked at the bath mat but it was still hanging on the towel rail. The floor outside the shower had been dry before he dripped all over it, but there was something else. The shower had been dry when he got into it. Why would Jade say she had a shower if she hadn't? What had she been up to? He reached out and felt her towel hanging on the rail. It was damp. Maybe he had been mistaken, or it was just something to do with the oppressive humidity. It was too much for his alcohol-affected brain to deal with and he pushed the thoughts aside. He hopped back under the water and lathered up, enjoying the sensation of the water streaming down his back. Within minutes, he had totally forgotten his concerns.

Brent left Jade to her own devices and headed out to the car to drive to the station. Strangely, the seat seemed a bit damp but it had been raining all week according to the boys. Maybe some damp had built up over that time. He thought nothing more of it.

Brent phoned Jade at ten am and reported in a whisper, 'We've got the warrant. We're going in.'

'Good luck!' Jade said. 'Let me know what happens.'

It was after lunch before Brent found an opportunity to call her back. He told her elatedly about the boarding passes, the bags, the notes, and their belief that Jennifer Morley was alive. She didn't know that part of his light mood was relief that it seemed to clear her of involvement. 'We haven't been able to locate Jennifer Morley though. She only rented the house a few days ago. Maybe she saw us there and she's hiding out until the heat is off. We'll check again over the next few days.'

Brent was more keyed up by the time he got back to the motel that night. He told her about the letters they had found. 'We haven't pieced it together yet, but it ties Angelo to here. The fact that Jennifer Morley was in possession of those letters and the post office box key indicates he may have been using the name Julianne McGuire as an alias to keep in contact with her. We're going to do some further searches on that name and see what we come up with.'

The local police still intended to keep the house under surveillance to catch anyone out if they were game enough to go back. If the theory about the insurance fraud held true, then they figured anyone else involved might lead them to Jennifer Morley. He knew that the local police were more objective than he was. They were not in love with one of the suspects. But he felt confident Jade wasn't involved.

Jade reached over and hugged him. 'I think this calls for a celebration.'

'You're damn right it does! Let me take you out on the town.' He lifted her and spun her around with youthful exuberance.

'Then again, maybe we should stay in and celebrate?' he said cheekily as he dropped her on to the bed, falling gently on top of her.

Before Jade fell asleep that night, she turned and watched Brent breathing evenly beside her. His sleep seemed burden-free and she envied him the naivety of his age. It had been to her advantage. He had given a lot away to her about the case, that as a police officer seemed to be a conflict of interest given she did still represent the convicted murderer. It made her wonder if his emotional immaturity was leading him to play more the role of a man in love than that of a cop. Where was the line between the two, and what would it take for him to cross it? She hoped she would never have to find out.

TWENTY

The next morning Hunter told Jade he planned to question the real estate and post office staff and nose around some of the stores Jennifer Morley had shopped in. Jade begged him to let her accompany him. She was not aware when he agreed that he still had orders to investigate her involvement in the Morley affair.

'I guess it can't do any harm, so long as you let me do all the talking.'

Jade intended to remain in the background. It had been over three months since she was in Cairns. It received thousands of tourists so she doubted anyone would remember her, especially since she had been careful to disguise herself. Even so, she put her hair up which made her look entirely different and donned a pair of sunglasses quite different to the ones she had purchased in Cairns.

They began at the stores at the Pier. As she had anticipated, most of the sales staff could not recall the transactions from three months prior and many of the casual staff had changed in that time anyway. They certainly could not recognise the photograph of Jennifer Morley that Brent flashed in their faces, since she had never actually been there. There was one store however, that concerned her. She had purchased a one-off designer garment that the woman might recall selling. This one transaction could be her downfall. She remembered having a lengthy conversation with the middle-aged owner about all the comings and goings of the tourists. The woman had told her she never forgot a face. As they entered the store, Jade busied herself by looking through the racks of clothing with her face turned away from the woman. Brent marched up to the storeowner, flashing his badge then began asking questions about the transaction. He had a photocopy of the sales slip and the woman's eyes lit up. 'Yes,

yes. I adored that piece. I was almost saddened to sell it. But it went so well with her long dark hair.'

'Dark hair?' Brent asked. 'Are you sure?'

'Yes, I remember she had the most beautiful shining black hair.'

'Was this her?' He handed her the photo of Jennifer Morley.

Jade stole a sideways glance as the woman stared at the photo. She had a confused look on her face. She felt her stomach tighten.

The woman handed the photo back to Brent. 'Well I can't be entirely sure, I have a lot of people through here you know? But yes, I think that could have been her.'

Jade hid her smile in the rack of clothing. So much for never forgetting a face!

Brent asked her a few more questions before heading toward the door. Jade turned then followed him discreetly out of the store.

Their next stop was the real estate office. The property manager was an attractive woman in her forties. Brent turned on his police interrogator persona and questioned her on the details of the rental transaction. He did so in the presence of the real estate principal and she was obviously afraid to admit she had never met Jennifer Morley and had handed over the keys to someone else. Jade deduced it was this fear of retribution that led her to agree that the photograph was indeed the woman she had rented the property to, although in truth she had only seen the photograph of Jennifer Morley on a faxed copy of her licence. Not one to follow the news, she had never seen Jennifer's photo in any of the newspapers. Brent was very interested to learn the woman had been in regular contact with Jennifer over the previous few months. He asked her to produce the contact details she had been using.

Jade felt herself suddenly riveted to the spot. The woman had been contacting her on her mobile phone so if Brent called the number... She hoped he would not immediately recognise it. She turned on leaden feet then reached into her bag in order to turn the phone off without him noticing. Then she heard the woman say, 'I've probably thrown out the piece of paper I wrote it on, but it will be on the lease.' Jade felt a surge of relief. She had put a fictitious number on the lease. She took her hand out of her bag and turned back more lightly. This woman's testimony, if she stuck with her story, would undoubtedly add to the proof Jennifer Morley was alive.

Their next stop was the post office. Jade let Brent walk in first and stride to the counter, holding back and looking for the boy so she could warn him not to act as if he recognised her. Brent was talking to a woman at the counter when the boy came out from the back office.

It was too late. He saw her, waved, and shouted out, 'Julianne.'

She turned her back and pretended not to hear him, looking through the items on the shelf. As he moved toward her, Brent turned around and took interest in what was taking place.

The boy reached her and touched her on the shoulder. 'Julianne,' he said again. She could see Brent looking at her questioningly.

'I'm sorry. You must have me confused with someone else. My name is Jade. Jade Sheffield. From Brisbane.'

She looked at him pleadingly. He seemed to sense something was up. She wanted him to think it had something to do with her hiding from her father. She had told him she used one alias, why not another? He cottoned on quickly.

'I'm so sorry. I thought you were someone else. But I can see now…your hair is quite different. I hope I haven't embarrassed you. Is there anything I can help you with?'

'No thank you,' Jade answered flashing him a grateful smile.

She walked over to Brent who, despite having heard everything that went on, was not showing the slightest hint of suspicion toward her. It had been a narrow escape but she could obviously do no wrong in his eyes. The whole day's exercise had only served to prove further that Jennifer Morley was alive.

By mid afternoon, the rain had abated and heat had become a stifling blanket cast over the town. Brent and Jade were sitting in a bar overlooking the water, sipping frozen martinis in an attempt to decrease their body temperatures. As they discussed the findings of the day, the national news came on the television screen in the corner of the bar. A news-breaking story caught their attention. A shark fisherman had snagged a body in the Nerang River on the Gold Coast.

The newsreader went on to report that the woman's body had been weighted down by concrete and, a likely murder victim, may have been in the water for some time. It was typical of the news to sensationalise the event. They had not even identified the woman.

'Wow!' Brent whistled. 'Concrete boots? Sounds like something out of a mafia movie and I'm stuck up here missing it all.'

For the second time that day, Jade felt herself freeze. The body of a woman? Weighted down by concrete boots? Mafia? She remembered the news cuttings. Could it be Jennifer Morley's body? She suddenly felt ill, ran to the bathroom, and vomited. The once familiar feeling of panic started to rise in her chest as she looked at herself in the mirror. *How did you ever think you would get away with this?*

Jade was breathing so rapidly she felt faint. She forced herself to slow her breathing and think rationally. If the body was that of Jennifer Morley, then it could have been in the water for over three months. Would it even be identifiable? She recalled having just read in the previous weekend's newspaper shark numbers in the river had increased as they had moved up river to breed. They had probably had a good feed on the body. Who *was* Jennifer Morley anyway, if that was even her real name? Was she someone that Angelo had just picked up off the street? It was possible that the body could remain a Jane Doe indefinitely. By the time she joined Brent again she was feeling a bit calmer.

As she returned, Brent was just closing his mobile phone. He placed it back in his pocket. 'Are you OK?'

She noted his look of concern and gave him a quick peck on the lips. 'I'm alright. I think it must just have been the heat.'

'Will you be OK? I need to go back to the station.' He pointed to his pocket where he had just placed his phone.

‘I’ll be fine. You go and do whatever you have to do. It’s not far. I’ll just walk back to the motel.’

‘OK, but you’re sure you’re feeling alright?’

‘Yes!’ Jade said it with more force than intended. The shock of the news report had more impact on her than she cared to admit. Brent looked hurt by her abruptness.

‘I’m sorry.’ She reached over to stroke his cheek. ‘I guess everything’s just getting to me. I’ve been defending someone I truly believed in and to have found out the whole thing was just a deceit from the start…’ Her words trailed off as she realised how true they were.

‘Oh Jade, I’m sorry. I haven’t really thought about how all this is affecting you. How about I take a day off tomorrow? I was watching the weather report while you were in the bathroom and the forecast for tomorrow is fine and sunny. Maybe we could go out and see the reef since we’re so close to it?’

Jade’s face lit up. ‘That sounds wonderful. I could book us onto one of the boats when I get back to the motel. They had lots of brochures there. We might be able to go snorkelling on the Great Barrier Reef.’

Brent seemed happy his suggestion had excited Jade. Jade was just happy she would be able to get away from her thoughts for a while.

‘I’ll see you back at the motel tonight.’ He kissed her gently and headed out to his car.

As Brent got into his car, he reached for his cigarette packet in his pocket. He fumbled the lighter and it slid from his fingers and landed on the passenger side floor, just out of his reach. He cursed and got back out of the car, walking around the other side to retrieve it. As he leaned in to pick up the lighter, he noticed something else on the floor. It was a credit card. Concerned it may have fallen out of Jade’s bag and she would not be able to pay her bill, he picked it up. He was about to take it to her, when another shiny plastic card halfway under the seat caught his attention. He picked it up and stared at it. The photograph startled him. It was Jennifer Morley’s face. He knew it well from the many hours he had spent poring over the photographs in the police file. The name on the licence was Julianne McGuire. He took a closer look at the credit card in his hand. The cardholder's name was Jennifer Morley. He felt under the seat and pulled out another credit card. This one was in the name of Julianne McGuire.

What the hell was going on? How did they end up in his borrowed car? There was a nagging voice in the back of his head that he had missed something. He had a mental block and could not quite grasp hold of it. Instead of going back to the station, he drove the car down and parked along the waterfront looking out to sea. It was high tide and a flock of seagulls swooped toward the water chasing a school of baitfish. The tranquil scene might bring some clarity to his mind while he tried to piece the puzzle together.

Brent got out of the car and leant on the bonnet, lighting up a cigarette. As he exhaled the smoke into the air, he let his mind wander back and forth over the past few days. It stopped at a moment earlier that day. 'Julianne?' the boy in the post office had addressed Jade. Was that really just a co-incidence? Was there some connection? He had been at the counter making enquiries about the post office box in the name of Julianne McGuire. The post office was right next to the real estate office. The real estate woman had positively identified Jennifer Morley. He needed to speak to her again. He took one last drawn-out drag on the cigarette then crushed it heavily under his boot. He got back in the car then headed for the real estate.

When he left the real estate agency for the second time that day, Brent walked with his head hung low. He had been in luck to find the principal had left the office for the day. Once he had applied pressure to the property manager, she had admitted that she had arranged the entire transaction by phone and electronic means. She could not identify Jennifer Morley in person. Anyone could have rented the property in her name. This bothered him because it meant that Jade was no longer in the clear.

The other thing that bothered him was that Jade was the only other person who had been in his car.

Jade ordered another drink from the bar then wandered out to the deck. Cairns really was a beautiful place. It was high tide and the water hid most of the mud from sight. She let her thoughts drift over the blue water and meet on all sides with the tropical green mountains. You could just disappear in a place like this. She was sure many of the people living up here had done just that.

Brent was being so damn considerate. It annoyed her. Not because it wasn't nice, but because she knew she didn't deserve it *and* because she was using him. She did not have any real feelings for him. Angelo had seen to it that she had locked that part of herself securely away. She doubted she could ever allow herself to be that vulnerable or gullible again. She was acutely aware that Brent's feelings for her were very strong and growing. At some point, she would have to pull the pin on it. He would be hurt, but she could live with that. She had lived with worse. In fact, she was living with much worse, and doing just fine. She passed over an hour and more than a few drinks looking out to sea lost in her thoughts.

Finally, she settled her bill then headed back to the motel. Along the street, she came across a swimwear shop. Remembering she had left the new bikini at Jennifer Morley's rental property, she stepped inside and began browsing through the brightly coloured garments. She tried on a few and settled on a plain pink bikini that was flattering but not too conspicuous. Should she dare trying to use Julianne McGuire's credit card? Why not? They might think she was still hiding out somewhere in Cairns. If the store asked any questions, she would just say she had changed her mind and leave.

She put her hand into her bag to unzip the side pocket but it was already open. She felt inside for the credit cards. There was nothing there. She dug her hand in a little deeper until she could feel the seam in the lining. Nothing. She placed her handbag down on the counter and began searching frantically for the cards in the rest of her bag.

‘Is anything wrong?’ the cashier asked.

‘No, not at all,’ Jade replied not wanting to draw attention to herself. She pulled out her purse and paid for the purchase in cash. The cashier put the pink bikini into a branded bag and Jade snatched it from the stunned girl then ran off at breakneck speed down the street.

Holy fuck! Holy fuck! The words repeated in her mind as she raced down the street. She remembered upending the contents of her bag last night to find something. It really was ridiculous that women carried so much of their lives in their handbags. *Think! Think!* She was sure she had picked everything back up. Unless something had fallen off the bed and she had inadvertently kicked it underneath. She had to get back to the motel before Brent got there.

She turned into the driveway and was relieved to see Brent’s car was not in the parking space. She unlocked the door and went straight to the bed, ripping the covers off and shaking them in case anything had lodged between them. Then she got down on her hands and knees and poked her head under the bed, feeling as far as she could with her flattened palm. Jade was so intently involved in her search she did not hear the door open.

Brent walked into the room to find Jade head down, rear poking out from under the bed. At another time, the sight would have turned him on. She bumped her head as she came out. ‘Shit!’ she cried holding her head, then caught sight of Brent’s shoes between her knees. She lifted her head but remained on her hands and knees, trying to regain her balance while the blood rushed back toward her oxygen-starved brain. Then she turned around and looked up at him, trying to hide the panic in her eyes.

‘Is this what you’re looking for?’ Brent asked. His tone was icy.

Jade could not really see much from her position on the floor but she instinctively knew what Brent held in his hand were the credit cards and licence she had been looking for.

‘What have you got there?’ she asked knowing her shaky voice did not make her sound at all convincing.

His eyes narrowed. 'I found them on the floor of the car, Jade.'

Jade managed to pick herself up off the floor and seat herself precariously on the side of the bed. Her feet wanted to run but Brent's solid frame remained in the doorway. How could she have been so careless? After all the hard work she had put into the ruse that Jennifer was still alive, it had taken one stupid slip up to ruin it all. She must have forgotten to re-zip the side pocket in her bag and the cards had slipped out. She had not even thought to look down on the floor. *Stupid! Stupid! Stupid!*

Brent was just staring at her, as a disappointed parent would look at a child who had just gone against the family's values.

'I've been sitting in my car all this time just trying to make myself believe it Jade. But it makes sense. There was that boy at the post office who called you Julianne. That wasn't a co-incidence, was it?' He waited for her to respond but she stared at him blankly. He answered for her. 'No, it wasn't. Because he knew you as Julianne McGuire. He probably organised the post office box for you. And about that post office box. Someone had to have collected the mail and placed it in the house *allegedly* inhabited by Jennifer Morley some time between the real estate giving out the keys and us finding the letters at the house the next day. And if we were to go one step more and say Jennifer Morley is *not* in fact alive, then someone had to have used her credit cards, rented her a house and put her things in it.' There was a rise in the level of his voice. 'And the person who seems to have had the means to do all that was you!' He waved the cards in front of her face.

Jade said nothing, her head lowered. She was thinking over her options. She could attempt denial, but she did not think Brent would buy that now, no matter how infatuated he was with her. He had switched to detective mode and the evidence was stacked against her, but the feelings he had for her were in her favour. She still had her feminine charms on her side.

'I know you went out yesterday morning in the rain, Jade,' Brent continued. 'You thought you fooled me, but the shower hadn't been used. You've had other opportunities since we arrived here, but given you lied to me I suspect you went to that house while I was asleep and planted those things. Am I right?'

Jade met his eyes with an expression begging forgiveness, while still trying to buy herself time to think. 'I did,' she said quietly.

'Is that all you have to say for yourself? Because the next obvious question is how you came to be in possession of a dead woman's credit cards and her identification? Jade, I have to tell you the department has had you under suspicion for a while. It's why I agreed to bring you up here. I needed to know if it was true.'

Jade stared at Brent, feeling exposed and naked to her very core. Did he already know the truth? She felt a little dazed, but she had to force herself to follow the plan in her head. The truth was now her only option. She would have to play on his sympathy. She induced tears into the corner of her eyes and let them trickle slowly down her cheeks. She put her hands over her face and dropped her head into her lap.

It worked. Brent instantly switched from bad cop back to protective lover. He sat beside her and put his arms around her. 'Jade, please. Tell me what's going on? Did someone force you to do this? Was it Angelo Morley? Did he threaten you in some way?'

Jade was astonished. He was giving her the benefit of the doubt - and a plausible motive. The lies had become second nature to her. After so many months of playing this charade, it would have been easy just to go along with Brent's suspicions. His unfaltering faith in her made it even easier. For a split second, those thoughts almost allowed her conscience to get the better of her, but it was far too late to let her conscience guide her. She pushed the voices aside.

Brent lifted her head gently with both hands and looked into her eyes. 'Jade, you know you can tell me anything. I love you.'

She had him! It was a strange time for him to admit it, but it was an emotionally charged situation. She felt confident she could pull it off. Her father had once told her, *'Never start a game you can't win!'* Jade looked deeply into Brent's eyes and with as much sorrow as she could muster, she lied. 'I love you too Brent'. She hesitated while the words sank in then continued, 'There is something I have to tell you. It was me. I killed Jennifer Morley.'

It was a relief to finally say it. She waited for Brent to react but he just stared at her dumbly as if he had not heard the words. She thought he had worked it all out, but it did not seem at all what he had expected to hear.

'It was an accident. You have to believe me,' Jade pleaded. 'I swear on my life I never meant to kill her.' By this time, the tears were streaming down her face. They were almost real.

'What? How?' was all Brent managed.

'You see, I think you were on the right track. I believe Angelo must have plotted to fake his wife's death. There was all that evidence in his apartment. Somehow, I found myself a witness to the whole thing. I saw him put the bag in his boot, so I followed him. I saw Jennifer get out of the car and he just left her on the side of the road. I thought they might have had a fight so I approached her to see if she was OK, but she went crazy and started to attack me. I just picked up a rock and hit her over the head to stop her. I didn't know it would kill her. You have to believe me.'

That fact was true, if not the motivation. Jade was trying hard to win over Brent's sympathy, the confession punctuated by sobs.

'So why didn't you call the police?' he asked.

She shrugged her shoulders. 'I just didn't know what to do. I panicked and got in my car and drove away. Then I didn't think anyone would believe me, especially after I just left her there on the side of the road. What kind of person does that? I know it was wrong and you can't imagine how bad I've felt about it all these months.'

'You should have told me Jade. I could have helped you.'

It was too late for anyone to help her. She had already committed murder once and got away with it. There was no way she was going to let anyone destroy her life and career, least of all another man! Brent had betrayed her too. He had lied to her to get her up here just to catch her out, and he had succeeded. The hurt of Angelo's betrayal resurfaced and the two moulded into one dark ball of hate twisting in the pit of her stomach. Then something happened. It was as if a void suddenly opened up inside her and she disappeared completely into the abyss. She lost all sense of right and wrong. Her burning single-minded focus on her own survival was the only instinct that guided her now. She knew what she had to do.

Jade would murder her lover.

The words that followed came with a renewed sense of determination. 'Oh, Brent. I wish you were around then to help me. What should I do?'

'I haven't filed my report yet. It would be better for you if you turned yourself in. I'll stand by you, of course. If you give evidence against Angelo in the fraud case, and claim self defence, I'm sure it will go in your favour.'

Jade had anticipated Brent's response. He was, after all, a man dedicated to law enforcement. She was furious at him and at herself for letting this happen, but she had to force herself to think clearly now. She had to buy some more time.

'You're right Brent. I will. Let's go down to the station first thing in the morning. It's the right thing to do and I should have done it a long time ago. You will come with me, won't you?'

'Of course. I promise I'll be right there beside you.'

She looked into his eyes and spoke in a child-like voice. 'I'm afraid, Brent. Hold me?'

Brent put his arms around Jade and she snuggled into him. 'I love you,' she whispered into his ear, blowing gently on his neck to in an attempt to arouse him.

'I love you too, Jade.'

She started to plant kisses down his neck and in the next moment, Brent's lips were crushing hungrily against hers. The raw emotion of the situation seemed to have heightened his senses, and the sheer physicality of their lovemaking was as intense as Jade had ever experienced. She retained a stony detachment from the experience. A sudden involuntary shudder ran through her as she again felt his betrayal cut deeply into the centre of her being.

She lifted herself resolutely from the bed. 'I'm going to have a cup of tea. Would you like one?'

'Mmm, yes please.'

Jade filled the jug and put tea bags into two cups. Brent was lying on the bed with his eyes closed, lost in his own world and not paying any attention to her. She took a blister pack of sleeping tablets out of her bag. She had obtained them on prescription when she first had trouble sleeping through the strange dream. She put four of them into one of the cups and added two spoons of sugar to mask the taste. The jug clicked off indicating it had boiled. She filled the cups with water, crushing the tablets as she stirred in the sugar. She handed the laced tea to Brent and sat beside him with her own cup while he sipped the brew.

'Does your tea taste alright?' Brent asked.

'Yes, why?' Jade replied, trying to sound casual about it.

'Just tastes a bit funny but it could be that the teabags are slightly stale. I hate the way they leave them out in the open.' Without further comment, he drained the cup and handed it back to Jade with a wink. 'Thanks. I'm just going to have a shower.'

'Why don't I run a bath for you? You look like you could do with a bit of relaxation.'

'You might be right,' he smiled as he watched her head toward the bathroom.

By the time Jade left him in the bath, Brent was yawning. She had placed a rolled towel under his head and made sure he was lying back comfortably. While he was in the bathroom, she washed the cups with hot soapy water to remove any traces of the drug. When she came back into the bathroom, Brent was asleep and snoring loudly. She watched him for a long while to ensure he was in a deep slumber. She was amazed at how peaceful he looked. He had no idea these were the last breaths he would take. She did not feel any remorse for what she was about to do. The first murder she had committed had plagued her mind for some time, but the second time it seemed somehow easier. She had already dealt with the emotions of guilt and fear, and locked them safely away.

She had cut the cord from the iron and hairdryer she found in the wardrobe. She used these to tie Brent's arms and legs together in case he woke. Then she straddled him and leant heavily down on both sides of his body, pushing his head under the water. His eyes suddenly opened and he stared up at her through the water, looking confused in his groggy state. As the realisation of what she was doing dawned on him, his survival instincts set in and he began to flop around like a stranded fish. Water spilled over the edges of the tub and his head breached the water allowing him to draw in a quick gasp of air. He was still powerful enough to thrust Jade sideways into the wall and she cried out as her head slammed against the tiles. She crushed her buttocks into his throat and sat hard on him, plunging his head under the water as he continued to thrash about. Eventually the bubbles from his breathing subsided. She had anticipated a further struggle, but his heavily drugged body finally accepted its fate. After he was still for a while, she felt for a pulse. His heart was silent.

Jade worked quickly, pulling the spare blanket from the wardrobe and spreading it across the bathroom floor. She rolled Brent's body out of the bath and wrapped the blanket around it. This was much cleaner than the bloody scene Angelo had staged, and would not leave traces of blood in the car. Struggling to drag the body toward the door, she opened it slightly and peeked outside. The humid night was eerily still. Brent had backed the car into the carport. It would make things easier for her. She still strained to lift the bundle into the boot of the car. His body was a dead weight. Funny how he had not seemed so heavy when he had collapsed onto her earlier after his sexual release.

She could not allow herself to have those thoughts about him now. She had to focus on disposing of the body without alerting any suspicion. It needed to look like an accident or the police would pursue the case relentlessly, and possibly her since they may discover she was in Cairns with him. She decided upon a boating mishap.

Jade packed up her things then double-checked there were no traces of her presence left in the room. She left the blister pack of sleeping pills beside a glass at the sink so it looked like they were his, knowing if they found Brent's body they might detect traces of the drug. Leaving Brent's possessions in the room, she put hers into the car so she would be ready to leave at dawn.

She flicked through the tourist brochures once again, and phoned one of the operators to book a small charter yacht for the following day in the name of Julianne McGuire. She then phoned the motel reception desk posing as Brent's assistant, booking him on one of the tourist boats that sailed out to the reef each day. She asked if they could slide the ticket under his door, as he would be working late that night. Finally, she called the airline and booked herself a flight home the following evening. Setting the alarm for 4.30am, she lay down to try to get some sleep in preparation for the task that faced her the next day.

A steely calmness seemed to take over as she drifted off into a contented sleep. It was almost over. By tomorrow she would be safe and on her way home.

TWENTY-ONE

Jade woke to the sound of the alarm. She had been in the middle of a nightmare but this time the demon had looked familiar to her. He'd had Brent's face and it was Brent's voice that chanted to her, 'You will become what you are meant to be'. As she wiped the wisps of the dream from her eyes and surveyed the room, she remembered the events of the previous evening. Had it just been another bad dream? If only it had been. She jumped quickly out of bed and dressed. It was time to go sailing.

Taking one last glance around the room to make sure she had not missed anything, she picked up Brent's tour boat ticket from under the door and slipped silently out to the car. She wanted to load the yacht before there were too many people around. The operators had agreed to allow her to pick up the keys at 5am. It was not unusual for people to get an early start out on the water.

Trolleys were available to transport the boaties' gear from the car park to the dock. Jade heaved Brent's body onto the trolley. Having been locked in the boot of the car in the humid climate, an unpleasant smell had begun to permeate the blanket she had wrapped him in. She tried to ignore it and was so focussed on her task that she did not hear the old boatie until he was right behind her.

'Need a hand, love?'

She froze. Her heart hammered mercilessly in her chest and her feet would not move. Had he seen anything? Did he know? She couldn't turn her body to face him. A seagull suddenly squawked above her head. The sound broke her out of her stupor and she swung around.

'Pew,' he said holding his nose. 'That's pretty ripe. What you got in there? Dead fish?'

Her skin went cold again and she looked at him blankly. He pointed toward the trolley.

'Um…err…' she stuttered. 'It's just some bait. I guess I should have put it in the fridge last night.'

'Damn right love. But it should make good burley for them fish out there.'

She managed a weak smile. 'Thanks for the offer, but I've got things under control.'

He tipped his sea-worn hat to her. 'Good fishing to ya!'

As he headed off, she packed all her other gear around Brent's body as quickly as she could then wheeled the trolley out to the small boat. She tipped it up so its contents slid onto the deck, feeling a twinge as Brent's body crashed heavily to the deck. Why she wasn't sure. It was not as if he could feel anything. She jumped down onto the deck and pushed him into the hold. It was difficult. He was a lot stiffer than when she had loaded him into the boot and the unpleasant smell made her gag.

She drove the car further up the dock and parked it close to the tourist boat moorings. Her eyes scanned the crowd. She picked out a man of about twenty-five who looked about the same build as Brent and seemed to be looking longingly out to sea. He seemed to be alone. She approached him with a smile.

'Hi there, how are you enjoying Cairns?'

'It's a beautiful place, ain't it?' She had picked correctly. He had a strong Cockney accent and was clearly a tourist.

'Look, I have this ticket for that boat there.' She pointed sadly. 'I bought it for my boyfriend but we broke up, so I kept the ticket, since I paid for it. I can't bring myself to go now, but it's a shame to waste it. Would you like to go out on that boat for the day?'

'You're joking, right? I'd surely love to! Could never afford to go out on a boat like that meself.'

'Well, here you go.' She handed him the ticket and he thanked her profusely. 'I doubt if anyone will ask for your name, just give them the ticket. But if they do, it's Brent Hunter, OK?'

'Okay. Brent Hunter it is. Hey, is he related to that Crocodile Hunter o' yours?'

Jade forced a laugh. 'No relation, mate.' Although they did have something in common, she reflected. Both were going to have met their deaths in a boating mishap.

'Have a great time,' she called to him as she walked back toward her charter yacht. The tour operators would do a head count. So long as someone was on the boat in Brent's place and handed in the ticket, they would assume he got on the boat. When he failed to turn up in the next few days, they would likely assume the headcount on the boat's return was flawed and they may have left him behind.

There was one more call she had to make. It was only 6.30am so the night operator's shift had probably not ended. She dialled the number. The woman's voice that answered the phone sounded tired and bored. She would possibly have ended her shift by the time Jade's message was passed on.

'Could I leave a message from Brent Hunter for the Senior Sergeant please?'

'Brent Hunter, how do you spell Brent?' the bored voice asked.

'B-R-E-N-T,' Jade replied.

'OK, and your message?'

'Need a day off. Going out to the reef on the Quicksilver tour.'

Jade could hear her typing the message on her keyboard. It would appear as if Brent had phoned it in. She doubted if the bored operator would even remember that a woman had left it.

She boarded the boat and her mind was suddenly flooded with memories of sailing with her father. As she untied the thick ropes from the bollards, she remembered his weathered hands guiding hers when she was too small to have the strength to separate the knots. She felt his hands on hers while she held the wheel, teaching her how to feel the wind. She had learned the lessons well and captained the yacht skilfully out of the harbour.

The azure water lapped along the hull of the boat as the wind blew through her hair. Jade abandoned herself to the sheer majesty of the blue expanse before her. It gave her an indefinable sense of belonging to something bigger. The sun had broken through the few lingering clouds and she could feel its warmth on her face, making her feel more potent under its dazzling glare. It singled out the tips of the waves and they shimmered into the distance. By the time the yacht had picked up the breeze, she was lost in her reverie and allowed herself to forget about her cargo and the purpose of her trip. For a long while, it was just her, the sea, and her childhood memories.

The sight of the slick Quicksilver boat brought her out of her reverie. Although it had left the dock after her, its powerful motors had allowed it to catch up and it now sped swiftly past her small craft. They would both end up at the same destination. She had no desire to get there in a hurry.

It took Jade some time to reach the area in which the larger craft had anchored. By this time, many of the tourists had already left the boat and were snorkelling over the shallow reef. She pulled up a safe distance from the group and dropped anchor to wait out their departure. About midday, a horn sounded summoning the tourists to lunch and they started to swim toward the boat. Jade's rumbling stomach made her wish she had packed some food.

After another hour, Jade heard the roar of the boat's engines starting up and it pulled up anchor. It sped past her once again, on the way to its next destination. This time she had no intention of following. She could see other boats, but they seemed so distant she felt like she was alone on the vast ocean.

Jade had brought along a pair of Brent's swimming shorts. She dragged him up from the hold, reeling at the pungent smell that escaped from the small space. Her motions were mechanical as she tried to ignore who he had once been and slide the swimming shorts up his stiff legs. She wished she had done it the night before when his body was more pliant.

Jade pulled up anchor and manoeuvred as close to the reef as she could without risking damage to the hull of the boat. She dropped Brent's cold stiff body into the small rubber dinghy supplied with the yacht. Attaching the oars, she rowed over the reef and dropped his body into a chasm between the brightly coloured coral. His body sunk into the space, already made heavy by the water in his lungs. She used one of the oars to wedge it under an outcrop of coral, wanting it to remain there until the tour boat returned the next day. The harsh sunlight struck his blonde hair with a ghostly glow beneath the water and for a moment, she imagined his eyes were staring at her. She blinked and they became lifeless again. It was unfortunate that the discovery might cause trauma for some poor person, but that was of minor concern to her after all she had endured.

The situation had posed a fleeting danger to her well-calculated plan but it turned out to be a glitch she had yet again shown the strength to handle. It was time to go home. The wind was with her all the way and she made better time getting back to the dock. After handing in the keys, she called for a taxi and headed to the airport leaving Brent's car behind in the car park.

As the plane flew out over Brent's watery grave, Jade sat back in her window seat and watched the mountains disappear from sight along with the undesirable memories. She turned her attention to the present and contemplated her next steps. She would destroy the cards before they got her into any more trouble. She had searched through Brent's belongings but had not been able to find any of his notes from his investigations in Cairns. She could only assume he had left them at the station. He had told her he had not filed his report. His notes would show all of the evidence they had gathered over the past few days to indicate Jennifer Morley was still alive and had been living in Cairns these past months. It was unlikely anyone would connect her to Brent's death. She was not registered as a passenger on the cruise boat nor was she registered at his motel. She had no reason to suspect that they would check for her presence with the airlines as Brent had assured her he had not told anyone she had come with him. She was in the clear once again. She commended herself on how she had managed to get everything back on track.

Jade felt physically and mentally drained. Laying her head back against the seat, she felt she should probably feel some kind of remorse for Brent's death. It seemed that a solid brick wall had built up in her mind, blocking any emotions other than hate and anger. She was barely aware of how the negative emotions had consumed her and her ability to discern right from wrong. There was only one right for her now, and that was to seek justice for what Angelo had done to her. With thoughts of revenge swirling in her head, she fell into a fitful sleep for the rest of the journey home.

PART THREE

PENUMBRA…

For a long time there was only the light…impenetrable white light, shining like a beacon through the surrounding darkness.

Yet another moment passed…

Between the zones of illumination and complete shadow, a fringe of partial shadow lingered. While it remained, it tarnished all that which fell into its grasp.

Slowly the darkness began to pass… and eventually the light returned.

TWENTY-TWO

Self is the only prison that can ever bind the soul.
- Henry Van Dyke

Angelo was seething. Who did that slimy little creep think he was? He had not bothered himself with any kind of retribution after the knifing attempt. He wanted to keep his record clean prior to his imminent release. After they returned the kid to his section of the prison, he had simply avoided him and let the incident go. The punk was no threat to him. He was just some young wayward musician who was in on drug-related charges. He went by the nickname of 'The Horn' as he was supposedly some shit-hot saxophone player. Angelo was sure he enjoyed the name for more conceited reasons. Probably made it up himself.

He had heard The Horn had been bad-mouthing him. Big-noting himself and telling all who cared to listen that Angelo was a big pussy and was afraid of him. At first, Angelo tried to ignore the jeers from some of the other prisoners. They did not understand why, with his reputation and mob connections, he had just let the smart-arse kid get away with his attempted murder. How could they? They didn't know about his plan. After what Frank had just told him, the time had come to teach the kid a lesson.

The Horn was conscious that most people considered him one of those types with an annoyingly obnoxious personality, developed through years of bullying at school. He had always been kind of a runt with a bright orange crop of hair, which accentuated his freckled skin. The only time he became someone was when he held his saxophone to his lips. His fingers danced over the keys, and the sound was pure magic. He was a very talented musician and rued the day he became embroiled in the drug culture of the music industry. When he made it out of this place, he certainly would not be making that mistake again. He had ambitions to make it big in the jazz scene where, in his view, the sax player was always seen as the hottest member of the band. He resented the other prisoners, because he felt he did not belong among them. He resented Angelo even more, because he was involved with the people who supplied the drugs that dragged him down and were responsible for him being there.

The prison had numerous programmes aimed at rehabilitating the prisoners and developing their non-criminal talents. The Horn was heavily involved in the prison's music programme, and had been practising relentlessly for weeks for the upcoming inter-prison eisteddfod, which was set for the following week. He was determined to bring his prison band in at number one. If returned with a victory, it might help improve his popularity and make the buggars leave him alone. Prison life had been tough for a small guy like him. They repeatedly took advantage of him once the lights were out. He had already created a bit of a stir with his assertions about Angelo's weakness, and the other prisoners were starting to talk about him in a more positive light.

Angelo was sure the kid had probably had a rough time growing up. In other circumstances, he may have felt sorry for him since his childhood has also been fraught with tragedy. However, the kid had chosen to take out the chip on his shoulder on him personally. Angelo was not going to stand for that.

He had maintained his control until now, but Frank had just told him some of the other prisoners were talking about contesting Angelo's position in the prison order. It was time to re-assert his position and put the little pain in the arse musician back where he belonged. If that was not enough to cajole Angelo into action, The Horn had now started to make derogatory comments about his mother. That was the one thing that evoked real emotion from Angelo. The emotion he felt right now was wrath. He snarled as he passed The Horn locking away his prized instrument under the supervision of the prison guard. The prisoners kept issued belongings in the lockers that the guards did not allow in their cells. They had heavy metal doors to discourage anyone from taking what did not belong to them. It gave him an idea.

Angelo did not want to get into any serious trouble, so after lights out that night he lay awake devising a plan that would show everyone else he had exacted retribution, but at the same time could be construed as a genuine accident. It was well after 2am by the time he finally drifted to sleep.

Before they left their cells the following morning, Angelo shared his plan with Frank. Frank was more than willing to lend a hand. His respect for the law was less than healthy and he could be confident that the way Angelo had planned the incident would not really implicate him.

During mess that morning, Angelo pushed his way through the crowd to be in line after The Horn. As the kitchen hand placed food on the kid's tray, Angelo bumped him and the plates went crashing to the floor. The kid turned around to confront him but Angelo glared at him in a threatening manner, challenging him to take him on right there. The air crackled with hostility and a silence had descended upon the room as the prisoners anticipated the fight. A guard suddenly appeared between the two of them and moved the kid on up the line before anything more could transpire, but Angelo had achieved what he wanted. He had gained the attention of the crowd. They witnessed his challenge. Now they would know that anything further that happened was intentional, whether it appeared to be an accident or not.

Angelo had visited the library that day and sat engrossed in some legal books relevant to his case. He knew The Horn attended band practice during this free time and he would be heading to the locker room in about ten minutes. Angelo scooped up his collection of reading matter and headed for the checking desk. 'I'd like to borrow this one for a few days,' he advised the librarian.

With his book under his arm, Angelo headed toward the locker room. He had seen the kid head into the room moments before him, and Frank was just rounding the corner behind him. Their timing was perfect.

'Just want to keep this in my locker overnight,' Angelo said to the guard. 'My cellmate has been giving me curry and I don't want him to take out his annoyance with me on your library books,' he winked.

The bored-looking guard waved him into the room where another guard was handing out keys and supervising. Frank had entered the room. With several long strides, he was beside Angelo as he neared the kid's locker. Then Frank was yelling at him.

It all happened so quickly the kid had no time to react. Frank pushed Angelo so hard that he hit the locker door just as the Horn was extracting his arms from the cabinet. The heavy metal door crushed down on his fingers and Angelo heard the crunch of bone as they shattered.

The kid dropped to the floor, howling and gripping his fingers in agony. Roused from his apathy the guard, who had witnessed the whole incident, started running toward them. He pushed Frank and Angelo aside to see what the fuss was. He almost gagged at the sight of the bone protruding from one of the kid's fingers, and the blood that was dripping onto the floor below him. He signalled to the other guard to call for medical attention.

Frank stooped down and looked The Horn right in the eye. 'Sorry about that amico,' he sneered. 'You were just in the wrong-a place at the wrong-a time.'

The guard pushed him away. 'Get out of here,' he demanded. Frank sauntered off gloatingly. The kid was a wimp. He had heard people plead for their lives with less cowardice. He had seen brains splattered on the pavement. The little pool of blood on the floor was nothing. Why was he being such a cry baby?

Angelo knew why he was howling. It was not the pain in his fingers. They had taken away the thing that meant the most to him. There was no chance he would be playing in the eisteddfod the following week. No chance he would be bringing his band home to victory. No chance he would be enjoying the popularity of being the hero.

Angelo glared at the kid and gave him a defiant snicker. The look he returned indicated he understood.

The kid's fingers were broken so badly it was going to take months of rehabilitation before he had the use of them back. Angelo was not concerned about the kid's future. A means to an end. That's what the incident was to him. There was a lot of talk over the next week as to whether The Horn would ever be able to play again as well as he had. But there was definitely no more talk about where Angelo stood in the prison order.

TWENTY-THREE

It was all over the news. *Body Found on Reef,* one of the headlines read. *Tourist Abandoned*, another declared. The young English backpacker picked up the newspaper left on the bus stop seat beside him with curiosity. He had been out on the reef the day before the discovery thanks to the generosity of a stranger. There was no mention of the identity of the tourist but it was definitely the same boat. There was a large picture of it on the front page, with an inset of the owner of the company. The story alleged the cruise company had been negligent by leaving the tourist behind on the reef. He tried to picture some of the faces of the people he had travelled with, and felt a small twinge of sadness that such a beautiful day could have turned into such a tragedy for one of them. The bus pulled into the stop and he put the newspaper back down then alighted the stairs. He was on his way to the airport for the long flight home. He took one last look around Cairns and thanked his lucky stars the unfortunate tourist had not been him.

In another part of the state, Jade switched on the TV to catch the morning news. Low-lying grey clouds had begun gathering outside and she wanted to check the weather report before she chose her attire for the day. She did not plan to spend much time in the office that day and it might still turn out to be hot and humid. As the opening sequence to the program ended, the picture that flashed up on the screen beside the newsreader's head made her catch her breath. She had been expecting it, of course. It was still a shock to see Brent looking vibrant and alive with his clean cut looks and neatly cropped blonde hair.

She brought her attention back to what the newsreader was saying. *The body found on the reef yesterday has been identified as that of Detective Brent Hunter, a member of the Gold Coast police force. Detective Hunter was in Cairns taking part in an investigation, but had apparently taken the day off to do some sight-seeing. The circumstances of his drowning are not clear, but it is alleged the cruise company left him behind on the reef. Whether he was alive at that point is unknown. Investigations are continuing into his death.*

The picture switched to a video of the large white vessel cruising on the shimmering blue ocean, then a local reporter confronting the owner of the cruise company for his comments on the incident. The distressed looking man put his hand up to the camera in an attempt to avoid them filming him then rushed away with the words 'I have no comment at this point.'

How many more people would she affect by what she had done? The man looked like he could handle himself though, the way he pushed past the media and jumped confidently into his black Jaguar. With a car like that and a company such as his, she had little doubt he would be able to afford the kind of legal representation which would see this as just a blip on the radar that would eventually be sunk far out to sea. Jade was relieved she had not been contacted by the police. She assumed it meant they did not believe there were any suspicious circumstances surrounding Brent's death. She switched off the set, forgetting that she had intended to check the weather report.

When she arrived in her office that morning, she was still thinking about the news report. She phoned the police station to find out who was taking over the Angelo Morley case. Now the police had discovered Brent's body, she could go about digging up some of the evidence they had found in Cairns to indicate Jennifer Morley was alive. It was time to get to work on Angelo's appeal. She was informed that Brent's former partner, Martin Andrews, who she had heard about but never met, had taken over the case. She made an appointment to meet with him that afternoon.

Jade cursed as she ran from the car toward the police station. It had started to drizzle on her way over and the rain had now become heavier. She should have taken the time to listen to the weather report and then she would have been prepared and have brought an umbrella. She was preening the water from her hair as Brent's former partner approached her in the waiting area.

Jade took an immediate dislike to Detective Martin Andrews. When he spoke, his eyes spent more time focussed on her chest than her face. She felt a droplet of water drip from her hair and watched as his eyes followed its path down into her cleavage. That was not such a bad thing since his beady eyes were too close together and she felt like they were penetrating her thoughts when he looked directly at her, and also because she knew his type. It would make it very easy for her to manipulate him. She wanted to get the information about Jennifer Morley out of him so there were no questions as to where she had obtained it or anything that could lead back to her involvement in the incident in Cairns.

They were discussing the unfortunate incident on the reef. Andrews informed her that at this stage, the police were still investigating a few anomalies, but he did not elaborate.

Jade leant in toward him and conjured up a smile. 'Detective Hunter and I had a very close working relationship.' Andrews noticed her implying tone, and she could see she was drawing him in. He seemed eager to get close to her as well. 'I know he was in Cairns to follow up a lead in the Jennifer Morley case,' she urged.

'Yeah, I guess if he hadn't been up there searching for Jennifer Morley then this tragic accident would never have happened.'

Jade sat up straight in the chair. 'I'm sorry. Did you say searching for Jennifer Morley? Is that what his lead was? Are you telling me she's still *alive*?'

'I mean searching for evidence in the Jennifer Morley case.' He squirmed in his chair but they both knew it was too late. He had let the cat out of the bag.

Jade railroaded him. 'You may as well tell me. You know it will come out anyway. Just help me out a little here. We're both on the same side. Neither of us wants to see an innocent man punished for something he didn't do. Do we?'

'No, of course not.'

She smiled invitingly as she waited for him to think the situation through.

'Just wait here a moment,' he said as he walked through the door to another room. He returned carrying a thick folder. As he opened it on his desk, a photograph of Jennifer Morley stared up at her. Even after the time that had passed, the sight still caused her to catch her breath. There was a large yellow envelope in the file and the detective opened it and took out the contents. Jade recognised Brent's handwriting.

Andrews began speaking. 'Hunter was in Cairns following up a lead that Jennifer Morley had been residing there. As you know, we never discovered her body. So, while it was unlikely that she was alive based on the evidence we've got for the murder charge, it wasn't entirely impossible.' He gave her a brief account of the evidence Hunter had gathered. 'He didn't get time to write up a formal report on his findings before his death, so all we have are his notes. I can't really let you see them. Procedure you know?' He turned up his palms in a helpless apology.

Jade looked at him curiously. Why was he teasing her, putting them right there in front of her, if he did not intend to let her see them?

'You look a bit cold. Would you like a coffee?'

Jade nodded her head, looking down to see that the coolness of the air conditioning was causing goose bumps to form on her damp flesh.

'Damn coffee machine is down the end of the hall, it will take me about ten minutes,' he said with a wry smile.

Jade cottoned on to his meaning quickly. As he sauntered off down the hall, she started leafing through Brent's notes. She was not interested in his findings. She already knew what they were. What she wanted to ascertain was that her name was not mentioned anywhere, nor his suspicions that she had been involved in the death of Jennifer Morley. There seemed to be nothing in his notes to implicate her. The real estate file was among the documents. She skimmed over the papers until she came to the rental application form. She flinched as she recognised the handwritten number on the form. It was her office number. She could not remove the form as every page in the file was listed in the index. She had to think quickly. She picked up the blue pen on the detective's desk and changed the number one in the prefix of the phone number to a four. The blue pen was a perfect match and that number would be in a completely different suburb. It would be enough to put them off the track if they tried to call it.

Satisfied, Jade closed the file. She was sitting quietly waiting when Andrews returned with two steaming cups of coffee. Her head dropped as if she had been asleep and he apologised for startling her. She hadn't been asleep, just lost in the eddy of her thoughts. They made some more small talk over the coffee then Jade thanked the detective for his time and made to leave. He caught her arm and his beady eyes pierced into hers again. 'Perhaps we could have a drink some time?'

'That would be nice,' Jade lied to appease him. She turned and walked away quickly. She braced herself to run through the rain again but when she got to the door, she could see that it had cleared and the sun was beginning to break through the clouds. She took it as a sign that she had just managed to clear some of the gloom from her own predicament.

Andrews made a quick perusal of the file to ensure nothing was missing. He did not want to land himself in hot water, even for such an alluring woman. He had been happy to help her out though. He had had been through the file thoroughly and it did appear that Jade's client may have been wrongly convicted of murder, although the theory remained he may still be guilty of insurance fraud.

Andrews had never been made privy to suspicions of Jade's involvement in the affair. Hunter had asked them to keep that information to a limited few, and specifically from his big-mouthed partner. As Jade seemed to be in the clear based on Hunter's investigations, the information had never been recorded.

Andrews decided he needed to step up the investigation. The search for Jennifer Morley was still underway and if she were out there, which it certainly appeared she might be, they would find her eventually. It might gain him some brownie points with the lovely lawyer if he were able to find the woman. It might also give him a reason to spend some more time with her.

He was definitely looking forward to spending more time with Jade Sheffield.

TWENTY-FOUR

Jade sat across from Angelo in the prison meeting room and delivered the news that the police had reason to believe Jennifer may still be alive. She explained the information Andrews had given her about how they had tracked her to far north Queensland, the use of her credit cards, and how she had allegedly rented a house recently in Cairns. She purposefully did not mention anything about the letters or Julianne McGuire.

The relief displayed on his face seemed almost real. He certainly was a good actor. Almost as good as she was. He took her hands in his and looked mercifully into her eyes. 'She knew about us Jade. I can't believe she would go to this much trouble just to get revenge on me. I thought I knew her, but it seems I didn't know her at all.'

'Can we ever really know anyone?' Jade looked deeply into Angelo's eyes as she spoke the words but their unfathomable darkness gave away nothing.

She squeezed his hand to feign support. 'It's not over yet, Angelo. They haven't found Jennifer so we still have to go through the appeal process. Given the circumstances, I've managed to secure a trial date for Tuesday week so we'd better get cracking. We should have more than enough evidence to prove reasonable doubt and overturn the murder conviction at the very least.'

He moved his hand on top of hers. 'Thank you for believing in me, Jade.'

She ignored the sentiment and took her hand away slowly. 'They're still going to try to pin a fraud charge on you. They think this might have been a set up engineered by you. There appears to have been a very large insurance policy set up recently.'

‘Of course. It was something I’d planned to organise since our wedding but you know how it is? Never enough hours in the day, especially in my profession. I don’t think the sum is out of place given my prominent status in the medical world.’

Jade could not believe the size of his ego. What had she ever seen in him? She choked the feelings down as she continued, ‘Then we need to find Jennifer, and hopefully she can corroborate your story.’

After Jade left, Angelo reflected on her visit. She definitely seemed to believe that Jennifer was responsible for his predicament. He had to work out his next step in light of the information Jade had just presented. He had not counted on Jennifer being so damn stupid as to use her own identity, nor had he anticipated that the police would be so efficient. The plan was still salvageable. This just sped things up. It was time for Jennifer Morley to make her re-appearance.

Angelo took out some paper and wrote a letter to Julianne McGuire care of the post office box in Cairns, letting her know his appeal date was set and he would appreciate a visit during the proceedings. He was sure Jennifer would be checking the box regularly given that the trial date was looming. He was not aware the police would seize his letter before it even left the prison and one of the likely places it would end up was in the hands of the investigating detective.

A few hours later, Detective Andrews stood at the fax machine at the station. He had just put the phone down after receiving the call from the prison and he was waiting for the machine to whir up and a copy of Angelo’s letter to appear in the tray. They had been planning to question Dr Morley about the letters found in Cairns but this new development was cause to alter that plan. As the prison officer had read the contents of Angelo’s brief letter to him, Andrews’s crafty mind had been at work. There was a chance this could lead Jennifer Morley right to him. Andrews wanted to be the one to crack this case, the first big one since his posting to the Coast. He read the fax then called the prison, authorising them to post the letter.

The Cairns police had gone off the boil on the Morley case, leaving it with the Gold Coast team who had jurisdiction over the original crime scene. They had left the post office box open and intended to check it periodically. He could almost bet they had not been near it since their first visit. He should ask them to monitor the box until Jennifer turned up but then he would miss his chance to apprehend the suspect himself. No, instead he would alert the prison to keep an eye out for Jennifer Morley. If she turned up there as instructed by Angelo, he would get them to detain her until he could question her and arrest them both for fraud personally.

It could all work out very nicely. He would receive a commendation for his part, and Jade Sheffield would be thankful that her client was acquitted of murder because of him. He would have to charge Angelo on the fraud count, but that may give him a further opportunity to be involved with his lawyer. The thought caused a swelling to stir in his pants.

The red post office van arrived at the prison at 6pm that night, and Angelo's letter to Julianne McGuire made its way into the van amongst the other despatches for the day. Within hours, it had been through the sorting machines at the mail centre and was on a plane destined for Cairns. When it arrived the next day in a bag of mail for the Cairns post office, it was the job of the young mail clerk to sort it and place it in the post office boxes. When the boy saw the letter addressed to Julianne McGuire, he stopped. He was not really clued in on what had happened but he knew there had been police there asking about her post office box and he suspected her father may have reported her disappearance to the police. They now had a key to the post office box and came in about once a week to check it. Julianne had not been near the place, or if she had it had been after hours. At any rate, this was the first letter that had arrived for her and it was marked from the prison where she had said her father worked.

It might be some sort of trap. Instead of placing it in the box, he put it in his pocket. Later that afternoon, when he was safely out of earshot of the other postal workers, he called Julianne.

'Jade Sheffield,' the professional voice answered.

'I…umm…I was after Julianne,' he said hesitantly.

Jade recognised the voice. 'Hi, I'm sorry. It's me, Julianne. Just being cautious, you know and using my assistant's name.'

He accepted her explanation readily and spoke in a conspiratorial whisper despite the fact that he was alone. 'I just wanted to let you know a letter arrived for you today. It's from the prison where your father works. I don't know if you know but there have been cops nosing around here about you, and I thought he might be setting up some kind of trap.'

'Wow, thanks! You don't know how grateful I am to you for letting me know. I haven't checked my box for a while. I've been so busy with my new job. Is there anything else in there?'

'No, this is the first letter that's arrived for you since I saw you last.'

'Look, I'm down at the Gold Coast for work all this week. Do you think you could have it re-directed to me?' Jade begged. 'I really want to know if my Dad's on to me.'

'Sure, no problems. What's the address?'

'She gave him the address of her office. Can you just re-address it to my assistant, Jade Sheffield.' She spelt out the surname for him. 'And write on the envelope *Private and Confidential*?'

He scribbled down the details. 'I'll put it in the mail to you first thing tomorrow.'

'Thanks again. I owe you that coffee.' Jade rang off before she had to make any firm arrangements to keep that promise.

She was intrigued. So Angelo had written to Jennifer again. She had not mentioned the letters. She did not want him to know she suspected anything. What was he up to? She would just have to wait until the letter arrived to find out.

True to his promise, the boy marked the letter with the details Jade had given him. He dropped it in the mailbox the next day with a smile, fondly remembering the mesmerising woman and hoping she would be pleased. He also hoped he would see her again soon.

Danni brought the envelope to her with her other mail two days later. Her assistant normally opened and date stamped all of her mail, however the envelope had been marked in big red letters 'Private & Confidential' so she had delivered it unopened. Jade tossed the other mail items into her tray and tore the envelope open in anticipation. She smirked as she read the letter intended for Jennifer Morley. So he wanted Jennifer to return now? He still believed his little plan was on course. Why wouldn't he? Jade was the only person who knew otherwise. She would love to see the crushed look on Angelo's face if she could let him know. Unfortunately, she could not enjoy that satisfaction. She still had to protect herself. She picked up a blank sheet of paper and began writing a reply to the letter in Jennifer's handwriting.

When Jade's letter arrived at the prison addressed to Angelo, the prison staff opened and photocopied it. They immediately faxed the copy to the police station for the urgent attention of Detective Andrews. When it was handed to him, he tried to contain his building excitement as he scanned the contents of the letter. It appeared Jennifer Morley was indeed alive and would be making her visit to the courtroom during the appeal proceedings.

He looked at the photocopy of the envelope they had faxed to him along with the letter. The postmark indicated Jennifer had posted the letter locally. She must already have acted upon Angelo's instructions and arrived on the Coast. It could not be easier. They had played right into his hands. What neither of them would be aware of was that Andrews would be waiting at the courthouse to apprehend Mrs Morley as she arrived. She would never make it into the courtroom.

The detective picked up the phone and instructed the prison staff to deliver the letter to Dr Morley and to watch for any suspicious behaviour or visitors in the ensuing week leading up to the trial. Jennifer might attempt to make a visit to the prison and if so he could have her picked up there. He secretly hoped that would not eventuate. The high profile case had attracted a lot of attention. It would be much more dramatic for him to apprehend Mrs Morley on the stairs of the courthouse. Even better if the media were around to capture the event and hail him as the cop who blew the case apart.

What Andrews was not aware of, was that Jennifer Morley would not, and could not, appear in that courtroom. Her unidentified body laid in a morgue drawer just a few suburbs away from the police station.

There was another person who knew Jennifer Morley would never reappear in life. He picked up the phone and placed a call to Jade Sheffield's office to make an appointment to meet with her. The time had come for the mob to avail themselves of the services of the talented lawyer. The appointment was set for 12.30pm.

It was almost midday. As Jade perused her appointment diary for the rest of the afternoon she decided to grab a quick bite before the arrival of the new client. He had not left a contact number so she had no way to prepare for the meeting. She would just have to wait and see what kind of trouble he was in, and she could not be sure how lengthy the appointment might be.

She was just finishing off her sandwich at her desk when Danni buzzed to let her know the client had arrived. She took a quick look at the diary to remind herself of his name, threw the packaging of her sandwich into the bin and then re-applied her lipstick.

Jade extended her hand to the man as she stepped out of her office into the waiting area. 'Mr Cloak.'

'Ciao Miss Sheffield, it is-a pleasure to finally meet you.'

The gravely Italian voice was unmistakeable and Jade froze. She felt the bile rise in her throat and was suddenly worried her sandwich might end up on the man's impeccably polished shoes. She was looking down at them, marvelling at their shine in an attempt to distract her mind and not give away her fear, which she knew must be showing in her eyes.

Without meeting his eyes, Jade forced a smile and turned toward Danni. 'Danni, could you show Mr Cloak into the meeting room.'

'I will be with you in just a moment,' she managed to say in a slightly shaky voice without looking up. She took a few steps back into her office and closed the door.

Jade's heart was pumping wildly. Her reaction surprised her after all this time. What did the man want from her? Why had he appeared now? As much as she wanted to take flight and not face the situation, there was only one way to find out. After everything else, she could handle this. She gathered her nerve and walked back toward the door, legal pad in hand.

'Mr Cloak,' she addressed the man as she sat down across from him at the small round meeting table. It struck her as an odd name. The words cloak and dagger shot through her mind. 'Is that your real name?' she asked feeling more brazen now. He was a paunchy yet imposing Italian man, greying at the temples where there had obviously once been thick black hair. He sat with an air of importance, as if he was used to giving orders and having them obeyed.

'It-a will suffice for our purposes,' he replied.

'And what exactly are our purposes?'

'Miss Sheffield, you seem a little disturbed by-a my presence, and understandably so. Let me ease-a your concerns. We are-a not interested in your private affairs and they shall remain exactly that - private. We are-a only interested in engaging your professional services.'

'What kind of professional services?' Jade asked guardedly, still not trusting the man. There had to be some kind of catch. They had covered up a murder for her.

'Miss Sheffield, I am-a man with varied business interests. It is-a very important to me to protect those interests. As you will-a no doubt understand, we sometimes have to employ methods which may-a be deemed by others as unlawful in-a our society in order to protect our own interests.'

He hesitated and Jade shuddered. Did he know about Brent? Had he had someone following her all this time? She attempted to relax her tense shoulders, realising she was probably just being paranoid.

'But why, Mr Cloak, did you take such an interest in the Morley case? I didn't win. Angelo Morley is in prison.'

He became stony-faced. 'Angelo Morley is-a no longer one of us.' It was a blunt statement, lacking emotion.

The statement staggered her. What did he mean by 'no longer one of us'? Angelo had been one of them? This whole mess also had something to do with him? What kind of trouble was she in now?

She itched to ask what he meant by that statement but his sinister glare told her the topic was not up for discussion.

'We have-a our own laws, Miss Sheffield, that date back far further than those of-a this society. Protection. Honour. Retribution. And we have our own law enforcers. It is-a one of them I have come to speak to you about today.'

'I'm not sure they are laws I can help you with, Mr Cloak.'

'Ah, but you are-a wrong Miss Sheffield. I don't intend to elaborate on the nature of our laws with you. I just expect you to-a accept what I tell you. From time to-a time, there will be certain cases in which we will-a require your support. You would be in our gratitude if-a you found it within your power to assist.'

He delivered the request as a demand and Jade fully understood his meaning. 'In our gratitude' meant they would continue to hold her secret. Hold it right above her head, like a gun. It did not appear she had much choice but to comply.

As insurance he added in a tone with an intent that she could not misunderstand, 'You have a young-a sister? Pretty thing, śi? It would be-a sad for you to lose her and become-a the only one.'

Jade swallowed hard. Her sister was the only immediate flesh and blood she had and she had sworn to protect her. She nodded slowly. 'What exactly is it you need me to do?'

The man extracted a file from his briefcase. It was a legal file, compiled by another law firm. The title on the file read 'Zuliani, Frank'.

‘I’d like-a you to familiarise yourself with this case, Miss Sheffield. Unfortunately we have lost the previous lawyer who was-a working on the case.’

Lost? It was a strange term to use. She pictured the previous lawyer wandering out into the desert disorientated, not able to find his way back. Then the picture in her head morphed into a bloody scene, a gun held to the man’s head execution style, before he slumped to the ground as the red ooze slowly seeped into the desert sand. She shuddered as she pushed the vision aside.

‘Mr Zuliani is one of our-a best men. His appeal date is set down for this-a Friday. He is currently in-a prison on a murder charge that your predecessor was unable to quash.’

His tone clinched it. Jade did not have any desire to be ‘lost’. Whatever this man wanted of her, she intended to make sure she did a damn good job!

‘The eyewitness who testified at the original trial has-a changed his story and this is the basis of our appeal. You will find that some-a new evidence is about to come to light. We need someone who can think quickly on-a their feet. I would like you to take over the case.’

‘What kind of evidence?’

‘Read through the file and if you’re as-a good as your reputation, I’m sure you will-a figure it out.’ With that the man stood, indicating the meeting was over. He shook Jade’s hand firmly and turned toward the door.

Before he left the room, he turned and said one word. ‘Omertá.’

Jade walked back to her office in a daze. Danni had gone to lunch so she did not have to hide her distress. She opened her browser and tried to Google the word he had spoken. She misspelled it but the browser asked, *Did you mean omertá?* She clicked on the first link and read about the mafia’s code of silence. It was a warning that she should not speak to the police. The police were the last people she intended to talk to about anything remotely connected to Jennifer Morley’s murder. But it confirmed her suspicions as to who ‘they’ were. She had lived on the Coast for ten years and had never considered the area a gangster's paradise. Until now.

She opened the case folder and began to read from the back of the file forward. Frank Zuliani had a colourful criminal past, beginning with time in a juvenile detention centre at the age of fourteen. He was no stranger to the institutional process but for the last ten years, his record was clean. Essentially, it appeared he had been a reformed man.

That was, until the crime he was currently convicted for. She thought she was beyond shock until she realised that the case before her was for the murder of the Asian family in Nerang that Amy had been involved in. How could they expect her to defend a man that had carried out such atrocities? She read the eyewitness accounts of two people who had identified him. They had witnessed him throw a gun into a bushland tract in Nerang. The eyewitnesses, a prostitute and her unlucky client, had both disappeared prior to the trial and neither had been available to testify. She was not surprised with what she now knew about Mr Zuliani's employer.

The prosecutor had then managed to pull a surprise eyewitness. One of the family's neighbours, who had been unwilling to come forward in the beginning, had witnessed Zuliani leaving the crime scene while he was taking out the rubbish. He had only come forward after his conscience got the better of him. Reading on, Jade discovered that during the trial the defence had argued the new witness's vision was impaired due to the darkness, and he could not possibly have identified his client with any degree of certainty. His argument had not been convincing enough to sway the jury. It was noted on the file that he had now withdrawn his statement.

Jade found herself intrigued as to what Frank Zuliani was like. She pictured the traditional hitman as portrayed in action movies, suave and good-looking. She guessed he was neither. He was probably a burly and thuggish looking man like those seen in gangster movies. It was no wonder the jury were not inclined to take his side.

As she read on, the file became more interesting. It seemed the police had recovered the alleged murder weapon and had submitted it for DNA testing. Somewhere along the line, the gun had gone missing and the police never performed the DNA tests.

If this had been of the mob's doing, it had also been their undoing. The prosecution had used the lack of DNA evidence in its favour. The defence were unable to rule out the suspect. The disappearance of the evidence backfired on them when the jury found Frank Zuliani guilty based on the eyewitness account. They had brought home a unanimous guilty verdict within the first hour of deliberation.

What if the missing evidence were now located? Jade recalled her visitor's words, 'New evidence is about to come to light.' What else could it be? If they somehow intercepted the weapon in the first instance, then they could surely return it. She could bet her bottom dollar it would come back in an entirely different state. Well, her job was just to present the evidence as it stood and not to question its authenticity. If it was in the interests of her client, then that is what she would do.

Jade picked up the phone and dialled the prison to arrange to meet with her new client. It turned out that Frank Zuliani and Angelo Morley were housed the same section of the prison. She was not aware they were cellmates, but she assumed they knew each other.

Perhaps she could kill two birds with one stone. She made separate appointments to meet with both of them the following day.

TWENTY-FIVE

Jade arrived first thing the following morning to meet with Angelo. She disliked the unwelcoming environment of the prison and she shuddered as the guard led her down the corridor through the cold steel barred doors. She was eager to see Angelo however. She was interested to find out if his attitude had changed. He would surely have received the letter by now and be under the false belief that Jennifer would turn up at his appeal to secure his innocence.

As expected, he was in a cocky mood. Jade tried to talk to him about the strategy for the fast approaching appeal, but he showed little interest in what she had to say. His mind was somewhere entirely different.

'How would you feel about owning a vineyard,' he suddenly asked interrupting her speech.

'What?'

'A vineyard. In Italy or France. We could just leave this all behind Jade, and run away to Europe.'

'And how do you propose we get the money to buy a vineyard?' Jade asked, playing along on the chance he might reveal something about his plan to her.

'When this is all over Jade, we will be able to do whatever we want. Now what were you saying about my performance at the appeal?'

Jade acted exasperated, and scolded him like a naughty child. 'Angelo we are less than two weeks away from the appeal. I need you to take this seriously! I can present all the evidence and we can hope the jury sides with you. Or you can listen to my advice and we can play this jury for sympathy and cast doubt in every single one of those juror's minds.'

There was a flash of hate behind her eyes, suppressed at once before he had a chance to see it. Jade could not believe she would be standing in a courtroom fighting to get this man off. If there was a way she could safeguard her own future and leave him to rot in prison, she would do it. Her hate for him, like acid, ate through every fibre of her being and threatened to distort her thinking.

Now she had Angelo's attention she went on. 'I am going to attempt to have a predominantly male jury. I want to put you on the stand first because I need you to appeal to those men, to make them believe your wife was a scheming, conniving woman who would stop at nothing to see you ruined. I want them to know it, to feel it, and to share your angst. We are then going to use the strength of the jury's loathing to create a sense of uncertainty. We can discredit the expert witness with evidence that Jennifer is still alive. Let him explain to the jury how a dead woman could seemingly carry on a whole life in another part of the state.'

'OK, I get it.' He had a wry smile on his face.

'Angelo, I've said it before. This isn't over yet. Jennifer is nowhere to be found, and believe me they have pulled out all stops to find her from what I can gather. The defence counsel could try to establish identity theft, or they may go along with the evidence and try to pin this fraud charge on you. I have no way to tell how they'll play it, so while we have to be ready for all those scenarios we also need to have a plan that will get you off this murder rap regardless.'

Jade knew he did not really care about what she was saying. He had his own strategy to get himself off the murder charge. But she went through her strategy for the appeal with him as if she believed it was in his best interests and was convinced wholeheartedly of his innocence.

As he rose to leave, she took his hand and looked lovingly into his eyes. 'The vineyard sounds like a lovely dream, Angelo.'

Angelo smiled as if all his dreams would soon be coming true.

Jade waited in the room for Frank Zuliani with a mild sense of anxiety. She had never met a hitman. Would he be as frightening as she had imagined? She also knew how important this case was in terms of her future. It could determine if she even had a future. She was fearful of how deeply and unwittingly she had become involved with these people. Mostly, she was unsure of how she could elicit information from him about Angelo without raising any suspicion. She was determined to know more about Angelo's connection with the mob.

She rose as he entered the room and shook his hand. 'Mr Zuliani. My name is Jade Sheffield and I have been engaged by your employer to represent you at your appeal on Friday.'

His grip was firm and his smile was full of gratitude. Her visions were not too far from reality. Frank Zuliani was a large intimidating man with short curly hair and a prominent scar that extended from his left cheekbone down to the base of his chin.

He grinned and took her hand. 'Ciao Bella. It's a pleasure to meet-a you. What's-a pretty lady like you doing in a profession like-a this?' His voice was as gruff as his appearance and she felt her skin crawl where he had touched her hand.

She ignored his offhanded compliment. 'I've read through your file, Mr Zuliani. May I call you Frank?'

He winked with a nod. 'Śi. You call-a me whatever you like.'

Jade continued unperturbed by his flirting. 'I'd just like to hear the story in your own words. Let's start with what you were doing in Nerang the night the murder occurred.'

'Like I told-a the cops, I was having a piss.' A blush appeared which looked out of place on the big man's face but Jade understood where it came from, having read about their code to respect women. 'Spiacente...sorry, I mean-a...relieving myself. I didn't throw-a nothing in those bushes.'

'Come now, Frank. It's me you're talking to now. I know what you do for a living.'

His eyes narrowed. 'I'm-a in security.'

Jade played along, a hint of sarcasm in her voice. 'Of course you are. So were you taking a break from a security gig at the time of relieving yourself?'

'No, I was-a on my way home. You know how it is when you got-a go?'

'OK, I guess we have to stick to that lame story since it's what you told the police. Now the question is *how* are we going to get the jury to believe you?' She was sounding him out to see if he knew anything about the alleged new evidence.

He smirked. 'Don't think we're gonna have to worry about-a that.'

'Ah, the new evidence?' Jade coaxed.

'You know about-a that?'

'Your boss mentioned it.'

Frank dropped his guard and seemed to relax a bit, obviously believing she was in the know. In a whisper he said, 'There was no time to do anything with the gun but-a toss it. Damn police found it.' A sly grin played across his scarred face. 'Pity it got-a lost somewhere along the way. But now it's found, they're gonna know it wasn't me.'

She had been on the money. The weapon was going to resurface and they would be forced to release her client to continue his killing spree. Jade checked herself. She was no longer one to make judgements about a murderer. But if it was so clear cut, why did they need her? Were they just using her to add legitimacy to their case? Was this case just a warm up? There would be no easy release from this trap she had allowed herself to be snared in.

'You're right, Frank. There's really not much we need to do. We'll have you out of here by Friday.'

It was time to drop it in. 'It's a pity my Angelo Morley case isn't so straight forward.'

She watched for his reaction. He did not seem surprised to hear she was representing him too. 'I believe you two are associated?'

'He tell-a you that?' he asked, screwing up his face.

'He respects you a lot.'

'Really?' Frank's scowl turned to a proud grin. 'Well he bloody well-a ought to. I got him out o' a few scrapes.'

'You go back a while, hey?'

'See this-a scar? That's his handiwork. Patched me up-a nice, śi?'

Jade looked closely at his face. 'I hardly even noticed,' she lied. 'But I thought he was a heart doctor.'

'He helps out when-a we need him. Part of the deal.'

'The deal?'

'Śi, you don't think they paid his-a way through med school for nothin', do you?'

'No, I guess not.' Jade played along, pretending she knew what he was talking about.

'We all got-a pay our debts, and for that we all-a get to share in the rewards.' His grin widened. 'Tit for tat.'

'Tit for tat,' Jade repeated. That was how it worked. Jade did not yet know what was to come but as an alternative to prison, she did know it was the favourable option. She suddenly felt more secure than she had in a long while. So long as she kept up her end of the bargain and did her job well, it appeared that she was going to remain safe.

TWENTY-SIX

Friday arrived but Jade had still not received any news relating to the new evidence. Was there something she had missed? She read the entirety of the Frank Zuliani file for the fifth time, but nothing obvious jumped out at her. All she could do was to forge ahead with the appeal, and wait. She had instructed counsel based on the information she had.

Jade sat in the docks with her fingers crossed waiting for the appeal to begin. A clerk of the court entered then tapped the Crown Prosecutor on the shoulder and whispered something in his ear.

'Your Honour, may I approach the bench?' the Prosecutor addressed the judge. He motioned for him to approach.

'Your honour, it appears some new evidence has come to light which may have a bearing on the outcome of this appeal. I would like to request a stay until that evidence is able to be examined and presented.'

The judge motioned for Jade's counsel to approach the bench. He returned and delivered the news to Jade that while in the evidence room looking for something for an entirely unrelated case, a young constable had come across a box without any case label. Curious, he opened the box and found the weapon. He took it to one of the senior detectives who immediately recognised it as the gun that went missing prior to the Zuliani trial.

It was what she had been waiting to hear. She acted surprised at the news that the weapon had been found. The judge had agreed to adjourn the appeal to the following week to allow for DNA tests to be completed.

By the time the re-scheduled date for Frank's appeal had arrived, Jade had obtained the forensics report on the gun found in the Nerang bushland. Her client was acquitted and released from prison. The DNA evidence proved undisputedly that the man who had fired the weapon that killed the family was not Frank Zuliani. The DNA turned out to be that of the male eyewitness who disappeared prior to the trial, who had willingly given a DNA sample early in the piece to eliminate himself as a suspect. It tied things up very neatly, providing a motivation for his sudden disappearance. Jade was hardly surprised. She had no doubt Frank Zuliani had carried out the execution but with no eyewitnesses to testify the DPP no longer had a case to link him to the crime. This just confirmed her suspicions the mob had been responsible for the disappearance of the eyewitnesses since the DNA of one of them turned up on the weapon. It also demonstrated to her what they were capable of if she did not comply with their requests.

A large bouquet of white roses arrived at her office that afternoon with a note of thanks from 'Mr Cloak'. Jade had not had a lot to do with the outcome of the case. All she'd had to do was co-ordinate it. It seemed they wanted to convey their appreciation anyway. She was sure there were bigger things to come.

She stared at the tight white buds with a growing sense of confidence. Her fears about what they would do with the footage of the murder had dissipated. She had secured her innocence by simply doing her job. It was not as if she hadn't represented guilty clients before, and permitted herself to bend and twist the law to win a case. It was the nature of her profession. The man, or woman, with the best case won regardless of innocence or guilt. It helped to apply those ethics to her situation. She was not the first guilty person to get away with murder, and Angelo was not the first innocent person to be convicted of murder.

Now she was feeling more assured of her own welfare, her mind turned to the viability of losing Angelo's appeal. There was one sure way to make that happen. Find Jennifer's body. If they were not going to turn her in, then there was no longer a reason to fear the discovery of the body. She remembered the news report in Cairns. There had been no further reports about the body discovered weighted down in the river. What was the possibility that it was indeed Jennifer Morley's body?

She picked up the phone and dialled the police station. An hour later, she was sitting at a coffee shop with Detective Martin Andrews.

'I'm so glad you could meet me on such short notice, Martin.' She used his first name to personalise things.

'It sounded important.' She thought he would have dropped everything regardless. He seemed eager to meet with her again.

'It is. I have some information I'd like to share with you. I recently represented a client, Frank Zuliani. You might know of him?'

'Yeah, we all know the story. Quite convenient how that gun was found during the appeal.' He did not sound convinced it was a co-incidence.

She dropped her voice and spoke from behind her hand. 'Well I'm sure you also know he is allegedly a mob hitman.'

'That may very well be the case, but unless he commits a crime we can actually hold him on, there's not much we can do about it.'

'It's not Frank Zuliani's case I want to talk you about. I trust this conversation is off the record? It creates a conflict for me to be telling you this, but I couldn't just let it go. Whatever you choose to do with this information, I can't be associated with it.'

'Of course,' he agreed.

'Frank Zuliani inadvertently mentioned to me he had connections to Angelo Morley. Apparently, Angelo is also on the mob payroll.' She raised her eyebrows. 'Something about them paying his way through med school in return for certain 'medical favours'.'

Jade waited while he absorbed the information. 'I guess you're wondering why I'm telling you this since Angelo is my client.'

'Yeah, you got me wondering.'

'A few weeks ago there was a body discovered weighted down in the Nerang River. A young female, who I assume remains a Jane Doe in some morgue somewhere. Don't ask me why, but my gut instinct keeps telling me that woman could be Jennifer Morley, and since I have come into the possession of this information about Dr Morley I felt compelled to tell someone. I figured you would be the best person.'

'Your gut instinct?' he asked with a hint of sarcasm.

It wasn't much to go on, her gut instinct, but she asked anyway, 'Can you do anything about finding out?'

'I didn't have much to do with that case, but from what I've heard the body was so badly decomposed it couldn't be identified visually.' She sensed he wanted to please her. 'I can make some calls and check on medical and dental records. It's worth a shot. But I thought you were under the impression Jennifer Morley was still alive?'

'We are all under that impression. But what if we're wrong? What if it's all just been a set up? I could be way off track but I just thought it was worth investigating. The appeal is set down for tomorrow.' She looked at him imploringly. 'The way the evidence is stacked, I'm going to be able to establish reasonable doubt. It's my job to do that. Angelo Morley could be back on the streets within days. If he was involved in the death of his wife, then I don't want to be the one responsible for making that happen.'

She had hooked him. 'Well then, I guess I better get onto it straight away. Thanks for coming forward. Do you want me to let you know what I find out?'

'I'd rather not be involved from this point. I've done my duty. I'm going to leave it in your capable hands.' She smiled her most alluring smile. 'But a simple yes or no might be nice.' She handed him her business card, brushing her hand gently against his as she did.

Jade stood and shook his hand. She walked away feeling quite smug. The detective had fallen for her story. If her instincts turned out to be correct, then Angelo Morley would find himself in a situation from which there was no escape. With a body to corroborate the murder, his well-planned scheme and the evidence he had planted would sustain his guilt and keep him in prison for a very long time.

When Andrews got back to the station, he called one of the junior constables to his desk. He would have him follow up the lead as he had promised Jade but he did not think it was worth wasting his time chasing up a notion based on her gut instinct.

Clearly pleased the detective had handed him the task, the young constable set off eagerly to make some calls. Within a few hours, he had tracked down the dentist that Angelo had arranged to repair Jennifer Morley's teeth. The dental x-rays were on their way over to the morgue by courier. He spent the rest of the afternoon familiarising himself with the case, and was excited to learn there were blood and DNA samples available for comparison. If the teeth were a match, then he would have the information sent to the coroner and he could be responsible for proving beyond a doubt whether the Jane Doe was Jennifer Morley.

By the time his shift ended, the eager constable had made five calls to the coroner's office to see if the x-rays had arrived. On his last call, the receptionist advised the package had arrived and the coroner was in receipt of it. He decided to detour home via the coroner's office hoping there would be some news by the time he got there.

He was in luck. When he arrived and asked to see the coroner, the receptionist shuffled him into his office. The middle-aged man peered at him through his wire-rimmed glasses then stood to shake his hand. 'Congratulations, young man! We have an I.D.'

'You're kidding!' he beamed. 'That's fantastic news. The boss will be pleased.'

'He has already been informed, and is faxing me the DNA records of Jennifer Morley as we speak. If you would like to hang around while I compare them, we can have a resounding answer today.'

'You betcha!'

'Is this your first time in the morgue?'

'It is on a real case,' the eager constable replied.

'Would you like to see the body?'

'Sure, that would be super.'

The coroner chuckled and the constable knew why. He had heard about green police officers reduced to convulsing and sometimes even vomiting when presented with their first real body. They toughened up of course. It was a line of work in which you had to.

The beep of the fax machine interrupted his thoughts.

'First things first,' the coroner said as he picked up the fax and carried it to his desk. For the young constable, time seemed to stand still. He could feel his heart pounding in his chest. This was the reason he had joined the force: to solve murders and put away the murderers. He was about to do just that. He knew it.

'Yeeesss,' the coroner drew out the word. 'Definitely a match. About ninety-eight per cent certainty.'

'Ninety-eight?'

'That's more than enough, my boy. Blood type and dental records match. This woman is Jennifer Morley without doubt!'

Andrews received the call back at the station with astonishment. He had doubted it, but Jade's gut instinct had been right. He hated the idea he was going to have to pass the information on to the Crown Prosecutor and she was now going to lose the appeal tomorrow. Then, she had given him the lead in the first place, so perhaps she would be happy with the outcome. He was going to shine all round on this one.

He started typing up the report, taking full credit for the theory and subsequent discovery of the body of Jennifer Morley.

TWENTY-SEVEN

Angelo sat beside Jade in the courtroom, a conceited smile on his face. Any time now, Jennifer was going to walk through the large timber doors and put an end to the proceedings. It was then the real battle would begin. Once Jade saw Angelo had not really murdered his wife, he was sure she would be even more determined to help him to bring his plan to fruition. The knowledge that he would soon be a very wealthy man comforted him even more.

Jade sat beside her client equally as conceited. She smiled as she recalled the one word sent by text message to her phone late last night. It read simply, *Yes*. At some point, someone *would* walk through the large timber doors and put an end to the proceedings. It was not going to be Jennifer Morley, as Angelo smugly believed. How much time and energy was she going to have to waste on defending him before she could watch him crumble as his plan fell apart before his eyes? She was going to relish the moment of his defeat.

It was a long morning and Jade had performed well, presenting a strong case that Jennifer may still be alive. She could tell Angelo's performance had moved the jury when she put him on the stand, particularly the men. He had done well under her coaching. They listened intently to the police evidence presented on the investigation in Cairns and she could sense they had begun to sympathise with her client. It would have been Brent on that stand had things turned out differently. She did not let those feelings persist, moving quickly on to the next witness.

Jade was definitely in need of a break. She had been feeling increasingly tired over the last few weeks and put it down to the stress of her involvement in the Frank Zuliani case, and the preparation for Angelo's appeal. She was definitely going to take a break when it was all over. She could do with some rest and relaxation, somewhere by a pool in the Whitsundays where the waiters brought you frozen marguerita and the biggest thing to worry about was not getting sunburnt.

By mid-morning, her exhaustion had begun to wear on her and she was starting to feel a little irritated. She just wanted this to end! She had expected somebody would have turned up by now with the news of the discovery of Jennifer's body and it would all be over for Angelo. He still seemed to have that smug look, and she wanted to just reach out and strike it off his face. She was enjoying the pleasure of the thought when an unexpected bout of nausea caused a knot to form in her stomach. She felt the bile rising in her throat and a tingling sensation suddenly struck her tongue. She clapped one hand over her mouth and with the other pointed to her stomach as she raced from the courtroom toward the bathroom.

She only made it as far as the basin before the contents of her stomach erupted violently from her throat. She had been feeling a bit off all morning so had only had a coffee for breakfast. She was thankful for that now. Maybe she had been coming down with something and that is why she had felt so tired all week. Entering one of the vacant cubicles, Jade sat down on the toilet until her head cleared. She headed back to the courtroom to discover the judge had called for a morning break.

It was a good opportunity to grab a quick bite to eat. Her previously unsettled stomach was now craving food. As she reached the cafeteria, the slight feeling of nausea returned. She settled on a packet of plain salted potato chips. The salty chips seemed to settle her stomach and by the time she had to return to the courtroom she was feeling much better.

The guards led Angelo back into the courtroom and seated him beside her. He had not said much to Jade, having remained in a relaxed mood for much of the morning. He seemed to have become more anxious since the break and turned toward the door every time a sound came from that general direction. Whenever he looked toward the door Jade followed his gaze, though both of them had different expectations of who would appear.

Detective Andrews strode through the large doors finally answering Jade's prayers. He mouthed the word 'Sorry,' as he waved a file in his hand. It must have taken longer than expected to execute the paperwork. He headed toward the front of the dock, behind the prosecutor's bench. The Crown Prosecutor stepped toward him. After whispering in his ear for a moment, Andrews handed over the file and took a seat. He glanced over at Jade and winked at her. She felt the relief seep into her body and the tension she had felt all morning began to subside. Her shoulders relaxed and she sunk into her chair with a contented smile on her face ready to watch the scene unfold before her. She glanced across at Angelo, who had no idea of what was about to take place. She smiled at him and he returned the gesture.

The Crown Prosecutor stood, but instead of commencing his cross-examination of the witness, he held up the file and removed a piece of paper encased in a plastic sheet. 'Your Honour, I would like to submit this into evidence.' The judge motioned him to approach the bench.

'Your Honour, new evidence has just been brought to my attention.' He handed the document to the judge, who perused it then nodded his approval.

The Crown Prosecutor called Martin Andrews to the witness box. After he was sworn in, he asked, 'Detective Andrews, can you tell me what the document is that you have just delivered to the court?'

Andrews turned toward Jade and Angelo so they could clearly hear the words he was about to speak. 'It is a death certificate issued by the Coroner's office this morning for Jennifer Morley.' He paused for effect as a collective sigh rose around the courtroom. 'Her body was discovered several weeks ago and a positive identification has been made using DNA results and dental records.'

Jade had waited so long for this moment. She fought the desire to let her smile widen into a triumphant grin. After months of bottling up her anger and hatred for Angelo, she looked sideways and let the full extent of her contempt for him show.

At first, Angelo did not react. It seemed to take a while for the information to sink in. Then he jumped from his seat. 'No-oo,' he screamed. 'This can't be right. You don't understand. I didn't really kill her.'

The judge ordered Angelo to refrain from his outburst, while Andrews continued. 'The Coroner's report indicates Jennifer Morley's death was a result of a blow to the head, consistent with the evidence held against Angelo Morley. The body has been in the water for some time and this has had an effect on the decomposition rate, but it is also estimated the death occurred around the same time period as Dr Morley is alleged to have murdered his wife.'

Jade watched with amusement as Angelo's emotional state wavered. She didn't want to miss the point of realisation where he knew he was damned.

Angelo was confused. He had been in contact with Jennifer just the week before. At least he thought he had. He tried to think clearly. Who else could it have been? The prosecutor's words 'body has been in the water' replayed in his head. He remembered the news segment a few weeks back about a weighted-down body found in the Nerang River. Who else knew about his plan? Of course. The bugs in his apartment! They must have heard it all and arranged Jennifer's death. All this time he thought things were going along perfectly but they were just stringing him along. But why? He did not even need to ask that question. Nobody crossed the mob and got away with it. He should have known they would never let him go.

His confusion turned to bewilderment. He had planted evidence that irrefutably proved *he* murdered Jennifer and now she was dead! He jumped from his seat again. "You *have* to believe me. I didn't kill my wife. It was them. It was the mob! You have to believe me!'

The judge raised his voice. 'Dr Morley, you will refrain from this outburst immediately or you will be removed from this courtroom.'

Angelo ignored the directive and continued to protest his innocence. The judge motioned for the guards to restrain him. As they surrounded him, he tried to push them away and struggled as he continued to rave like a madman. They managed to cuff him and attempted to lead him away.

He pulled toward Jade and pleaded, 'Help me. *Please!* I didn't do this. You of all people *have* to believe me! Help me get out of this.'

Jade looked at him with no emotion on her face. It appeared she also now believed he had murdered his wife. Who could blame her? Evidence did not usually lie. A stony disillusionment descended upon him. It seemed he could do nothing now to avoid his fate. The guard led Angelo out of the courthouse in handcuffs, where the completion of his life sentence awaited him.

When he stopped at the door and looked back, Jade had turned her back on him.

TWENTY-EIGHT

Jade sat at the table forcing a smile. She had felt obliged to accept the dinner invitation from Martin Andrews but was now ruing the fact that she had to put up with the smarmy man's company. He had chosen a table in the back corner of a cheap restaurant. She stared at the flocked wallpaper peeling from the wall behind him to avoid having to make eye contact. She had been preoccupied by her discomfort so had not really been paying attention to his conversation, dropping in a 'yeah,' and 'really,' from time to time. He seemed to like the sound of his own voice and hardly even noticed her inattentiveness.

Andrews suddenly said something that made her sit up in her chair. He told her that since the police had established Angelo's connections to organised crime, they had launched a new investigation into Brent Hunter's death.

'What have they got to go on?' she asked.

'The autopsy showed traces of drugs in his system, which initially set off alarm bells,' he said, 'but they found some sleeping tablets in his room. That in itself might not have been suspicious, but the water they found in his lungs was fresh water, not salt water. So he couldn't have drowned out on the reef.'

Jade stiffened, feeling the colour suddenly drain from her face. She hoped he had not noticed. She had made a fatal mistake. How stupid of her not to think of it!

Andrews continued, 'That's not all. They found bruising on his wrists and ankles indicating he'd been tied up.'

Jade suddenly felt ill. 'I'm so sorry, I think I'm going to be sick.' There was no time to make a dash for the bathroom. She picked up her empty bowl and vomited into it right in front of him. She was slightly embarrassed but at least it gave her an excuse to end the awful evening.

Jade hadn't slept well after what Andrews had revealed to her at dinner the previous evening. What if they somehow discovered she was in Cairns? Would they connect her to Brent's death? The possibility had troubled her all night.

She stared at her desk calendar. It was exactly one week after the appeal. She should have been happier about the victory but it had left her feeling flat. She was still feeling a little off colour and had brought up her breakfast again that morning. Maybe she had eaten something bad and the bug was still in her system. She would get Danni to make her an appointment at the doctors if it persisted much longer.

She knew that was not the only thing that was wrong. There was something missing that she usually took away from a victory. Her whole existence for the past few months had revolved around getting revenge against Angelo. Somehow, revenge didn't seem as sweet if the person you directed it at didn't know where it had come from. If only there was some way she could let Angelo know of her role in his downfall without him being able to do anything to incriminate her.

She decided to go out to get some lunch to clear her head. She was standing in the queue at the takeaway shop when an idea suddenly jumped into her head. There was a way she could wrap the whole thing up nicely. The idea left her strangely calm and with none of the apprehension she had been feeling all day. When she got back to her office, she phoned the prison and asked to meet with Angelo Morley that afternoon.

Jade arrived at the prison feeling jubilant. She had stopped trying to rationalise her behaviour. No emotion was rational where revenge was concerned. This would be the last time she would ever have to lay eyes on Angelo Morley. Knowing how he had toyed with her heart and betrayed her in his ploy to become wealthy, she detested the idea of even having to look at him but the reward would be well justified. She would finally have the satisfaction and closure she longed for, and she felt sure the evil demons plaguing her dreams would disappear.

A prison guard oversaw the meeting. He stood at a respectful distance so that if they spoke quietly, he could not really decipher what they were saying to each other.

'Hello Angelo,' Jade said in a blunt and unemotional tone. Angelo sat back, obviously sensing she was not there to offer him her support.

'Jade. I'm so glad you came.'

'You are? Why is that?'

'I wanted a chance to speak to you. To let you know I didn't kill Jennifer. I was surprised when I heard you wanted to see me. I thought you'd turned to the other side and any effort to convince you of the truth would be hopeless. It's not like I'm an angel, but I *did not* murder my wife and I was bothered that you'd believe I did.' He reached out to take her hand but she pulled away.

Jade wanted to make this as quick and direct as she could. 'I know you didn't kill Jennifer, Angelo.'

He seemed to sense the contempt in her voice. A confused look crossed his face as he recognised the hate in her eyes.

'I also know all about your plan, Angelo.'

'My plan?' he whispered so the guard would not hear him.

'Yes, your plan.' She spoke quietly but resolutely. 'You know the one? We all had our roles to play. You were the leading man of course, Jennifer as your wife, me as the lawyer.' She spat the last words at him. 'I'd say we all played our parts very well. But you forgot to cast one role.'

Angelo eyed her nervously now.

'The Murderess!' Jade snarled.

'Murderess? Jade? Do you know who killed Jennifer?'

Jade's tone turned sugary sweet. 'Of course I do, Angelo. You killed Jennifer.' She smiled at him innocently.

Her sudden change of demeanour worked in startling him. A moment ago, he had been the target of her scorn. Now she was smiling sweetly at him. She was enjoying playing games with *him* for a change.

Jade continued in the same sweet tone. 'Unfortunately, Detective Brent Hunter found out about it, so you had him killed too.'

‘Who told you that?’ Angelo retorted, slamming his hands down on the desk. The guard made a move toward them but Jade waved him away.

‘Whoever wrote this letter, because we both know it wasn’t Jennifer.’ Looking over to check the guard was not watching, Jade removed a blank sheet of paper and a pen from her pocket. She smoothed it out before her and began to write in Jennifer Morley’s handwriting.

Dear Angelo,
The execution of Brent Hunter was been carried out as per your instructions. We will be in touch regarding payment.
Humbly yours,

She signed the note with Julianne McGuire’s signature. As Angelo looked on, she saw the realisation dawn on him. She had written the letters. She had known all along that Jennifer was dead. He looked into her eyes, which were again filled with contempt, and she knew he understood that she had played the part of the Murderess.

That was all Jade needed. She put the items quickly back into her pocket and stood up alerting the guard she was ready to leave. Before she walked away, Jade whispered to Angelo, ‘This letter will arrive in the mail this week. Though I expect they will intercept it before it gets to you. They are already investigating your connection to the mob and Detective Hunter’s death.’

As she moved to leave, he grabbed her arm. ‘You won’t get away with this Jade. I’ll tell them the whole story.’

She pulled away then turned up her palms. A deep laugh, not unlike his, rose up from her throat. ‘Who is ever going to believe you, Angelo?’ There was an icy sharpness in her voice reflecting her hate for him, which she now made no effort to conceal.

Angelo’s face became impassive and she could not read his look. ‘Jade, what have you become?’ His tone resembled sadness but his eyes did not show any sign of the emotion. She found the question rather hypocritical. He was a true narcissist, a man with little empathy or conscience who used others as a means to his own end. She had simply played him at his own game.

'We all hide a part of ourselves away from the world, Angelo. You of all people know that.'

She turned on her heel and strode from the room.

Back at her office, Jade again stared at her desk calendar. She flipped the pages and counted off the months since this dilemma had begun. It was finally over. The evidence would implicate Angelo for both killings and she could get on with her life and put it all behind her. As she flipped over the calendar pages, Jade noticed the red mark she had made on each page marking her monthly cycle. There was no red mark on the calendar this month. She counted twenty-eight days from the last red mark. Her finger landed on a date two weeks prior. She had been so distracted by what was going on around her she had not even considered the possibility. The tiredness and nausea, it all suddenly added up. She was pregnant!

Two weeks later Jade stood outside the women's clinic but could not force herself to take the steps required to get inside. She reached for the rail as a familiar wave if nausea washed over her. By her calculations, she could have conceived on the night she murdered the child's father. Maybe this was her penance. She had believed she had made the right decision to terminate the pregnancy but as she placed her hand on her stomach, she felt an instinctual connection with the tiny being growing inside her. As she grappled with this new and surprising emotion, the glass door of the clinic swung open in front of her and a young woman walked through it. Her face was a picture of distress. She passed Jade in anguished confusion, hardly even acknowledging her presence on the stairs.

Jade felt compelled to run after the woman, 'Are you OK?'

'It's...over.' She choked on sobs as she felt for her stomach and hurried off up the road.

Caught up in her own pain, the encounter had a profound impact on Jade. She looked down to where her hand remained on her stomach and a pang of guilt struck her so sharply she stopped breathing for a moment. Perhaps fate had dealt her this hand to allow her to make amends for what she had done. She took one more glance toward the closed clinic door then headed in the same direction as the woman who had just retreated.

EPILOGUE

Four years later

Jade left the courthouse via the back entrance, flanked by two police officers. At the same moment, the Crown Prosecutor ducked the camera flashes erupting around him at the front of the building. For months, the media had swarmed over the high profile case against the mob but it was finally over. Having been one of the star witnesses, they would soon relocate Jade under the witness protection program. It was a small price to pay to break her bond to the mob. She had been bound to them for several years and had thought that she always would be. They had continued to call in favours whenever they deemed she could be of assistance to them. She had initially accepted this as her punishment. She often lamented in a way she had been in a similar position to Angelo in that she had committed an act from which there was no escape. It had been her jail sentence.

But she had found an unlikely ally in Frank Zuliani. A task force set up to investigate organised crime on the Gold Coast had kept him under close surveillance and they had convicted him of another murder he committed about six months after his release. This time the police had been very careful not to lose any of the witnesses or evidence. The DPP had coerced him into breaking the Omertá, the mob's code of silence. He had turned state's evidence in exchange for a reduced prison sentence and they had conditionally released him to gather evidence against the mob. In the process, he had secured the only existing copies of the DVD that incriminated her in the murder of Jennifer Morley. He had returned them to her secretly under some strange sense of indebtedness to her.

It gave her the opportunity she needed to close out the dark side of her life and help expose the organised crime that was taking place on the Coast. In a covert operation, she began to work with the task force to bring down the notorious mob leader she had once known as 'Mr Cloak', a code name she still used to refer to him although she now knew his real name. Cloak had not known of her involvement until she testified; by which time there was little he could do to stop her.

The police officers escorted her home where she picked up what few personal possessions she still needed. Her son and sister were already in protective custody and she was eagerly waiting to join them. She took one last look around the room, saying a quick goodbye to her old life then picked up the bag and followed the officers out the door.

Another year later

The young boy climbed to the top of the play gym as his mother sat watching him from the park bench. The sun glistened off his golden blonde hair contrasting it against the blue spring sky. It was a sky that reflected the deep blue in his enthusiastic eyes.

'Look at me, Mummy,' he called out as he waved to her.

Jade smiled fondly and waved to her son, once again reminded of how he was the image of Brent. A twinge of guilt often struck her in these moments and would probably never leave her. The boy would never know his father, and Jade was the one who was responsible for that. She had committed herself to motherhood and making sure she brought the child up in an environment of unconditional love and support. She owed him that.

Looking up at the wind whispering through the leaves of the tree above, she could almost hear the words of one of her favourite authors, Anne Frank. *The final forming of a person's character lies in his or her own hands.* She looked down at her hands. She had made the fateful mistake of letting that control leave them. She had allowed circumstance and emotion to eclipse her entire personality and her values. It had been a difficult lesson. There were things she had done that would haunt her for the rest of her days and she was sure that one day she would be called to atone for them. But the thing with an eclipse is that the darkness passes and the light returns. Now, she had a much stronger reason to go on, a much stronger desire for self-preservation. She was now responsible for another person. It was her second chance. She had learned the only person who could shape your future was you. You became good by being good.

Jade had not given up her aspirations to become a good criminal lawyer, and arrangements had been made to convert her qualifications into her new name. She juggled her family and career responsibilities commendably. Her new role allowed her to be choosy with her cases, so she tried to the best of her ability to only to take on clients that she believed were innocent. Her track record of wins for her clients was testament to her commitment.

She did not think much about Angelo these days. She had been concerned for a while that he may come after her someday looking for his own revenge, or send someone else to do it for him. But she felt safe from him now that she had a new identity.

Her young son ran toward her and launched himself into her arms. She swung him around in a circle and watched as his face lit up like a million stars. The words she had once heard in her dreams ran through her head. *You will become who you are meant to be.* She looked into her son's smiling face and knew in her heart who she was meant to be. She had once believed that the dream was about giving in to her darker side. That was not who she was meant to be.

It never was.

About the Author

Born in Australia in 1970, Lea Scott resides by the Brisbane River in sunny Queensland. While not writing, she divides her time between exploring other parts of the world and spending time with friends by the river, while encouraging her two sons in their own artistic endeavours.

With a degree majoring in Commerce with studies in Communications and English Literature, Lea could be coined a true 'creative accountant'. She founded her lengthy accounting career in Insolvency – an area steeped in corporate crime. During this time, Lea faced adversaries both in court and at the end of a gun barrel. Threats of bodily harm came with the job. It was this experience that first whetted her appetite for crime stories.

Her first crime novel, *The Ned Kelly Game*, received outstanding reviews. With an interest in psychology and the delicate balance of the mind, Lea intends to continue to deliver crime thrillers that explore the many facets of the human psyche.

Lea devotes most of her writing time to crime and suspense stories, but some of her poetry has been short-listed for several awards. She has published short stories and poems in the collective anthologies, *A Pocket Full of Wry* and *A Twist in the Tail*.

To find out more, visit

www.leascott.com